Emily's Mistake

Emily's Mistake

Sasha Fenton

Stellium Ltd

Published 2019 by Stellium Ltd
22 Second Avenue, Camels Head
Plymouth, Devon PL2 2EQ
email: stelliumpub@gmail.com   web: www.stelliumpub.com

British Library Cataloguing in Publication Data:
A catalogue record of this book is available from the British Library

ISBN: 978-1-912358-00-7

Cover design by Jan Budkowski
Images: Adobe Stock Images

Typesetting by Zambezi Publishing Ltd
Printed in the UK by Lightning Source UK Ltd

About the Author

Sasha Fenton became a professional dancer, actor, singer and acrobat at the age of twelve, "retired" at twenty to live a suburban life as a wife and mother. She then became a professional astrologer, palmist and Tarot Reader, spending the next three decades giving consultations.

To date, Sasha has also been a prolific writer, with 134 books to her name, international sales of over 7 million copies, and translations into fifteen languages. She has written many astrology columns and thousands of articles on mind, body and spirit subjects for various magazines and newspapers.

Interspersed with regular radio and television broadcasts, Sasha has somehow managed to find time to serve on the Executive Council of the Writers' Guild of Great Britain, as Chair and Treasurer for the Advisory Panel on Astrological Education (APAE), and as President and Secretary of the British Astrological and Psychic Society.

Writing fiction has always been on Sasha's mind, and now that she has finally started, she finds herself thoroughly enjoying the process, as a totally new literary direction.

Sasha is married with two children and four lovely grandchildren. She was born in London, but now lives in Plymouth. As hobbies, she has a knack for languages, can fly a plane, play golf, dance the tango and catch trout on a fly. She grows veggies and makes excellent chicken soup! However, she can't knit and she's hopeless with mobile phones.

Dedication

For Helen and Riccardo

Acknowledgements

Thanks to:
Sarah Jane Field - otherwise known as Sal

and

Harcourt Brace Jovanovich,
the publisher of
By the Rivers of Babylon

Contents

Cast of Characters

Name	Age	About
Emily Cromwell	24	Daughter of Sir James Cromwell and niece of Sir David Cromwell. Slightly mature student at the start of the story.
Sir James Cromwell	56	Palaeontologist at Cambridge University
Sir David Cromwell	53	Director of the BBI (British Bureau of Investigation)
Thomas Hatherleigh	43	Director of TUDOR
Sophie Hatherleigh	39	Head of Special Department at TUDOR
Rosie Hatherleigh	5	Daughter of Thomas and Sophie Hatherleigh
Baz Baverstock	43	Deputy Director of TUDOR
Margie Baverstock	40	Wife of Baz, works in a hospital office
Shelley and Taylor Baverstock	14 & 11	Daughter and son of Baz and Margie
Jack Duquesne	34	Head of Intelligence Department at TUDOR
Steven Byers	45	Deputy Director of TUDOR
Kate Byers	45	Sister of Thomas Hatherleigh
Robbie and Harry	13 & 6	Sons of Steven and Kate Byers
Carlo Hatherleigh	34	Joint Head of TUDOR West
Lucy Hatherleigh	23	Joint Head of TUDOR West
Danny and Josie	5 & 3	Son and daughter of Carlo and Lucy
Raj Patel	41	Head of Technical Department at TUDOR
Jill Standish	49	Secretary to Sir David Cromwell at the BBI
Ryan Andrews	27	Secretary to Thomas Hatherleigh
Emma Willis	26	Secretary to Baz Baverstock

Cast of Characters

Name	Age	About
Colonel Alec Blitz	41	The Mossad
Captain Shimon Sobieski	28	The Mossad
Paolo and Rivka Rossi	34 & 32	Sister and brother-in-law of Shimon Sobieski

PROLOGUE

The world is a book, and those who do not travel read only a page.

SAINT AUGUSTINE.

Debile principium melior fortuna sequentur.
It's stupid to depend upon fortune.

The Tudorland Series

The series starts with 'Sophie's Inheritance' and follows with 'Lucy's Dilemma', while 'Emily's Mistake' is the third story. The saga kicks off in 'Sophie's Inheritance' when Sophie Mason inherits a fortune and a contraption called *The Project*, which encourages her to rescue Sir Thomas Hatherleigh from certain death. Thomas had been the Director of 'The Office of State Security for England and Wales', reporting to Sir Thomas Cromwell and Henry VIII, but in New London he eventually returns to his old career as a member of TUDOR, working for Sir David Cromwell.

In 'Lucy's Dilemma', the emotionally fragile Lucy Sanders joins TUDOR and discovers the strange nature of the organisation. She meets Thomas's younger cousin, Sir Charles (Carlo) Hatherleigh, which lands her with an impossible choice.

Now read on to encounter new faces and places, including Emily Cromwell, Janine Weston and a new set of problems.

Part One

A Historical Timeline

Something as curious as the monarchy won't survive unless you take account of people's attitudes. After all, if people don't want it, they won't have it.

HRH PRINCE CHARLES

What a brilliant quote that is! (With grateful thanks to Brainyquote.com)

So, while 'Sophie's Inheritance', 'Lucy's Dilemma' and 'Emily's Mistake' can hardly be termed history books, they are based on the history of the 1540s, which though a much-trawled era, still fascinates us. I started 'Sophie' when I was in very bad place in my own life, and I set about researching the background of the story to give myself something to focus on other than the misery and loss that I was living through at the time. Writing has always been my salvation, as has psychological astrology, as both are about people. So now, let me take you through a brief timeline of the real Tudor history that sits behind the imaginary world that I created for the Tudorland stories.

* * *

When Henry VIII came to the throne at the age of eighteen,

he was tall, slim, and by the standards of the day, good looking. Henry was active, sporty, well-educated, charming, musical and intelligent, and he had a deep knowledge of theology, which was important in those days. The country took to the lad and he got off to a good start. His older brother, Arthur, had been the original heir presumptive, but he'd died at the age fifteen, soon after being married to Catherine of Aragon. Arthur was sick, very young, very ill, and he may not have been able to work up much passion for the Spanish princess who he'd been fixed up with, so it is likely that Catherine's assertion that the marriage had never been consummated was true.

So when King Henry VII died at the age of fifty-two in 1509, it was Henry VIII who was crowned king, and Catherine came along as part of the package, because it was important for Henry to maintain the union between England and the massively powerful Spanish Empire.

A royal marriage was supposed to produce heirs, so even if a King disliked his Queen, he only needed to visit her once in a while to do what was necessary – rather like visiting a sperm bank – but as it happened, Henry and Catherine got on surprisingly well together. Catherine was a few years older than Henry, and she was more knowledgeable about world affairs, so he often turned to her for advice. Kings and Queens led separate lives in those days, and Henry spent most of his time with his male friends, riding, hunting and playing sports, although he was also busy at times with matters of state. Unfortunately, Henry had inherited a genetic disorder called *Kell blood*, which meant that he could make a woman pregnant with one healthy child, but thereafter she would have miscarriages, stillbirths and babies that died in infancy. Catherine produced one daughter but no sons who lived beyond infancy, despite several pregnancies. The Tudor family had a somewhat tenuous claim to their throne, but Henry's situation would have been greatly helped if he had a couple of healthy sons, and the opportunity for this started to loom over the horizon when he met and fell in love with Anne Boleyn.

Anne came from minor nobility and her father was extremely ambitious. For some years, he'd been the English ambassador at the French court, and while there, he had pimped out Anne's older sister Mary. Mary had made it to the top slot by becoming the girlfriend of the French King, and now that papa Boleyn was back in the English court, he kept up the pressure, so Mary did the rounds, even becoming Henry's girlfriend at one time. When her father proposed the same course of action to Anne, she was having none of it, and she made it clear to all concerned, that if King Henry wanted to sleep with her, he'd have to marry her first. Once Henry had decided upon Anne for his next wife and the mother of his future sons, he had his own reasons for avoiding sex with her, because he didn't want to risk having an illegitimate son. He already had one of these who he acknowledged, supported and may even have loved, but an illegitimate son couldn't sit on the throne.

Henry's first step on the road to divorce was to ask his First Minister, Cardinal Wolsey, to contact the Pope and get him to grant him an annulment. This wasn't such an outrageous suggestion, as the Pope had granted this to one of Henry's sisters, but despite all the Cardinal's efforts, a combination of bad luck and a new and less helpful Pope meant that Wolsey didn't get anywhere. Wolsey gave up and retired to his home in York, but Henry ordered the Cardinal back to London to be tried and probably executed, but the Cardinal deprived Henry of revenge by dying on the journey.

The first king to elevate competent commoners to the

top posts - rather than use the nobility for this purpose - had been Henry's father, Henry VII. He needed to keep the wealthy and arrogant nobility away from any real power, to stop them from trying their hands at a coup d'etat.

Henry VIII followed his father's example by keeping the nobility away from the real business of government, so after Wolsey, the butcher's son, left the scene, Henry opened the door to another brilliant and capable commoner.

* * *

Sir Thomas Cromwell's father was a blacksmith and publican who had several business interests in Putney in south London. He was a clever man, but also a hard man who sometimes sailed close to the wind of legality. Thomas Cromwell was one of three children, but the only boy. His mother was an intelligent woman who valued education, so she saw to it that Thomas was well educated. At some point during his teens, Thomas Cromwell fell out badly with his father, so he left home and travelled to Europe. He re-emerged several years later as a sophisticated and educated man, with a good knowledge of the law. I wouldn't be far out in suggesting that an older woman could have been at the back of his transformation. He may even have inherited some useful money from her. Who knows? However, he returned to London, came to court and worked his way up the ladder of success, taking over as First Minister after Wolsey.

Like his predecessor, Cromwell was a very able man, and he set up the first proper bureaucracy in this country, which amazingly, is still in use today! He pretty much ran the country on behalf of Henry, but unlike Wolsey, Cromwell wasn't a priest, and there is no evidence that he was particularly interested in religion, so when Henry urged him to find a loophole that would allow Henry to obtain a divorce, Cromwell managed it. The unexpected side-effect was to break with Rome, the Pope and Roman Catholicism and Henry's declaration of himself as the head of the English Church. As it happened, Henry genuinely felt that God had ordained him to take on the job, and we can also speculate that he was heartily sick of sending money to the Vatican and having the Pope interfere in his foreign policy – apart from stifling his plans to marry Anne. Up until a couple of hundred years before Henry's time, splitting from Rome would have been unthinkable, but circumstances had been slowly building the emergence of Protestantism throughout northern Europe.

Where Anne Boleyn is concerned, my personal view is that she and Henry made a classic mistake that is still common today, which is to marry and try for a baby when a relationship is pretty much over. Once Henry had finally had got her first pregnancy under way, he drifted away from her. Her habit of picking fights and telling Henry what to do (never a good idea, as Wolsey and the Pope had already discovered) allied with the fact that her first child was a girl, and with her two subsequent pregnancies ending in miscarriage, meant that it soon became time for Henry to move on.

It wasn't going to be so easy for Cromwell to get the marriage annulled, so he had to find something with which to accuse Anne, as a way of getting rid of her. Whether Cromwell was trapped into what he did, or whether he did it out of dislike for Anne (there was no love lost between them) or whether it was no more than expediency, is hard to say. In the event, he concocted a story that Anne was sleeping with five men, including her own brother, and this allowed Henry to purge Anne and at the same time, get rid of the faction who surrounded her.

Henry married Jane Seymour, and it really was third time lucky for him, because Jane pulled off the much-needed miracle of giving Henry a healthy son – but this is where we really get to understand Henry. Apparently the labour was awful, and when a midwife sent a message to Henry as to whether she should try to save the child or the mother, Henry said, 'Save the child. A new wife can always be got.' Bearing in mind that he didn't even know the sex of the child at this point and that Jane was probably his favourite of all his wives, we can see what a selfish, cold-hearted man he'd become. In the event, Jane died a few days after the birth.

Now we move forward to 1540 and to a moment in time when Cromwell finally overstepped the mark. The situation with France and Spain was becoming increasingly tricky, so Cromwell decided that it would be a good idea for England to form an alliance with one of the new Protestant North German states, and the easiest way of doing this was to marry Henry off to a German princess. This was a dangerous course of action as Henry hated people interfering in his personal life, but Cromwell sent the painter Hans Holbein to Cleves to make a small portrait of Anne of Cleves in the hopes that Henry would choose to marry her.

Holbein must have wanted to please his King, so he made the poor girl look very pretty, and it worked because Henry was captivated by the portrait. The all important betrothal, or perhaps actual marriage, took place in absentia, but when Anne arrived in London, Henry took one look at her and decided he couldn't go through with it. She was plain and she couldn't speak any of the languages that Henry spoke, so it would be impossible for him to have any kind of relationship with her. Henry swiftly annulled the marriage. This situation, along with malicious whispers that his many enemies were putting out about supposed treachery, led to a fatal tragedy for Cromwell. To the delight of the Howard family, of which Anne Boleyn had been a member, Henry now married Katherine Howard, and he did so on July 28th 1540, which was the day of Cromwell's execution.

* * *

This much is fact, but now we bring the fictional Sir Thomas Hatherleigh into the picture in his position of Sir Thomas Cromwell's head spymaster. We show how Sir Thomas Hatherleigh had nothing to do with the destruction of the monasteries, due to being out of the country when Cromwell set this up, and he also had nothing to do with the execution of Anne Boleyn. Thomas was far from squeaky clean by our standards, but he wasn't vicious or unreasonable. His job was to keep the country safe from foreign and domestic terrorism, and that's what he did. In 'Sophie's Inheritance', we see that, when Cromwell was condemned, Thomas was also due to be executed, partly because of his association with Cromwell, but also perhaps because he had too much insider knowledge of Henry's affairs.

* * *

When we reach the second book, 'Lucy's Dilemma', we see how magnanimous Henry becomes during the Abbey affair, when he learns that Thomas and his friends saved Henry's life, but we also see how law and order is breaking down in Tudor England, with Carlo and Lucy getting the rough end of that situation.

By the time we reach the third book, 'Emily's Mistake',

we visit another country and another era; we also return to Tudorland and meet Thomas's cousin, Sir Francis Diall which shows us how by the mid-1540s, the wheels of state were coming right off, and how close the country was to revolution, but we leave Francis in Tudorland, keeping an eye on his family and spending weekends with his lover, Jannie. This situation is too difficult to maintain for long, but the solution to that problem will doubtless come about in another book; likewise with the investigation into the 'is he or isn't he a spy' issue at the Home Office, the Parmian satellite problem and more dealings with Tudorland and other places and other eras – maybe this time the Elizabethan court or the Spanish Armada – when your long suffering narrator, Sasha Fenton, gets down to it.

1:

Emily Borrows The Project

We travel, some of us forever, to seek other states, other lives, other souls.

ANAIS NIN

The Project shuddered, gave a little jiggle and came to a halt. Emily peered out of the window, but it was too dark to see anything. She'd timed the arrival of the machine for ten in the morning, so it appeared that the Project must have landed inside some kind of building. Wondering if she'd bitten off more than she could chew, Emily briefly considered abandoning the whole potty idea in favour of turning tail and going home.

'Don't be such a wimp;' she told herself, 'you're here now, so you might as well take a look.'

Emily stepped out of the car and immediately saw why it was so dark – the Project had landed inside a cave, but when looking around, she could see a distant source of light coming from her right. The air in the cave was warm and dry, but she could feel the heat increasing as she walked towards the light. She was so busy focusing on the light that she tripped over an uneven rock that jutted up from the floor of the cave, bashing her shinbone as she fell. Emily sat up and swore quietly to herself while she rubbed her shin and inspected the hole the rock had left in her trousers, but apart from the trouser damage, there didn't seem to be much to worry about, so she decided to carry on with her mission.

There were several dark blue barrels stacked near the cave entrance and as soon she'd passed them, she found herself out in the open air. The landscape was reminiscent of the programmes she'd seen on television about the area, as it was rocky with a few scrubby bits of bush and a range of golden hills in the distance. The sun was so fierce that she wished she'd thought to bring her sunglasses. Once outside the cave, she noticed several more barrels stacked in the shade of a nearby rocky outcrop, but as Emily began to walk away from the cave, a loud 'whump' was immediately followed by the sensation of the ground shaking beneath her feet.

For a moment, Emily was too stunned to work out what was happening, bur before she could make sense of anything, a strong pair of arms grabbed her from behind, lifted her bodily and dropped her, none too gently and face down, into a foxhole, after which, the owner of the arms climbed in and settled himself on top of her. Emily registered the smell of warm man, along with the slightly spicy aroma of an unfamiliar type of soap.

Emily gasped and tried to push the man off her.

The man spoke in an urgent and somewhat angry tone, Emily had no idea what he was saying, so stupidly perhaps, she asked the guy if he spoke English – and to her relief, he did.

'Stay down woman, they're tossing mortars over!'

Emily tried to twist around and get a look at her captor in an effort to make sense of the situation, but the man merely hooked his chin over her shoulder and pushed her back down. Emily was so frightened she couldn't speak, and worse still, she was extremely annoyed with herself because it was obvious that she'd keyed in the wrong data in on the Project's computer. Despite her attempts to push him off, her captor held her down even more firmly while shouting at her as though she was a stupid child.

'Keep your head down if you don't want to get us both killed! Those barrels contain gasoline and if a mortar hits them, our only chance of survival is to stay in this trench and hope the burning fuel flows *into* the cave rather than in our direction.'

It occurred to Emily that if the cave became filled with blazing fuel, her chances of getting home would be kippered.

'Who are you? Where am I? What's going on?' cried Emily, realising she must sound positively demented.

Giving her the benefit of the doubt, the man said, 'To answer your questions in the order given, I am Sergeant Shimon Sobieski of the *Israel Defence Force,* and in case you hadn't noticed there's a war on.'

'The Six-Day-War, I take it,' said Emily.

'The what?'

'What year is this?'

'1967 of course. What year did you think it was?'

'June 1967, is that?'

'Yes, of course.'

'What's the actual date?'

'The ninth.' Shimon wondered whether the mortar blast had given the girl concussion. She seemed very disorientated.

'Blast!' said Emily. 'Double blast!' Her keying in had definitely misfired, because it was obvious that she had arrived in Israel *during* the bloody war instead of after it. She suddenly realised with horror that she could get killed

18

here, and she wished she'd had the sense to double-check the date *before* pressing "enter" on the Project's computer. Meanwhile, another mortar landed but it seemed a little further away. Emily was shaking so hard by this time that she wondered how her captor managed to stay on top of her, but he merely repeated his instruction to stay down and didn't shift one inch from his position.

Emily noticed that the guy's voice was lightly accented, so she supposed his first language was Hebrew, but with a name like Sobieski, it could just as easily have been Russian, Polish or something. He'd pronounced his first name 'Shim*on*'. Was that Russian or was it Israeli? Also, he'd pronounced the "o" in Sobieski as in "hot" rather than as in "coat".

Another mortar 'whumped' but it sounded even further away than the last. Even so, her captor-turned-saviour continued to press her firmly into the bottom of the trench, with her nose now digging into the sand. His right arm was curled around her body and his hand happened to land on her right breast, making her jump when his thumb gave her nipple a speculative brush. Now, in addition to being so terrified that her teeth were actually chattering and furious with herself for her data-entry error, she was getting seriously irritated by Sergeant Shimon Sobieski.

'Saucy monkey!' she said. Even those two words were an achievement with a mouth dry with shock and hampered by the sand that was doing its best to work its way between her lips.

Shimon raised his head and looked around while listening for the sounds of battle.

'It looks as though they've moved off so I'll have to get back to my men, but before I go, I need you to tell me who you are and what you're doing here.'

Emily had to think quickly, and on balance, she was

19

pleased with the story she concocted.

'My name is Emily Cromwell, and I came from England to visit my friend who lives in the next village, but I hadn't realised that there would be fighting in this area, so I guess I became a bit disorientated with the shock of it.'

'I suppose that makes some sense,' replied Shimon, not commentating on the fact that the only habitation within miles was an ancient monastery.

Shimon climbed out and sat on the edge of the trench while taking a good look at Emily. Scruffy and sandy as she was, he saw a pretty girl in her early twenties with a mass of dark blond hair, eyes of an unusual golden shade and a really decent figure. She was wearing a pale green tee-shirt, tightly fitting navy cotton trousers with a rip in them and white sandals. Shimon decided that he wanted to know more about her, partly because he found all pretty girls interesting, but also because her story just didn't hang together.

Shimon contemplated taking Emily with him, but he knew he'd soon be too busy to take care of a passenger, and even if Emily turned out to be some kind of Mata Hari, there wasn't anything in the area she could damage apart from a few oil drums. Common sense and intuition told Shimon it was unlikely that Emily posed a threat, so he decided to leave her where she was. He did briefly contemplate how she could have arrived in the area and even whether she had some kind of vehicle hidden in the cave, but he really didn't have time to think about it.

'Look Emily, I have to go now, but when the fighting is over I'll be back with my unit. I can usually be found in the Whisky a Go-Go nightclub late on a Saturday night. It's near the King David Hotel in Jerusalem so come and find me there and we'll get properly acquainted. You can even buy me a beer in gratitude for saving your life.'

Looking at Shimon properly for the first time, she saw a slim tall soldier with very blond hair, a happy smile that dimpled his cheeks and gave him a boyish look, and a pair of sparkling blue eyes in a lightly tanned face. He certainly was a cheeky one and he looked like fun, but soon she would be back in her own time and place and she would have neither the desire nor the opportunity to search out Sergeant Shimon Sobieski in his Jerusalem nightclub. She merely nodded her head and watched him while he gathered up his rifle and strode away.

Emily clambered out of the trench and stumbled into the cave as fast as her wobbly legs would take her, promising herself she'd never leave home without a torch or a pair of sunnies in future. She also admonished herself for not thinking of the roll of safety rings in the Project's glove compartment. If she'd put one of them on, all she needed to do when she heard the first mortar was flip open the jewelled top, press the little red button inside and let it whisk her back to the Project.

'The safety ring is a great idea,' she admonished herself, 'and it would have been an even better one if I'd actually thought of using the sodding thing.'

She could still hear mortars in the distance, along with an insistent rat-a-tat sound that she took to be machine gun fire, but the fighting seemed to be moving further away. Her slow progress was getting on her nerves, but she soon reached the Project and clambered gratefully back into it. At least she'd had the sense to leave the Project on standby, so all she had to do was to tap the spot on the tablet that said "Mews" to get back to her own place and time.

The Project landed back in the Mews in darkness, and thankfully, everything was quiet, so Emily used her key to slip out through the side door without being noticed. The security cameras didn't cover the old doorway because it was thought to be redundant, but they did register someone walking away from the warehouse, and this triggered a warning on a distant computer. Emily knew nothing about this while hurrying down the alley to her car.

Back at her flat, Emily re-ran her adventure in her head, firmly telling herself to forget the intriguing Sergeant Sobieski, because even if she would now never forget what life was like in a slit trench under mortar fire, the fact was that she already had enough on her plate. She was in the middle of a course in modern history at the Central London University, and she'd been doing all right up to now, but she was finding the history of modern Israel confusing and hard to grasp, so she'd decided to take a trip back in the Project to see if she could discover anything useful about the Six Day War. Her problem had been that while she'd intended to land there on the *twenty-ninth* of June – which was *after* the war had ended, she'd missed the two off when keying in the data and had landed there on the *ninth* and thus in the middle of the war.

Sir David Cromwell had been the Director of the counter-terrorism and counter-espionage agency known as "TUDOR" before being given the job of running the much larger *British Bureau of Investigation*. TUDOR differed from other agencies in several respects. It was small and not overburdened by bureaucracy, and its agents could operate at home, abroad, with other agencies or independently. However, the main difference between itself and other organisations was its amazing secret – which was the acquisition of a technical innovation called the Project. The first Project had now been cloned into several others of different kinds, but all were time and space machines that could transport TUDOR agents wherever they were needed in a matter of minutes.

Most of the Projects were housed on the TUDOR

complex in Devon, but a couple of small ones that were used as shuttles lived in the workshop behind the Mews. Among them was the original Project, which was housed in an old Peugeot estate, and it was this one that Emily had borrowed. This wouldn't have been remotely possible but for the fact that her Uncle had given Emily the key to the old side door, and he'd done so way back before the Projects or anything else of a secret nature had been in the Mews.

* * *

Emily was doing well at college, but her personal life was a wasteland, so when the term ended and loneliness descended yet again, she decided to give herself a bit of fun by visiting 1967 Jerusalem to see if she could find the Whisky a Go-Go, and maybe even come across her golden haired sergeant. She considered that, while it was unlikely that she *would* find him, it would at least be an interesting trip.

She prepared herself by downloading maps of Jerusalem and by shopping around on the Net for old Israeli Lira and old US Dollar notes of the era. She checked for fashions for 1967 and discovered they weren't too different from what she could find in the shops now, so she dipped into her savings to buy herself a dress that wouldn't look out of place. The deep blue lightweight polyester had a slight brocade effect, which worked well on the fitted bodice and a tulip-shaped skirt that ended a couple of inches above her knees. A pair of navy blue, pointy stilettos and a small handbag completed the ensemble.

A few days later, Emily drove to the Mews and parked in the alley behind the workshop. Unbeknown to Emily, the CCTV at the back of the workshop had been replaced, and now it triggered an alert, which was picked up by someone who happened to be working late in the nearby Millbank offices.

2:
The Whisky-A-Go-Go

I don't know anything about music. In my line, you don't have to.

Elvis Presley

The Whisky-a-Go-Go was large and nicely decorated, and the dance floor filled with people moving to the music. Some were couples, but there were also groups of women bobbing up and down. The music was more melodic than in a modern club and the people were of various ages, with some of the older ones doing complex steps that Emily recognised as the jive. The place wasn't the least bit seedy and it looked like fun. When the music came to a stop, a voice announced something in Hebrew and the floor filled with people forming lines. They danced a group cha-cha-cha, turning and moving as one, with the fluidity and confidence of those who knew the steps well. Lucy watched the dancers for a while, but when they'd finished their routine and returned to normal dancing, she moved on.

Nobody in the club looked remotely like Shimon – but she hadn't really expected that had she? She'd already come to the conclusion that even if she found someone who knew him, they'd be sure to tell her that A) Shimon hadn't been seen for weeks, B) he only came to the club when there was a 'Z' in the month, or C) he was busy getting married to a supermodel. She was getting close to giving up her cockamamie mission and returning to her own era, when she decided to try the bar area for luck, then if nothing happened, at least she'd treat herself to a drink before going home.

She couldn't see a bar in the big room, but there had to be one somewhere, so making her way past groups of chattering people, she ventured further into the club, soon spotting an area off to the right that had small tables and chairs dotted about and a long bar at the back. When she got closer, she saw two long, curved banquettes against the far wall, each fronted by a large table and many chairs. The banquettes and seats were filled with young men who were talking, laughing and drinking beer from bottles. Some of the men were in uniform while others were casually dressed. The first group contained about a dozen guys, but none had fair hair, so she made her way towards the second group, which was closer to the bar, where the music was less intrusive. There was an even larger group of men sitting with their backs to her, but none looked remotely like Shimon, but then for one brief moment, Lucy caught a golden flash of light bouncing off a blond head at the back. The thought of approaching this gang of lads was more than she could cope with, so she stood rooted to the spot with her heart banging against her ribs. Pulling herself together, Emily told herself she'd gone through too much of a performance merely to scuttle away without a quick peak, so she edged towards the banquette.

At that moment, two men whose backs were towards her leaned away from each other, and a pair of smiling blue eyes rose up to meet hers.

'Emily!' exclaimed Shimon, 'you found me!'

Shimon's friends turned around to give Emily the once over. In this land of short, square bodied, hairy legged, brunettes who spent much of their time in army uniform, this tall fair haired girl with creamy skin, golden eyes and long legs, who was wearing an elegant London dress, was a true rarity. His friends concluded that as usual, it was Shimon who'd found the only truly hot-looking woman in the city that night. They continued to gape while Shimon worked his way off the banquette and walked slowly over to Emily, taking her into his arms and kissing her softly on her lips.

'Fancy a drink?' he asked.

Truth to tell, she needed a bit of Dutch courage, so she asked for a vodka and tonic. 'Do they have vodka in Israel?'

Shimon couldn't help laughing at her question.

'In a country, full of ex-Polaks and Russkies, what do you think?' He gave Emily a quick cuddle. 'Tell you what, rather than have whatever rubbishy vodka the barman wants to push, I'll get you a glass of Wyborova with lots of ice and a touch of water. It'll be interesting to see what a well brought up English girl makes of it.'

'How do you know I'm well brought up?'

'It's obvious.'

Shimon took Emily's elbow and guided her to the bar where they perched themselves on stools. Shimon ordered Emily's drink and a lemonade for himself.

'You don't drink?' she asked.

'I've had a couple of beers and I'd rather pace myself for the moment.'

Emily tasted her vodka. Her first conclusion was that the Polish drink had none of the harshness of Stolly or even the slightly rough edge of the far smoother Smirnoff – indeed, the Polish vodka slid down her throat like Devon cream. As she smiled in appreciation, a little of the vodka glistened on her lips and Shimon bent forward and licked it off. A rush of desire shot through Emily, catching her breath. She could feel her mouth falling open and her face reddening.

Emily hadn't given much thought to conversation, so she decided to stick to her cover story of coming to Israel to visit a friend, and then taking a little time to look around the country. She decided on the truth as far as possible, barring the teensy-weensy fact that she actually lived fifty years in the future.

Emily told Shimon about the illness and death of her mother and how later, she had used her small inheritance to rent a flat, buy a small car and enrol in University. She told Shimon her studies had made her want to look at the politics of modern Israel.

Shimon told Emily that his parents had originally lived in a small town called Sokolow-Podlaski in Eastern Poland, and that he and his sister had been born there. They'd survived the first couple of years of the Second World War because they were in the Russian zone rather than the area that the Germans had taken over. When the Germans eventually rushed in, the Sobieski family used their blond looks to pass as Poles, which had allowed them to survive, because if the Germans had realised they were Jews, they wouldn't have lived. Shimon said that his parents, sister and her family now lived in a pretty village near the Sea of Galilee.

Emily thought it weird to hear a name she'd only heard of in the context of Sunday school being a place where ordinary people spent their lives, so she resolved to see more of this fascinating country one of these days.

Shimon told her that when he left school, he decided against a desk job or work on a farm, and he'd joined the army. He knew he would be called up for National Service

28

sooner or later, so he decided to get in early and make it his career. His mother wasn't entirely happy with his decision, but she understood it. Shimon had also taken up further studies as he went along, so he understood Emily's desire to catch up with missed study, but now that the short war was over, he was back with his usual unit in Jerusalem.

'You say your parents are both fair haired and blue eyed. How does that happen? After all, when I look around in this club, most people have brown hair and some have really dark complexions.'

'Jews have been around for a very long time Emily, and many influences have crept in over the years. A child is deemed Jewish as long as his mother is a Jew, so if a woman becomes pregnant through rape or from an affair, the child is still Jewish. It's unusual for two such fair people as my mom and pop to meet and marry, but it just happened that way. We think part of our bloodline might have been Teutonic, Germanic, Swedish or some such thing, but as far as I know, my family has always been Jewish, so only the good Lord himself knows how a load of Krauts and Swedes managed to get their blood into our good Jewish veins.'

'What about religion though? Poland is a catholic country isn't it. Surely your parents couldn't have practised their religion during the war.'

'My parents behaved as though they were catholic, going to church and doing everything as the locals did, and my sister and I were both confirmed into the church.'

'Crikey!'

'My parents had been observant Jews before the war, but they realised they'd have to lay their religion aside in order to survive, so they taught Rivka and me everything they knew about Judaism in secret. In a way made the Jewish religion and its rituals more interesting than they might otherwise have been.

It occurred to Emily that she was having enough of a problem with just *one* rather large secret, so Shimon and his family must have been amazingly disciplined to cope with life under the Nazis.

Neither of them wanted any more to drink, so Shimon took Emily's hand and led her to the dance floor.

Emily found to her delight that Shimon was a good dancer, happily showing her how to dance the jive, the twist and other moves that were already passing into history in the late 1960's. Emily soon picked up the steps and had a great time, but when the music slowed and Shimon took her into his arms, she seemed to slide into a place that felt just right for her. Being close to Shimon was a disconcerting phenomenon – familiar but also new and exciting. Back at the bar after their dance, Shimon ordered orange juice for them both, along with some olives and a few small cheese biscuits. Emily offered to pay, but he waved her away, and soon they were back on the subject of religion.

'You say your surname's Cromwell. Wasn't there a Cromwell who brought in a severe form of Protestantism and cut off a King's head?'

'Yes indeed. That was *Oliver* Cromwell. He lived in the 17th century, but in the previous century, his great uncle, Sir *Thomas* Cromwell had been the First Minister to Henry the Eighth. Thomas started life as a Catholic, but became a Protestant in 1534 when Henry the Eighth declared himself the head of the English church. I am descended from both Cromwells, and while my uncle and his wife were catholic, my father isn't into religion at all, and neither was my mother, although they sent me to the local Church of England Sunday school so I would understand the nature of Christianity. I guess my official status is protestant, but I can't say I know anything about Judaism.'

'Well, fortunately we don't need to know anything about

it to dance at the Whisky a Go-Go, so let's have a final dance before I see you home. Where're you staying?'

Emily told Shimon that she intended to book herself into the King David Hotel for a night. Her real intention though, was to go into the hotel, wait until the coast was clear and slip out again before making her way to the car park. That would have been fine, but Shimon was determined to scupper her plans.

'The King David is horrendously expensive, so why not stay with me tonight? I've got two bedrooms, so your virtue will be safe.'

Shimon ignored Emily's protests, tucked her hand firmly under his arm and led her outside to his jeep. A short journey brought them to a small, square, white-painted house, whereupon Shimon ushered Emily into a cosy sitting room, brightened by colourful rugs spread over a terracotta-tiled floor. It had a kitchenette to one side. Shimon made coffee and took a cake down from a cupboard, but no sooner were they tucking into the cake than a banging noise outside the house put Emily in mind of the mortar attack by the caves. Shimon went to look out of the window and when he turned back, even in the low lamp light, Emily could see that his face was ashen. Shimon walked quickly to the back of the house and peered out of the bedroom window. It seemed that a group of hooligans were using the house as a shield while they tried to get at a second gang who were in the front. It seemed as though the house was now in the crossfire of some kind of turf war, and Shimon and Emily were about to get the worst of it.

'I have my pistol,' said Shimon looking around wildly, 'but I can't fight them all off at once. This is only a small house and the walls are thin, so it won't take much to destroy it. Worse still I wouldn't be able to summon help in time.' Shimon ran his hand through his hair. 'I'm so sorry Emily. It looks as though we're going to die in this mess. I wish to God I'd never brought you here!'

'We're bloody well *not* going to die!' yelled Emily, while her brain started to kick in. She asked, 'Do you have a special place where you keep important papers and stuff like that, Shimon?'

Shimon pointed to a side table and a battered metal box file that was parked under it.

'Grab it and keep hold of it.'

A startled Shimon did as Emily asked, and though so frightened that she could hardly think, Emily managed to get Shimon to tuck his arms round her and grip the handle of his box file in both hands behind her back, while she grabbed her handbag and wound her arms around him. They could hear the insistent sound of guns and another 'whump' as a mortar fired, but then dust and heat engulfed them as the side wall blew in and Shimon's gas cooker exploded. Fire raced across the ceiling and it looked as though Emily and Shimon were about to be cooked.

Emily spoke urgently to Shimon. 'I want you to stay exactly where you are and trust me completely.'

Without any other option on offer, Shimon did exactly as he was told while Emily sent up a heartfelt prayer and shifted her hand so it rested on the safety ring. She flipped open the jewelled cap and felt for the tiny button hidden beneath, and when her finger landed on it, she pressed firmly down.

The room went black, a rushing, whirling motion took hold and a few moments later, they were in the King David car park. Emily opened the car door and shoved a totally bewildered Shimon into the driver's seat, while running round to the passenger seat and climbing in. She opened the glove compartment, flipping the tablet down and watching its glowing screen come to life. Then she tapped her finger onto the word 'Mews', and with a slight whirring sound, the world went black as the Project carried them away from danger.

3:

Back To The Mews

If there are no stupid questions, then what kind of questions do stupid people ask? Do they get smart just in time to ask questions?

SCOTT ADAMS (AUTHOR OF THE DILBERT COMIC STRIP)

'What the hell....' yelled Shimon. He was both terrified and bewildered, and for the first time in his life, he couldn't believe his own eyes – or any other part of his body for that matter. Emily was slightly better off because she knew what was happening, but the whole evening had been so disconcerting that she doubted she'd ever be the same again. They both stayed where they were for a moment, but then Emily motioned to Shimon to grab his document case, while she plucked a small torch from the car's side pocket. She took Shimon by the arm and started to walk towards the old side door – but then the lights came on!

Leaning elegantly against the wall by the door was an extremely handsome, dark haired man in his mid-forties – and he was levelling a pistol at Emily and Shimon. His eyes glittered with fury.

'Emily!' exclaimed the man. He knew someone had taken the Project and he hadn't known what to expect, but

Emily's name wouldn't have been at the top of his list. He nodded at Shimon without taking his eyes off Emily. 'Who's your friend?'

'Hello to you too, Tom,' sighed Emily. This is Sergeant Shimon Sobieski of the Israel Defence Force, circa 1967. And believe me, I never intended for him to come here or to know anything about this.'

She waved a hand in Thomas's direction and introduced him to Shimon. 'This is Thomas Hatherleigh, Director of TUDOR. The name is an acronym for something like, '*Against Terrorism and Unprecedented Danger to Our Realm.*' Needless to say, TUDOR is a branch of the British security services, and the vehicle you've just travelled in is a time and space machine. Oh, and the current year is 2019.'

There were dozens of questions whizzing round in Shimon's head, but he knew enough about the security service mind-set not to open his mouth. Meanwhile, Thomas picked up a chair and ushered the pair towards a small office. Once inside, he motioned Shimon behind the desk and signalled to Emily to take the visitor's seat. He put the third seat down in front of the door, leaning back in the chair with his long legs stretched out in front of him. His pistol was no longer pointing directly at Emily or Shimon, but it was clear that Thomas wouldn't hesitate to use it. Thomas's face was set and his icy eyes locked onto Emily's. He said nothing.

'Where do you want me to start, Tommy?'

Thomas raised an eyebrow.

'I suppose I'd better begin at the beginning.'

The eyebrow stayed up.

'Oh well…' sighed Emily with a slight shrug. She took a few moments to gather her wits and then began to tell her story.

'I am studying modern history at Uni, and thought was doing all right until my tutor asked for an essay on the Arab-Israeli conflict in general, and the Six-Day-War in particular – and I just couldn't figure it out.'

Now Shimon's eyebrow went up.

'I had moved into my Brentwood flat a while ago, I was going through the last of the boxes of stuff when I came across the key.'

Thomas's eyebrow came down and his eyes narrowed. 'Key?' he asked.

He still looked irate, but no longer on the verge of putting a bullet through Emily.

'My aunt and uncle had never trusted Miles, so they'd given me a key to this place in case I needed a bolt-hole. TUDOR was just starting up at the time and it was being run out of the Mews. Remember, this was before the workshop had been tacked onto the back and before the main office had moved to Millbank. There were no Projects or anything of a sensitive nature here then, so I guess Uncle David thought it would be okay for me to have the key to that old, unused side door in case I needed somewhere to run to in the middle of the night. In time, I forgot about the key, but when it turned up again, I found myself looking at it while I made up my mind to borrow the old Project and take a look at 1967 Israel. I mean you have so many lovely new Projects these days that I figured nobody would be bothered if I borrowed the old clunker for a while.'

Emily's admission sent Thomas's eyebrow back up.

'Anyway Tommy, the people who work for TUDOR may be the best techies in the world, but I'm a history student and I'm not the brightest star in the universe when it comes to maths or computers. I did fairly well though because I reached Israel all right, but I cocked up the data and landed there *during* the bloody war rather than after it.

I have to say that the Project behaved perfectly, because I told it to find a place of concealment and it tucked itself away in a cave, but when I got outside, I was nearly creamed by mortar fire.'

Neither Thomas nor Shimon said anything, but Thomas was looking marginally less angry.

'The next thing I knew is that someone grabbed me from behind, chucked me into a hole and climbed on top of me. When the man realised I was English, he stopped speaking Hebrew, changed to English, and told me to keep my head down. He stayed on top of me so I couldn't see him, and anyway, my face was stuffed into the sand at the bottom of the trench.' Smiling slightly at Shimon,Emily said, 'The man was Shimon, of course!'

'When the mortar fire moved away and I could speak, I told Shimon I was staying with a friend, that I hadn't expected the war to be active in that area, and that I was on my way to do a bit of shopping. He seemed to accept my story, so he went on to do what he had gone to the caves for, which was to get some petrol from one of the barrels by the entrance. Before he left, he told me he would be posted back to Jerusalem once the fighting was over and that I could find him in the Whisky a Go-Go club in Jerusalem late on any Saturday night if I wanted to.'

Emily looked around at Shimon and a few small bottles of diet Coke on the shelf caught her eye. She gestured to them and Thomas nodded, so she took them down and gave one to Shimon and another to Thomas. He set his bottle down on the desk, while Emily popped her lid and took a welcome draft. Her throat was dry from the dust stirred up by the explosions earlier that evening, also from her state of nerves and all the unaccustomed talking.

'At first, I had no intention of searching for Shimon... after all, the whole idea was completely crazy; but my term had come to an end and I suddenly felt very alone and very fed up, so I made the spur-of-the-moment decision to give myself a fun night out – my first ever!'

Emily ran a hand through her dusty hair. 'I didn't expect to find the club, let alone find Shimon, but I decided to treat myself to a new dress and give it a go. I bought some old Israeli money and some old US Dollars on the Net, borrowed the Project and aimed it at the car park of the King David Hotel. I chose that location because Shimon had said the club was near the hotel, and it was the only place in Jerusalem I'd heard of – apart from the Wailing Wall, that is. I figured I could ask someone in reception to call me a cab, but the receptionist told me the club was nearby and she gave me directions. When I got there, I could see it was a nice place with lots of people dancing around. I didn't see any sign of Shimon: but then I hadn't really expected to. Then I had a brainwave, because I figured that a group of squaddies were most likely to hang out near the bar, so I decided it was worth a look. I worked my way through the room telling myself that I'd probably end up buying myself a drink and calling it a day.'

'When I got to the bar, I saw loads of dark haired guys, but when two lads who had their backs to me leaned away from each other, I was able to see the guys on the other side of the table and I spotted the light bouncing off Shimon's hair. I knew it was him right away, and when he saw me, he not only remembered me but he seemed pleased to see me.'

Shimon nodded slightly.

'We danced and chatted and I must say that it was a very nice evening. When it ended, I decided to let Shimon walk me back to the hotel. I planned to hide out in the loo until the coast was clear, when I would slip out and fly home. Unfortunately, Shimon insisted that I stay at his house for the night. He told me the hotel was very expensive and that he had a spare bedroom.'

Emily stopped and took a deep swig of the coke. Shimon was trying to smother a grin.

'Of course, I weighed up the potential problems – the kind that men never need to consider – like that Shimon might knock me about and rape me. Well I had learned what that felt like when I'd been living with Miles, so I knew I could survive it.'

Thomas looked aghast. He spoke up at last. 'Christ Emily! I'd no idea…'

'No one did, Tommy,' snapped Emily, biting her lip to stop herself saying too much.

'My second thought was that I might catch an STD.'

'An STD?' asked Shimon, speaking for the first time.

'A sexually transmitted disease,' answered Emily.

Now Shimon looked shocked, but Emily ploughed on regardless.

'I knew that STDs of the 1960s could be treated with penicillin so I reckoned I could cope if the need arose. As far as pregnancy was concerned, I'd gone on the pill when I was with Miles because I hadn't wanted to bring a child into that nightmare, and I'd stayed on it because it seemed to suit me. Anyway, while I wasn't actually looking for a new boyfriend at that moment, I figured that if I happened to meet someone nice, being on the pill would be a good idea.'

Emily took another swig of her Coke and then looked to her right while thinking for a moment.

'Another possibility of course, was that Shimon was a homicidal maniac, but nothing he'd said or done pointed to him being anything other than a nice guy – albeit a saucy one. He also made a point of assuring me that if I stayed with him, my virtue would be guaranteed.' Emily's face suddenly brightened as she gave Thomas a grin.

'Well, I may not be an ace interrogator like you Tommy, but even I know prize bullshit when I hear it, so I figured the worst that could happen is that I'd get a decent shag out of the situation.'

By now, both Thomas and Shimon were trying not to laugh.

'What does that make you, Emily?' asked Thomas.

Emily shrugged while Thomas and Shimon gave up trying to hide their grins.

Emily wasn't finished though.

'When Mum got ill, I looked after her and took over the housework. Dad helped as much as he could but he wasn't always there. He had his work of course, and he sometimes needed to check on events overseas – like when those fossils turned up in Wyoming and those oversized dinosaurs were found in South America. There were also times when he vanished for no reason, and if I asked him where he'd been, he wouldn't give me a straight answer. He seemed so shifty at times that I wondered if he was seeing someone else, but that just didn't fit his character. He loved Mum dearly, so whatever he was up to, it was unlikely to be a woman. It struck me then that Dad had always tended to disappear at times for no obvious reason, so something weird must have been going on over the years, but I had enough to deal with, so I just left it.'

Thomas made a mental note to look into this, because in his experience, there was always a reason for secretive behaviour, but in the meanwhile, Emily had more to tell.

'After Mum died, Dad became very depressed and I needed to get away from it all, so I went to live with Aunty Helen and Uncle David for a while. I got an office job, and one night I went out with the girls from work and one of them introduced me to Miles. I can't say I fancied him or even liked him very much, but whenever I left work, he was waiting for me. He seemed very enamoured and very solicitous, texting me every day, offering help, buying coffee and flowers and being very understanding about my sadness. All that was seductive to someone who was as lost and bereaved as I was at that time. One day he took me to his flat, and I didn't know how to rebuff him. He'd been so kind, and it made me feel obliged. A few days later, he told me to move out of Aunty Helen's and live with him.'

Emily took another sip of Coke and looked directly at Thomas. She wasn't finished with her story and both men knew it, so they waited quietly for the rest to emerge.

'It was a big mistake. I was never comfortable living with Miles, and after a month or two, he started getting really moody. According to Miles, my clothes were wrong, my hair was no good, I cooked the wrong food and I didn't clean the flat to his satisfaction. He got worked up if I talked to friends at work – even female ones – and he constantly accused me of looking at other men. One day, I was chatting with the postman about a package that had been misdirected, and Miles actually accused me of bonking the bloody man – I mean he accused me of doing it right on the *doorstep!* After that, he pushed himself onto me whenever he wanted sex and he began to slap me around. I realised that being with Miles wasn't making me even marginally happy and that I was in a classically abusive relationship, so I stuffed some clothes into bin liners, called a cab and decamped to Aunty Helen's.

Emily was now looking somewhere into the far distance and smiling slightly, while reliving the situation.

'Miles came to her house a couple of days later to find me, and didn't hesitate to make a scene. He grabbed me by the hair and bashed my head against the hall wall, and he tried to intimidate Aunty, but unfortunately for him, that was the moment when Uncle David came home from work.

Uncle grasped the situation in an instant, and a moment later, he'd got Miles in some kind of wrestling hold and dragged him into his study. I don't know what he said to Miles, but a few moments later I heard the front door slam and I never saw or heard from him again. I couldn't thank Uncle David enough.'

Emily came back to the present, smiled, took another sip of Coke and finished her story.

'A couple of weeks later, the money came through from Mum's will, so I rented a flat and started my course at Uni. More importantly, I now had the space and the peace I'd needed to get over it all, so I could properly mourn the loss of my Mum, and cry the tears that had been blocked up in my heart for so long. I looked back on her life remembered the good times as well as the sad ones, and I slowly recovered the worst of my loss. It didn't take too long for me to recover from the Miles episode, though I knew I wasn't ready to get involved with other men, so despite the fact that men asked me out from time to time, I ignored them, put my head down and got on with my studies.'

Emily gazed at Thomas. She spoke very quietly, 'Truth to tell, Tommy, I don't know what it's like to go on a proper date. And I haven't been within a hundred kilometres of anyone I really fancy – until now – if you see what I mean.'

Shimon was experiencing a mixture of emotions. He felt sad for Emily, anger at the man who'd used her so badly, but also joy at her final revelation.

Thomas wasn't surprised at any of it. Sir David had long since told Thomas what a useless sod Emily's father had been to his daughter, and he knew Sir David hadn't liked or trusted Miles. When Emily told Thomas about the safety ring, he was concerned about the danger Emily and Shimon had been in, but also relieved that the safety ring had worked so well. Thomas got up, walked out of the office and locked the pistol away in the gun cabinet, sitting down again before turning to Shimon.

Shimon knew what was expected of him, so he told Thomas everything he'd told Emily about his parent's background but with one small twist. 'What I didn't tell Emily was that I'd reached the rank of sergeant four years ago, but then I was recruited into a different branch of the military, given the rank of lieutenant and later promoted to captain.'

Emily noticed that Shimon pronounced lieutenant in the British style as *'lef*-tenant'.

Shimon went on. 'When war seemed inevitable, the army needed men and women with regular army experience, and as any student of history knows, it's the sergeants who run an army in war time, so I asked for a temporary reinstatement at my old rank.'

Shimon smiled slightly at Thomas.

'Now that it's all over, and I've got a couple of weeks' leave before I return to my post in Jerusalem as *Captain* Sobieski.'

'So, what's your regular job?' asked Emily.

'Emily, take a good look at him,' said Thomas quietly. 'Most men can't bear to sit still while someone talks, especially if the speaker happens to be a woman. They wriggle, fiddle with things and can't wait to stick their oar in. Your Shimon sat there like a bloody cat with his eyes narrowed and ears on stalks. Haven't you worked it out yet?'

'I'm afraid to say it, Tommy, but I think I have.'

With one voice, Thomas and Emily said '*Mossad!*'

Shimon's mouth fell open, and Thomas's smile widened as he addressed Shimon directly. 'The real reason you wanted to take Emily to your house was to question her, wasn't it? You knew her story didn't hang together and you wanted to get to the bottom of it. Oh, I don't doubt a bit of nookie would have been a nice bonus and I can't blame you for that, but you were just as interested in screwing information out of her as... well, you know what I mean.'

Now it was Emily's turn to look surprised. She turned to Shimon. 'Is that true?'

'Guilty as charged, my love.' He sipped some of his drink before going on. 'The place where I saw you is called *The Caves of Boronia* and there's nothing for miles around other than an old monastery, so you couldn't have been visiting a friend or popping to the shops. My jeep was low on fuel and I knew there was a small dump there, but before I could siphon the gas into my vehicle, the mortars started up. I knew I'd be back in the thick of it before long and I had no means of coping with a prisoner, so my choices were either to shoot you or leave you where you were. I didn't think you posed much of a threat to a few barrels of gasoline, so I chose to leave you to your own devices. I never thought you'd turn up at the Whisky a Go-Go though, but when you did, I knew I needed to find out who you really are – but I could never have imagined this lot,' said Shimon with a wave of his hand.

Emily shuddered at the thought that Shimon might have shot her, while Thomas's expression and the slight lift of one shoulder showed that he would have done it without a qualm. Emily felt the blood drain from her face.

Thomas turned back to Emily. 'So, what are your plans now?'

'Well, I haven't had time to make any, but I suppose I'll stick Shimon in the *Brentford Travelodge* and go home. Tomorrow I'll ask if I can borrow the Project and drop him back at the King David.'

'Why not take him to your flat? Your term is at an end, isn't it? You've both been through an ordeal, so why not

44

show Shimon around the 21st century in general – and your bedroom in particular. You can dump him back in Israel in a couple of weeks' time, and still arrive there the morning after you left – assuming you've discovered how to enter a date in properly.'

'Sarky bugger,' muttered Emily, pulling a face. 'Learned how to enter a date properly – and show Shimon round my bedroom indeed.'

Thomas gave Emily a wicked grin, while Shimon smiled happily.

'Look, I'd like to talk to Shimon again and I know Sir David would love to meet him, and he'll want to thank Shimon for looking after you. Why don't you both come to Millbank on Wednesday morning at ten, and I'll invite Sir David over from the BBI for a little chat.'

Both Shimon and Emily knew this was more than a mere suggestion.

Thomas left the office and returned a few moments later carrying a backpack. 'This is one of our men's emergency packs, Shimon. The underwear should fit and it contains men's toiletries and an electric shaver. You can keep the backpack.'

Then he handed a pile of banknotes to Emily, and when she saw how much was there, she remonstrated.

'Don't be daft, Emily love. Shimon will need clothes; and getting around London isn't cheap. You'll need to buy in kosher food and pickled cucumbers, too. God's teeth Emily, Sophie can drop £500 in Waitrose when her friend Margie and my sister Kate and all their kids come over.'

'Blimey,' muttered Emily. Her entertainment budget stretched to a large pizza and a couple of bottles of discount plonk.

'Now take your little friend home and sin no more,' said Thomas.

'Piss off, Tommy,' replied Emily cheerfully.

'Nice way to talk to the Director of the Home Secretary's favourite security service,' laughed Thomas, giving Emily a hug. 'I'll have that key though... and the safety ring if you don't mind. And next time you fancy time travelling somewhere for a quick history lesson, ask Sophie first.'

* * *

Emily drove over the bridge onto Brentford Dock, which, despite its down-market name, is a pretty island in the Thames with almost seven hundred attractive flats and houses on it. She parked in her usual space and walked Shimon over to one of the low-rise blocks.

'The flat's got a decent kitchen and a balcony off the sitting room. There's my large bedroom and a smaller one for a guest, but even that is a good size. The island is very pretty, and I'll show you round it tomorrow.'

Emily pointed to the guest room, but left Shimon in the living room while she headed to the bathroom to shower away the grit and dust from earlier that evening. She was luxuriating in almond scented shampoo and lather when she became aware of a warm body fitting itself around her and a pair of strong arms winding around her middle.

'Kerrrrrrist, Shimon!' she cried, 'Haven't you had enough excitement for one day?'

Shimon showered himself and Emily before swinging her up into his arms and carrying her into the bedroom.

'Your friend has saved me the job of questioning you.' said Shimon. 'So, all that remains is to conclude the unfinished part of the business... now that you've met someone you *really* fancy.'

'Cheeky monkey,' laughed Emily happily.

4:

Religion And Politics

It is wonderful how much time good people spend fighting the devil. If they would only expend the same amount of energy loving their fellow men, the devil would die in his own tracks of ennui.

HELEN KELLER

The TUDOR team sat around the boardroom table and scrutinised Shimon, while Thomas introduced the young soldier and told them a little about him. As it happened, Sir David wasn't able to be at this meeting, but Thomas and Sophie had decided to introduce Shimon to the team anyway. His presence led to a discussion about twenty-first century Israel, and this brought several sniffs of disapproval. Sophie put a hand on Shimon's forearm, saying quietly to him in Yiddish, '*Los es sein*', which means 'let it be'. Then, she spoke to her colleagues about the confusing situation.

'When it comes to Jews, people tend to mix up three different matters' said Sophie, 'these being Judaism, the Jewish people and The State of Israel. In years gone by, people thought that if a Jew converted to Christianity, he would become acceptable because it was his status as a "non-believer" that made him a pariah. Benjamin Disraeli is a good example, because it was only after his father converted to Christianity that his family could get ahead in politics. By the latter part of the 19th century, Darwin's discoveries made people begin to look at race and ethnicity rather than faith, and while this is a more accurate measure of Jewishness, it brought another set of problems that eventually led to the genocide of our people in the 20th century.'

My mother suffered from quite severe anti-Semitism when she was a small girl at school, and she said that it was particularly painful to be a five-year-old schoolchild whose classmates hated her on sight and blamed her for "killing Jesus". She didn't know what had made her different from them, and she had no idea who this Jesus person was. How could she? Nobody talked about Jesus in her parents' household and she certainly hadn't killed anyone. She was just a rather small and timid five-year-old, and she'd never met the man they were accusing her of killing. None of it made any sense – not then and not later either, when she began to be blamed for a place she knew nothing about – Israel.

'As far as the State of Israel is concerned, like most secular Jews in Britain I've never visited Israel, I have no relatives there and no special interest in the place. All I know is what I see on the telly and it doesn't always look good, but it also strikes me that the reports from the BBC are invariably biased against Israel, while Sky TV gives a more balanced view. However, I am the first to admit I don't know enough about the situation to make a balanced judgement, but I have read that Israel's policy is *defensive* rather than *offensive* – e.g. they aren't in the business of expansion, colonisation or taking over other countries. Their battles are predicated upon their need for survival.

Israel is small and its topography is long and narrow, so the Israelis always try to conduct their fights on *someone else's* territory rather than their own, and that doesn't go down well on the international newsreels. As far as I can see, they have been ruthless at times and the West Bank settlements are provocative and divisive, while those who attack them are by nature even more savage. However, do two wrongs make a right?'

'Added to this, people here think the population of Israel is entirely Jewish, but more than a third of Israelis are Arabs and there are actually two Arab parties in government. There are also Christians of every denomination and many other races and religions living there. Israel is a democracy with complete freedom of worship, and that makes their Arab neighbours uneasy, because an example of a modern parliamentary democracy sitting in the middle of their bailiwick don't suit them.

'There are also some weird misconceptions floating around – such as the bloke who I heard on a radio phone-in programme complaining that Britain should stop giving Israel "massive" financial support. I suspect the caller was confusing Israel with India, because Britain has *never* given financial support of any kind to Israel – massive or otherwise. We trade with Israel as we do with many countries, but it's a minute amount when compared to the trade we have with the oil producing countries.' And to finish my explanation, I doubt that every Jew in Israel agrees with the policies of the current government!'

You could hear a pin drop as the group digested Sophie's words, but then Raj spoke up.

'I know Sophie won't say much about this, but as a Muslim with Pakistani parents, I can tell you that even in this enlightened country, racism plays its part. I'm sure that being half Irish and half West Indian, Baz's wife Margie also knows this, as does "Martinique" Mike at TUDOR North. The holocaust is slipping into history and the old prejudices are re-emerging, and being such a small ethnic group and such a non-violent one, British Jews make an easy target.' Raj looked around the room and said, 'Do you know there are as many registered heroin users in this country as there are Jews? And that encompasses religious, secular Jews, and those married to non-Jews. There are twice as many Chinese and other eastern Orientals here as there are Jews – let alone the millions of Hindus, Pathans, Janes, Buddhists and Muslims.'

Sophie was surprised that Raj had gone into the subject so deeply, and she was grateful, but now she had something else to get off her chest.

'From what I have seen when looking into the situation in 1967, the majority of British people were firmly *behind* Israel in the Six-Day War. Anti-Semitism was at all time low here, while Britain saw a tiny nation, less than twenty years old, being attacked by a half a dozen large and powerful nations that were backed by a Soviet Union that was extremely hostile to the West at that time. Added to that, the protagonists also had the backing of all the extremely wealthy oil-producing countries.'

Sophie smiled for a moment before looking at the situation from the Israeli side. 'The event threw up several charismatic and magnificent figures though, such as Mordechai Hod, Moshe Dayan and those Mirage fighter pilots.' Sophie smiled gently, 'Although Yitzhak Rabin's froggy looks made him a lot less magnificent than the others.'

This brought a chuckle from the TUDOR team, but then Jack decided to end the discussion. 'Whatever we might think about politics of twenty-first century Israel, we can't blame them on Shimon. He's a member of his country's intelligence community in 1967 and he should be respected as such.'

Pushing the plate of biscuits towards Shimon, Jack waited until the others moved onto other topics before having a quiet word in Shimon's ear. 'I'd really love to come over to Israel for a visit – perhaps to your era. I've always wondered if those suntanned farm girls with strong thighs and short-shorts are as interesting as they look.'

Shimon couldn't help laughing while telling Jack that he'd tried a few of them himself and he would definitely agree about the thighs. 'It's all the scrambling up and down ladders and picking oranges that does it,' he said.

Jack crossed his eyes in feigned ecstasy while Thomas caught the whispered conversation and tried to pull off a disapproving look. He failed dismally, due to memories of the many girls he'd bedded during his time in the service of King Henry, including more than a few 16th century English farm girls with well-developed thighs of their own.

* * *

A few days later, Sophie was gazing at herself in her full-length mirror and she had to admit she looked good in her new dress. When Thomas spotted her and smelled her perfume, he wanted to abandon the party and take her straight to bed, but he satisfied himself with a deep sigh before getting on with the job of setting out ice buckets and bottles of Tattinger. Sophie set a large platted loaf on a board before placing a couple of bottles of kosher wine on the table. She fitted a pair of candlesticks with creamy candles, and laid a long silky scarf over the back of her chair. She was glad Thomas had insisted on buying such a large dining room table. She'd wondered why he was so keen on the idea at the time, but he'd reasoned that he'd always needed a large 'board' in Tudorland, so he was bound to need one now.

Sir David walked in, looking distinguished in his dark grey Savile Row suit and Lady Helen looked glamorous in a dark green velvet cocktail dress. The others drifted in and Thomas and Jack handed out aperitifs while Margie and Kate gave Sophie a hand with the food. When everyone was seated round the dining table, Sophie stood up.

'I'd like to welcome our friends, family and loved-ones to this eve-of-Sabbath meal, and I hope the Christians among us will enjoy the experience.' Turning to Shimon, Sophie said, 'I'm sorry to say that my Sabbath prayer won't be in your posh modern Ivrit, so you'll have to put up with my low-class Yiddish-accented Hebrew.'

'Same way my mum does it,' smiled Shimon.

Sophie gave a small nod, arranged the scarf around her hair, carefully lit the candles and waited to ensure they caught. Then she moved her hands in a curious gathering motion, as though collecting light and energy from the candles. She repeated the action twice more, then closed her eyes and covered her face with her hands, before reciting the Sabbath blessing, first in Hebrew, then in English.

'Boruch utoh adonoi elohenu melech ho-alom. Ushere kiddishenu vermitsvosov vertisivonu lahudlic nere shell Shabbat'

'Blessed art thou oh Lord, King of the Universe who has commanded us to light the Sabbath candles.'

Sophie dropped her hands and gave a small nod to Shimon who stood up, broke a piece of from the loaf and fluently chanted the blessing for bread in his beautiful Ivrit. Now he broke the rest of the soft springy challah loaf into pieces, setting the pieces on paper napkins and passing them to Steven to hand round. Shimon poured a good measure of wine, held up the glass and chanted the ancient blessing for wine before sending the glass around the table for everyone to take sip. Sophie was surprised at how quickly and easily their friends took to the ritual, but Thomas came up with an explanation.

Along with everyone else in England, Steven, Kate and I were Roman Catholics until 1434, and Sir David, Lady Helen and Val are modern Roman Catholics, so we're all familiar with this ritual as the act of communion. Baz, Margie and Jack are Protestant, but they have Catholic friends and relatives, so they are also familiar with the ceremony, while as Muslims, Raj and Janessa also have some understanding of both Judaism and Christianity.'

Shimon then amazed his friends by telling them that he'd lived as a Catholic for several years while growing up in Nazi occupied Poland, and he'd even been confirmed.

'God's teeth!' exclaimed Thomas, 'so you understand the Christian Mysteries?'

'I do indeed, my friend, but hopefully tonight the bread will stay bread and the wine will remain wine – because if they don't, we've all got a problem!'

When the friends had stopped laughing, Sophie said, 'With all these lapsed Roman Catholics in the room, is there anyone who can recite a Latin grace for us before we start on the chicken soup?'

Several hands shot up, including Shimon's, but Sophie chose Steven, because of his naturally priestly air.

Steven stood up, took a breath and intoned:

'Benedic, Domine, dona tua quae de largitate sumus sumpturi. In nomine Patre et Filii et Spiritus Sancti.'

Steven made the sign of the cross over the table and everyone said a hearty 'amen' before getting down to the serious business of eating, drinking and talking.

Shimon asked Sir David and Lady Helen whether they'd ever been to Israel, and they told him they'd taken a couple of holidays there and visited the Wailing Wall as well as the places that were holy to Christendom. Sir David also mentioned that he'd also visited the country several times on 'business.'

'I was also there on "business"', said Thomas.

'Really?' asked Sir David. 'When were you there?'

'I went to Jerusalem for your many-times-great-granddaddy Thomas Cromwell, in 1525, and I spent about a year and a half there. Thomas Cromwell wasn't First Minister then, but he was already involved in espionage and counter-espionage. I remember visiting the fortress Acre, the Abbey at Latrun and a big Crusader castle called Belvoir. There was a good deal of secret interaction between the Crown and the Ottoman Empire at that time and I remember several important meetings with the Turks in Jerusalem.'

'I guess the crusades were well over by then, but Turkey and the Byzantines were the big deals in the area, so that makes sense,' said Sir David thoughtfully.

'Do you speak Hebrew?' asked Shimon.

'Enough to get by, but the lingua franca of the area was Greek in those days, and sometimes Latin. I coped with the Greek well enough, but I speak Latin fluently, so that was often the easiest for me.'

Thomas could feel something lurking behind Sir David's eyes, so he quietly asked him what was on his mind.

David spoke quietly. 'I doubt that this is the last we'll see of Shimon, and I think TUDOR might have a little job for him before long.'

Thomas knew he'd hear more from his old boss when the time was right, but the familiar tingle of a coming adventure was sending sparks along his spine.

When the meal was over, Shimon offered to say grace, but Sophie pulled such a face that Baz asked her what was the matter.

'Have you ever heard the Jewish grace after meals, Baz?'

'What's wrong with it?'

'Nothing. Other than the fact that it's in Hebrew and it goes on for so long that you lose the will to live,' sighed Sophie.

'There's no need to suffer,' smiled Shimon, 'I'll just do the first verse – and in English at that. I wrote it out before coming here because I thought you might like it. And now that I've discovered this room is full of theology scholars, I know you'll appreciate it.'

'Fair enough,' said Sophie warily.

Shimon recited the opening psalm, and now that she was hearing it in English, Sophie was suddenly entranced.

'By the rivers of Babylon, there we sat and wept as we remembered Zion.

There upon the willows we hung our harps.

For there our captors demanded of us songs, and those who scorned us, rejoicing, saying,

"Sing to us of the songs of Zion."

How can we sing the song of the Lord on alien soil?

If I forget you, oh Jerusalem let my right hand forget its dexterity.

Let my tongue cleave to my palate if I will not remember you,

If I will not bring to mind Jerusalem during my greatest joy!'

This set Margie off, as she couldn't help breaking into the Boney M song, and soon Baz, Sophie, David, Helen and Emily were joining in the chorus. None of the Tudors had heard the song before and neither had Shimon, but it wasn't long before they too were clapping along to the lyrical melody.

'By the rivers of Babylon; there we sat down,
Yeah-eh we wept, when we remembered Zion.'

Helen, Emily, Kelly and Sophie kept up the chorus line while Margie's beautiful voice rose to carry the lead solo, smoothly taking on the African cadences of her Jamaican father. So, now another ancient culture permeated the room, as memories of suffering in the sugar plantations of the West Indies and the loss of an ancient African homeland were evoked.

The wonderful evening finally ended and Thomas called cabs for their guests. Soon he and Sophie were stacking the leftovers into the fridge.

'There's plenty left,' Thomas said.

'That's great, because it means I don't have to cook tomorrow.'

'Rosie's gone to her friend for the night,' said Thomas, his face taking on a mischievous expression.

'Oy vey? I might have known. I'm a bit tiddly Tommy, so I don't know what you'll get from me.'

'I like it when you're a bit drunk. Gives me a chance to try something different.' Thomas's blue eyes twinkled.

His loving spouse told him in no uncertain terms that he was a 'manipulative, Machiavellian, medieval monster', but it didn't deter him one bit.

All too soon, Shimon had to return to his own time and place and Emily needed to focus on her finals, dryly remarking between kisses that at least she now had a really good grasp of modern Israel. Shimon lay back and put her hand on his prick, telling her that she could grasp modern Israel any time she felt like it. Emily exploded in giggles before taking advantage of what was on offer. Emily knew she would miss Shimon dreadfully and she wasn't sure how she would cope without him, while for his part, Shimon knew his intelligence skills would be needed in the coming months, but he also knew that he'd feel like a rudderless ship without Emily at his side.

Soon Emily dropped Shimon back into his own place and time in the King David car park, and they kissed each other for the last time. Emily's last sight of Shimon was his golden hair, glowing in the lamplight before she powered up the Project and vanished into the night. Back at her flat, her heart was heavy and there was a nasty ache in her midriff. She tried telling herself this had been the equivalent of a holiday romance and that it was over. She told herself to be glad that something nice had happened at long last, but to put it into the past. However, before she turned her mind to the revising for her next batch of tests, she decided to pay a visit to her father.

5:

Steven Hears A Whisper

I am the wisest man alive, for I know one thing, and that is that I know nothing.

SOCRATES

When he heard a tap on his door, Thomas was surprised to find Steven in the doorway. The technical nature of Steven's job allied to his even temper meant that he was unlikely to bring petty matters to Thomas, so this had to be something important.

'Hello Steven. Problem?'

'Something's niggling me and I don't know whether it's important enough to bring it to your attention, but I thought…'

'Come in and sit down.'

Steven and Thomas headed to the casual corner of Thomas's office while Steven gathered his thoughts.

'You know that I run the GCHQ waveband in the background while I'm working – in the same way that Kate has the radio on while she's making dinner.'

'Yes, I do.'

'Well, I tune the chatter out for the most part, but this morning something caught my attention and… apparently

58

GCHQ picked it up somewhere, and...' Steven bit his lip for a moment. 'Sorry I'm being so vague.'

'Go on.'

'Someone mentioned Parmia.'

Thomas sat up. 'Parmia?'

Steven nodded.

'Anything else?'

'One of the messages mentioned a virus.'

'A *virus*? What, you mean a computer virus or something in the water or what?'

'Well, that's the problem, I've no idea, but I don't like the sound of *Parmia* and *virus* in the same message.'

'It might be something or nothing, but as you say, it's the combination of ideas that puts the hairs up on the back of the neck. Look Steven, keep your ears open and I'll get the lads to ask around.'

'Thanks Tom. I'd rather look a damned fool over a false alarm than discover it was important when it's too late.'

'Quite right. Get one of the youngsters to check the Net and see if anything shows up, and ask GCHQ to keep a sharp look out. You'll let me know if there's anything more on this one, of course.'

'I'll get young Julie to sit on the computer. She's got the patience for it.'

'Okay, Steven. Keep me posted.'

Thomas called Baz and Jack into the boardroom. 'Steven's heard something that's worrying him, and as you know, he's the last person to get his knickers in a twist for no reason. He hasn't got much to go on – assuming there *is* anything.'

Thomas gave them the gist of Steven's report and they agreed that they didn't like the Parmia/virus combination.

Baz said, 'I'll do a bit of legwork Tom. I still have a few contacts and it wouldn't hurt me to get out and about for a bit.'

Jack said he'd also look around a few old haunts and ask the techies to look around electronically. They agreed to meet in the boardroom the next morning and see what they'd got – assuming there *was* anything.

Something from Thomas's Tudorland days was ringing a bell, so he gazed out of the window at river traffic while trying to bring the memory into focus. In 16th century Tudorland there were hundreds of small ports where a man could come ashore unnoticed, but the small boats of those days weren't like today's ocean-going yachts, with their radio, radar, GPS and so on, so small boats couldn't navigate the oceans. Anyone coming in from afar would need to travel on an ocean-going ship, but even in those days, cargo and passengers had to clear customs before coming into the country.

The terrorist threats of 9/11, the liquid bomber, the underpants bomber and so on had all involved *airplanes*, but now things were moving to the sea, to railways and everywhere else, and did that make entry to the country by sea an easy option for terrorists?

He remembered a case in his early days in *'The Office of State Security for England and Wales'*, when a Burgundian gang had sailed in from the West Indies, bringing a box of wheat-eating insects and the intention of letting them loose in the fields of England. The ship's captain and crew had sensed that there was something wrong, so when the ship docked, the captain had sent a messenger to Thomas's office in Austin Friars to report his fears. It turned out that the insects hadn't survived the journey and couldn't have done any damage, but the intention had been evil, and that led Thomas to arrest the men, try them for treason and hang them. Thomas then remembered another case that was so horrifying that his staff, his Troopers and even the Yeomen of the Guard were still talking about it years later. It had involved a diseased corpse that someone had brought in for the express purpose of infecting the population. With all this milling around in his mind, Thomas strolled out to Ryan's work area, perched himself on his Personal Assistant's spare chair and told the young man what was on his mind.

'I've got a strange feeling that something or someone's coming in on a cargo ship. It's a hunch based on a couple of cases that I worked on back in Tudorland, and while it sounds crazy to link a modern case to something that happened nearly five hundred years ago, I still want to follow it up. I need you to contact the Port Authorities and ask them if anyone or anything has aroused their suspicion in recent weeks.

* * *

By the next morning, it was clear something *was* going on, and it was Baz who came up with the first tit-bit.

'The Asians in the Midlands are sick and tired of being turned over by the police every time there's a scare,' said Baz. 'They're actually coming forward and *offering* information – and telling us that this threat has nothing to do with the local Asian community. Parmia is being mentioned, along with one of those fanatic Irish groups, but the two situations may be unrelated.'

Thomas turned to Jack and raised an enquiring eyebrow.

'I've also heard about an Irish team,' said Jack. 'It seems they've joined a bigger team of anti-Brits, and I've also heard mention of Parmians and South Americans. The team seems to be gathering in the Midlands, but the target is London, and one of my informants thinks he knows what it might be.'

This made them all sit up.

'The idea is to drop a virus into the House of Commons during a debate on the economy,' said Jack. 'The House is always packed for those debates so it would do a lot of damage.'

'Well that gives us the where and when,' said Thomas. 'Anything about what the virus might be?'

Jack shook his head.

Thomas turned to Steven. 'Anything more from the airwaves, Steven?'

'Julie's picked up a few whispers, and GCHQ rang this morning. There's definitely a virus, and the idea is that it will be let loose here, although they haven't heard where or when. All I know is that the disease is coming from South America; possibly from Peru.'

Now Thomas told them about his Tudorland experiences of the insect case and the case of the diseased corpse. 'The woman had apparently died from the Sweating Sickness, and her body was wrapped in sacking and packed into the hold of a cargo ship sailing in from the Caribbean. The body was stored in a large lead-lined box and the crew hadn't been told about the contents, but when the ship reached Tilbury, the box was dumped in a brothel in Limehouse.'

'The Sweating Sickness used to break out during warm weather and disappear again when it got cooler, sometimes there wouldn't be any outbreaks for several years and then it would reappear for no apparent reason. Now that I have more knowledge of these things, I can see that each outbreak came in anew on ships from infected areas – normally unwittingly of course – but on that particular occasion, the disease had been *deliberately* imported. When the sickness broke out, King Henry buggered off to one of his country castles and much of the court scattered. The distraction allowed the Spanish to start a nice little war against some of our West Indian islands while King Henry and the government were distracted and away from the court – which of course, was the main purpose of the exercise.'

Thomas checked his notes. 'Anyway, on the off-chance that little has changed in the last half-millennium, I asked Ryan to contact the Port Authorities and amazingly, something's turned up. It seems that a ship came in from Chile last Tuesday, carrying a cargo of fruit and wine. These container freighters are huge, but they only need a small crew to operate them, and sometimes the ships also carry a few passengers. The crews quite like having passengers, because they give them someone different to talk to. It's an expensive way to travel, but there are people who prefer it to flying, and while cruise liners don't come to London from Chile, freighters do. In the case of the Chilean ship, there were three passengers, a middle-aged couple and a man in his late thirties. The couple seemed okay, but the man wasn't sociable and the crew felt uncomfortable about him, so they reported him. Apparently, the man had a Chilean passport, but the crew was certain that he wasn't Chilean.'

'Which port?' asked Baz.

Thomas gave a wry half smile. 'Tilbury.'

The room fell silent as the TUDOR team took in the implications. Thomas looked even more serious than usual, while both Baz and Steven were fiddling with their pens and chewing their lips in agitation, and at that moment, there was a light knock on the door and Kelly walked in.

Thomas raised an eyebrow. 'You're supposed to be on leave!'

'I've finished doing up the flat and I'm due back in a couple of days anyway, so I thought I'd come in early. To be honest, I'm getting bored at home, but that's not the real reason I'm here. You see, I heard something odd, and while I don't know how important it is, I felt I should come in and tell you.'

Thomas waved Kelly to a seat.

'You see Boss, I was on a girl's night out with a couple of friends from my old nick, and we were gossiping about work – or in my case, as much as I *can* gossip about. Then one of them said she'd heard a whisper about a *virus* being brought into the country, so I thought I'd better come in and find out if there was anything to it.'

At that moment, Baz's secretary popped her head round the door with a message for Thomas.

'The Home Secretary's on the phone, and she's not happy.'

'That's all I need,' sighed Thomas.

* * *

Frances Shulman liked being Home Secretary, but the position of Prime Minister would have suited her better. She knew for a fact that she could make a far better job of it than the long, tall, streak of piddle that was currently holding the position. For one thing, that cow, Angela Merkel, wouldn't put Mrs. Shulman in her place the way she did Simon Carlisle.

If Mrs. Shulman had met Margie, she would be even *keener* on the top job than she already was. Astrologer Margie had discovered that Mrs. Shulman's horoscope was almost identical to that of Margaret Thatcher, with the only difference being a few degrees of shift between their moon placements. Interestingly, Frances Shulman's moon in Cancer was even more *strongly* placed than Mrs. Thatcher's moon in Leo, and it clearly demonstrated the main difference between the lives of the two women. Mrs.

Thatcher's moon showed that she'd come into this world with a silver spoon in her mouth, while Mrs. Shulman's family had been as much help to her as a chocolate teapot. With a deep sigh, Frances Shulman accepted that for the time being at least, she would have to settle for her current position as Home Secretary – and she didn't settle easily for anything... Worse still, she became even more irritated when problems took her away from her usual day's work, which as she saw it, was to charm those who needed to be charmed to be smoothed over and terrify the rest.

Emson Barotse, Mrs. Shulman's beautifully dressed, smoothly urbane Permanent Private Secretary ushered Thomas into the 'presence'.

Thomas resisted the impulse to bow Tudorland style, while Mrs. Shulman took one look at him and came straight to the point.

'I hear some bastard's trying to poison us. What I don't hear is what *you're* doing to stop it.'

'We're looking for the perpetrators, Madam.'

'Well, bloody *find* them! And the sooner the better. We can't have this. Viruses in *Parliament?* It's not on!' The Home Secretary glared at Thomas. 'I hear this is the work of Parmians and South Americans or something. Didn't you get them all the last time? What do you lot do all day long? Make each other cups of tea?'

'The leader got away after the Westminster Abbey affair, Home Secretary. He's an Argentinean called Jose Lopez. We have no intel to suggest he's behind this job as well, but it may be so. Anyway, there's a new crew working out of Birmingham, so we're already working with the West Midlands police on this one, but they seem to think the terrorists have now moved to London.'

Slightly mollified, the Home Secretary said, 'If you want help from Five or any foreign governments, just let me know. Officially speaking, Argentina isn't keen on us since we blew up their terrorists' mountain hideaway after the Abbey nonsense, but unofficially, they don't want any more trouble. As long as we keep a low profile *inside* their country, they'll help all they can. Parmia is a different kettle of fish though – a law unto themselves and a potential threat to everyone.'

The Home Secretary picked up her notepad and scanned it quickly. 'If you get blocked or tied up in red tape, let me know and I'll get Emson to sort it out. If you need to send someone overseas, we'll bump up your budget. Do what you need to do first and worry about it later. The Chancellor of Exchequer will have a hissy fit if he thinks it'll cost money, but I'll sort him out; we all know the man's a wet.'

Not for the first time did Thomas wonder how her husband put up with her, but they appeared to be a happy couple. He left the building, muttering to himself, 'I guess there's a lid for every pot.'

6:

The Virus

I have never met a healthy person who worried very much about his health, or a really good person who worried about his own soul.

JOHN B.S. HALDANE

Thomas's meeting with Dr Prendergast of the *Health Protection Agency* wasn't easy. Prendergast was tall and skinny with a high-bridged nose, which he kept firmly stuck in the air. A few strands of mousey hair were spread carefully over a balding pate while a pale, pasty, pockmarked skin made up the unattractive whole. An overweight woman in her fifties, decked in an ill fitting grey-green tweed suit, assisted Prendergast by scrabbling around in a voluminous old-fashioned briefcase whenever he wanted something. Poor, fluttery Miss Crafthole was clearly ground down from years of working for her bullying boss.

Thomas waved Prendergast to a seat and told him as much as he could, asking the Doctor to tell him what health measures his office would recommend under the circumstances.

Prendergast decided to give Thomas a hard time. 'Do

you know what kind of virus this is?'

'Not yet,' replied Thomas.

Prendergast gave an irritated snort, while mentally deciding to bring his five-week Bavarian walking holiday forward and extending it thereafter until the threat has passed, but his first task was to show Thomas who was boss.

'It's obvious that you don't have a clue as to what you are dealing with here, Mr Hatherleigh. And until you do, my department won't be able to help you.' Prendergast sat back and glared at Thomas. 'I'm disappointed in the level of incompetence that I am seeing here, and it's obvious to me that your leadership skills are sadly lacking.'

A pair of vivid cerulean eyes locked onto the Doctor's. The voice was icy. 'Tudor isn't your local police station, Doctor, so don't think you can polish your ego by pushing us around. If you refuse to give us the advice that would enable us to handle something that is clearly a danger to the realm, we will ensure that you career comes to an abrupt end. And that includes suspending your Civil Service pension.'

Thomas gave Prendergast a minute to absorb this threat before handing him an even more worrying one. 'Whereas MI5 doesn't have the power of arrest, TUDOR does. So if you continue to obstruct us for your own amusement, we will arrest you and have you remanded in Belmarsh with no chance of bail. The charge will be aiding and abetting those who wish to commit treason. While we can no longer hang you, Dr Prendergast, we would have no difficulty in ensuring that you spend the rest of your life in solitary confinement with no opportunity of parole. Do you understand me?'

Prendergast looked shocked. The last time anyone had stood up to him was when a boy in the fourth form had taken an objection to his slimy bullying ways and socked him on the nose. He was about to remonstrate, but stopped himself just in time. He realised that Thomas was right, because in this situation he could easily lose his status-filled career, fat pension and even his freedom. Prendergast decided to back down and cooperate – for the sake of the nation – as he told himself.

Miss Crafthole's face was a perfect picture. On the one hand, she was delighted to see someone getting the better of her boss, but on the other, she was seriously worried, because if Prendergast lost his job, she would lose hers, and she was not only supporting herself, but also her elderly parents and her beloved cat, Mortimer.

* * *

Steven slipped quietly into the office, grabbed a seat from the other side of the room and set it down facing Thomas's corner seating area.

'I've just heard from the public health people in Chile,' said Steven. 'Apparently the virus can be something of an epidemic in Peru, South Asia and other hot countries, and it sometimes turns up in the USA. It's called a *Hantavirus*, and while some strains are no worse than a bad dose of flu, there is one that is a real killer. This kind of virus takes four weeks to incubate, so it gets passed on to many people even before the first person gets sick. However, the Chileans think the terrorists have synthesised a *fourth* variation. This is also a killer, but it has a much shorter incubation period, so in a way it's more containable than the usual virus because those who are incubating it don't have as much time to spread it around, but the downside is that those who become infected get sick too quickly to be helped. Children, the elderly and those with underlying health problems or those whose nutrition is poor all die within a few hours.'

Dr Prendergast decided to show that he actually knew what he was talking about. 'Your man here is quite right, Mr Hatherleigh. A Hantavirus is difficult to deal with because death comes on so swiftly. There are many account of people going out in the morning in perfectly good health, starting to sweat profusely and dropping dead in the street before arriving at their destination.' Prendergast looked around at his rapt audience. 'It used to exist in the UK, but died out four hundred and fifty years ago due to a change that occurred at that time in the northern climate. You see, the Hantavirus doesn't like cold weather, and as the sixteenth century came to a close the weather became progressively colder, and the country entered what was later called "the little ice age". The Hantavirus always *was* a summer complaint, characterised by copious sweating, which is where it got its common names, which were the summer sweats or the sweating sickness.'

Thomas blanched, and Steven shot him a look of concern. They both knew that the sweating sickness had killed Thomas's first wife and young son. Thomas had been away on business when the time so he'd avoided the infection, but he'd never forget the day he returned, to find his family wiped out. His boss at that time had been Thomas Cromwell, and he'd suffered a similar loss when the same ailment claimed the lives of his wife and two of his daughters within a few hours of each other. Thomas has always contended that the disaster had contributed to Cromwell's loss of equilibrium and common sense during his latter years in office.

Prendergast started up again. 'The virus is mainly passed on by rodent droppings that have dried out, but it can develop a pneumonic version that is passed on from one person to the next, and if that is what we're dealing with here, it would be very dangerous indeed. Unlike the plague, which is caused by a bacterium that can be treated fairly easily with broad spectrum antibiotics, this is a *virus* – and there is no antibiotic that can combat a virus. The only treatment is oxygen, intensive care and time, but it can only work if those who are infected can get to a hospital in time, and then not always.'

Prendergast decided to give Thomas and Steven the potential prognosis if the disease took hold. 'The sweating sickness was a terrifying disease in its day, and if it gets out into the wider population now, we'd be in no better straits than they were in the time of Henry the Eighth. With our high population, there would be mega-deaths and we would have to cremate bodies on pyres, much as they did to cattle during the outbreak of foot and mouth disease. Burning cattle was bad enough, but this would be people.'

Thomas looked distinctly green, but he decided to grasp the nettle. 'Okay Doctor, how do we deal with it?'

Prendergast twisted his thin lips into a slight smile.

'The best way to deal with a killer infection is to vaccinate. We can make a synthetic vaccine, but it will take time and it may not be effective enough. The quickest and best way is to get our hands on live antibodies and use them to create the basis of a vaccine.'

'Antibodies?' asked Thomas. 'How do you get hold of them?'

'We need to take a little blood from someone who has been infected with the virus, but who then *recovered*. The death rate is very high with a virulent Hantavirus, but there are always people who survive. For instance, there may be people who have recovered from this particular virus in Chile or Peru who we could use, but we would have to go to those countries and search the jungle to find them.'

'How much blood would you need?' asked Thomas.

'Very little. Just a vial or two would be enough.'

'Would the recovered person need to have been infected with this new strain or would someone who'd had the previous Hantavirus do?'

Prendergast gave Thomas his death's head grin. 'The virus exists in the USA, and we can certainly get antibodies from there, but the most virulent strains outside South America only existed in Medieval Europe and Medieval England. Unfortunately, we can't get what we need from old bones, so what we really need is a living person from Tudor times who had the sickness and recovered. In short, what we need is a time machine.'

Prendergast gave a nasty laugh that reminded Thomas of a death rattle. Meanwhile, the telepathy between himself and Steven was palpable.

'So this virus is initially rodent born?'

Prendergast nodded. 'It's carried by rats, mice, deer mice and other such rodents.'

'So if someone wanted to spread the virus, all they'd need are a few droppings from infected rodents?' Thomas asked.

'Exactly.' Prendergast collected his thoughts. 'As I said, a less virulent form of the virus occasionally turns up in the USA, where occasional outbreaks occur even today. The virus probably comes in on ships carrying fruit and vegetables from South America, and it's carried by rats that run off the docked ships in search of food. Ships nowadays carry their cargoes in containers, so the rats don't get much to eat on the journey, and being hungry, they rush down the anchor chains and into the port in search of food.'

'The local rodent population becomes infected and this gets passed onto other such creatures, such as deer mice. In time, the droppings dry out and break up, leaving miniscule particles to fly around unnoticed in the breeze. In country areas, campers, hikers and so on breathe in the dust and become infected. Several groups of Red Indians have become infected over the years, and Mexicans know the virus well. They call it "*Sin Nombre*" virus, meaning "the virus without a name". There was even an outbreak in Yosemite National Park a few years ago and it killed several people, so as you can see, even the slower acting and less lethal strain is very dangerous, while an enhanced version let loose in a crowded city… well, it would be a disaster.'

Thomas spoke quietly. 'So if someone wanted to infect a specific group of people, he could grind up infected droppings and leave them on a plate in front of an air-conditioning unit, thus ensuring the virus would blow around and infect those in the room.'

Prendergast nodded, and now his assistant started to consider arranging an extended visit to her cousins in the Orkneys. She wondered how her elderly parents and cat would cope with the long train and boat journey.

* * *

Once Prendergast and his downtrodden assistant had been ushered off the premises, Thomas sat staring into the middle distance.

'Something's coming back to me Steven. Wasn't there someone who went down with the sickness in Austin Friars and recovered? Thomas turned to Steven. 'Is this ringing any bells?'

'My housekeeper, Janie's sister Frieda got it. Janie was out of her mind with worry when Frieda fell ill and she spent the better part of a week on her knees praying. She said that's what had saved Frieda's life. She…'

Thomas broke in. 'Are you telling me that Frieda had the sweating sickness and recovered?'

Steven nodded.

Thomas loosened his tie and undid the top button of his shirt. 'You're sure it *was* the sweating sickness and not something else?'

'No question. Frieda lost several of her relatives to it on that occasion. Cousins of her late husband's I think. But she definitely had it – and got over it.'

There was no question in their minds that Thomas and Steven would have to go back to Tudorland to find Frieda, but now Thomas spotted a problem.'

'Are any of us skilled in taking blood?' he asked. 'I'm not and neither are you.' He thought for a moment and then saw the answer. 'We have a tame clinic on hand now and their staff don't ask awkward questions when one of us turns up with an arrow sticking out of us. We can bring Frieda and Janie here, and get the clinic to send us a nurse to take blood from them; then we can take it straight to the Ministry and give it to the Ghastly Prender.'

Steven broke in. 'I'm not renting a doublet this time, I'll buy a new one. I could do with popping back to see Wilf and Janie anyway, so it won't go to waste. You'll need to check that yours hasn't fallen apart Tom, and we'll need to get swords and so on.'

'We could go in modern clothes.'

'That's fine if we go at night, but it means getting there in the dark and frightening Janie and Wilf. You remember how Wilf nearly pole-axed me with a shovel when he found me creeping around in my old house last time?'

For the first time that day, Thomas couldn't help smiling.

* * *

Sophie and Raj decided they'd use the small van for the gig, and they were giving it a final check while Jessica stowed medicines, bottled water and gifts for Janie and Frieda and their family, in addition to packing whatever Steven and Thomas would need for themselves. The trip would be on a smaller scale than the one they'd undertaken during the Abbey adventure, as there would only be the two of them, and they'd only be away for a few hours at most. When Thomas asked Sophie if his doublet and trunk hose were still all right, she told them that they were really decrepit and needed to be replaced. Thomas and Steven took a cab to Angels and bought Tudor outfits that were suitable for 1541, which was a year after they'd left Tudorland for New London. They noticed that the fashion had changed slightly from their time, as the boots were longer and the trunk hose shorter and more defined. They cabbed the lot back to the Mews and changed, suddenly reverting to the upper class Tudor gents they'd once been.

Raj decided to pilot them himself, dropping them into Thomas's old office. Sophie always worried when her loved ones were on these jaunts, but she was comforted by the thought that they would soon be back. Ten minutes later, Raj was back, telling Sophie and Jessica that the brothers-in-law had commented that Thomas's office was a bit different now, but that Wilf and Janie had left space by the door for the Project, just in case. He had no other news though, because all they'd done so far was to unload the gear.

Raj went off again, and soon the van was back with Thomas and Steven, accompanied by two rotund figures, which to Sophie's delight turned out to be Janie and her sister, Frieda. When the women climbed out and fell into Sophie's arms, there was much hugging and crying. The two sisters looked healthy and happy and were obviously delighted to see their New London friends again. They hadn't had time to change, and they were embarrassed to be seen in their cooking clothes, but soon accepted that none of that mattered, because they would soon be wearing New London clothes.

'Where's Sir David? How are Jack, Baz and Kelly? How did Jack get over his injured side? The sisters were falling all over themselves with questions, but Sophie assured them they'd meet all their old friends in a day or so and they could catch up with the gossip for themselves.

'I expect you'll want us to have a good wash,' said Janie. She'd obviously heard abut the washing sessions from Steven's wife, Kate after her first trip to New London.

Sophie piled the sisters into her Jazz and took them home to get cleaned up. At first, the tubby sisters were scared rigid at finding themselves moving along the road in a car, but they trusted Sophie and soon relaxed and started to look around. Like Thomas, Kate, Steven and Carlo before them, they found it weird to see paved streets with no horses, cows, pigs and sheep wandering around. They also found the smell of the city very different, but couldn't make up their minds whether the smell of petrol and diesel fumes were an improvement to the Tudor stink or not.

Meanwhile, Sophie's secretary, Jessica, and Baz's secretary, Emma, went to Bon Marché to buy a selection of clothing in sizes eighteen and twenty. When the girls had bought up half the shop, they called a cab and schlepped their booty round to Thomas and Sophie's house in Tamerlane Square.

Janie and Frieda marvelled at the hot shower, and when they told Sophie they still had some soaps and shampoos left over from the team's previous trip to Tudorland, Sophie told them they would take even more gear back after this trip. Then Emma and Jessica arrived with the clothes.

Janie settled for pale blue slacks with a patterned blue shirt and a navy cardigan, while Frieda chose a long skirt in pale green with a white and pale green flower-patterned shirt and a darker green cardigan. They loved the low-heeled shoes and the modern handbags. Sophie trimmed their hair and neatened it for them. The two women were amazed to discover that respectable women could walk about with their hair uncovered, and they found it liberating.

Thomas and Steven changed back into their modern clothes and went back to Millbank, and when Sophie turned up later with Janie and Frieda, everyone crowded round, asking questions and answering them all at once.

'I understand we have to call Sir Thomas *Tom*, is that so?'

Thomas grinned. 'You can still call me Sir Thomas, and you can still curtsey to me. It will show this rabble that there was a time when I was treated with proper respect.'

Steven asked Frieda if she'd ever had the sweating sickness and she said she certainly had, but that Janie's prayers had brought about her recovery. When he heard this, Thomas felt his shoulders relax for the first time in days.

'Frieda love,' said Steven gently, 'we need you to help us. It means taking a little blood from your arm, very much like putting on a leach, but not as unpleasant, and it will be over much more quickly. The blood will be used to create a vaccine that prevents the sweating sickness from happening to us or to anyone else in New London, and it will save a lot of lives. Once the vaccine has been created, we can come back to Tudorland and administer it to all your family, which means that none of them will ever get the sickness, even if everyone around them went down with it. We will vaccinate you here Janie, although Frieda won't need a vaccination as she's already had the disease and has thus built up immunity to it. Are you willing to do this for us, Frieda?'

'Of course, Mr Steven. I am more than happy to help, especially as this means our loved ones in Tudorland can also be protected.'

Thomas turned to his PA. 'Ryan, get onto the Harley Street Clinic and ask them to send us a nurse who can take the blood, then we can get it to Prendergast at the Ministry.' Turning to Steven, he said, 'Prendergast might decided he needs more blood in a day or two so we'll put Frieda and Janie up at Tamerlane Square for a while just in case.'

Sophie jumped in. 'Kate and Robbie will want to see them, and Janie and Frieda will definitely want to see Harry and Rosie. Margie and her two will want to come over, so it will be lovely if the two ladies stay with us for a while.'

Thomas explained to Janie and Frieda that it wouldn't matter if they were away from Tudorland for a week or two, as they could still arrive back in the Project fifteen minutes after they'd left, regardless of how long they stayed in New London.

7:

Taking Blood

*Trust your hunches. They're usually based on facts filed
away just below the conscious level.*

JOYCE BROTHERS

The police rounded up the gang and settled them into
prison, whereupon Baz, Kelly and Jack questioned them
tirelessly. Breaking the gang turned out to be easier than
they thought, and even the ringleader had given up fairly
easily in the end. The Irish and the Parmians couldn't
stand each other, and neither could understand why the
South Americans had their knives into Britain. The only
problem was that nobody knew exactly where the infected
rat-poo had been stashed. The lad who'd taken it to
London had hidden in the house of a friend of a friend and
then gone out and spent his payment on drink. He couldn't
even remember the names of any of these supposed
friends – or where he'd stashed the stuff. Apparently, this
had led to several screaming matches among the gang, but
so far, no virus.

Thomas ordered Baz to bring the team back to Millbank.
Without the gang being able to get their hands on the virus,
the immediate urgency had diminished, but on the other

hand, leaving a dangerous virus lying around was still hazardous. Meanwhile, Prendergast's team were busy synthesizing the antibodies they'd obtained from Frieda's blood, making a small amount of vaccine to start with and preparing to authorise mass manufacture if the need arose.

* * *

Sophie invited everyone to Tamerlane Square for a Sunday lunch of roast lamb and all the trimmings. Kate was delighted to see her old friends and to catch up with their news, while Janie and Frieda had a great time playing with the children. They marvelled at how Robbie had grown and how well he was doing, and they just loved playing with little Harry. Both the sisters said they found New London exciting, but while they said they would love to visit from time to time, they would prefer to continue living in their old familiar Tudorland with their own families nearby.

* * *

Back at their home Baz, Margie and their children had settled for an old-fashioned 'high tea' of sandwiches and cake, but after putting the children to bed, Margie found herself in a funny mood. She couldn't settle and she wandered around the house in a state of distraction. It was during her third perambulation of their sitting room that Baz grabbed her and held her close.

'What on earth is it Margie love? What's bothering you? Everything's all right with the kids, isn't it?'

'Yeah, Baz, the kids are fine, but something is trying to contact me and I can't get a grip on it.'

'Sit down and relax and perhaps it will come.' Baz thought for a moment, 'How about getting your Tarot cards out. That often opens the door for you, doesn't it?'

Margie took her cards out of the sideboard and laid out six cards in a row, studying them for a while, slowly beginning to make sense of them.

The first card was *The Hermit*, the second, *The Page of Swords*, the third *Eight of Swords,* the fourth *The Moon,* the fifth *The High Priestess* and the final card was *Judgement.*

'This reading is all about something that is hidden, Baz.' Margie pointed to *The Hermit.* This card normally talks about going on in inward journey and tapping into one's inner spirituality, but in this case, I think it's to do with things that are hidden from sight, like something that's hiding in a cave. *The Page of Swords* can also hold secrets, but he'll reveal them when the time is right. *The High Priestess* and *The Moon* both shriek about things that are not yet revealed. *The Eight of Swords* can relate to prison among other things, while the *Judgement* card suggests that something will soon come to life, but it can also refer to trials and legal judgements.'

'Sounds about right, Margie. You seem to be tuning in well enough, but what we need to know is where the bloody thing has been stashed. How about asking your guides?'

Margie sat quietly with her eyes closed, taking herself on an inward journey just as *The Hermit* card had recommended. Soon, she started to feel a connection, enhanced by a sensation of cool air pooling around her back and shoulders. Spirit had arrived, and a man started to build in front of her. His feet and legs were the first to appear, and then inch by inch, the rest of him took shape until she could see him clearly in her mind's eye. This was not one of her usual guides: this was someone new. The man was middle aged and bookish in appearance, with thin cheeks and a ski-jump nose. He was dressed in black and wearing a short cape edged with a long fur collar. It took a minute for

Margie to realise the outfit was pure Tudor, so now she mentally asked him who he was. Thankfully, Margie was clairaudient as well as clairvoyant, so she could *hear* spirit as well as see it, and she wasn't overly surprised when this particular spirit started to speak.

'Canst thee not guess who I am, Margie?'

'No, I can't guess, I need some help.'

'My name is Thomas Cromwell, Margie, and I greatly desire to help thee and thy friends. They have done so much for England that it would be a shame if it were spoiled now. I also wish to impart my feelings to thee and to tell thee how much I despise that hideous sweating sickness. It took my wife and two of my children and while we're together, and it was partly that which made me so bitter and resentful towards others. If I can help thee now, it might allow me to redeem myself here against some of the unfair things that I perpetrated upon others during my lifetime.'

'Brownie points in heaven, Sir Thomas.'

'Brownie points?'

'Notes of good behaviour, perhaps making up karmically for the harm you did to innocent people while serving King Henry.'

'That might be true,' admitted the ghost, 'I do hope so. I've been in this cold place for such a long time, and now through your husband and friends, and my own former Director of State Security, I have been given this golden opportunity to save many more lives than I prematurely ended.'

'Sir Thomas, I will accept your help in good faith and I am sure the others will too. Can you tell me where the virus is hidden?'

'Relax thy mind, Margie my dear, and I shall take thee on a journey. I believe this will be called "remote viewing" in your day, so give me thy hand and allow me to carry thee with me.'

Margie's hand went out and her mentor grasped it. She found the hand that took hers surprisingly warm and human. As her mind cleared, she saw a street of narrow terrace houses appearing. It could have been anywhere, but then the word 'London' came to her, and then the words, 'Christina Avenue'. Now Sir Thomas Cromwell was showing her a house with a faded number 47 scrawled on a piece of board nailed over a broken window that was part of a chipped and scuffed dark green door. She felt herself drifting up the short path to the house and a moment later, she moved through the solid door and into the hallway, as though she were herself a ghost. She glided down a grimy hall and passed a massive bookcase on the left. The bookcase was overflowing with all kinds of junk. To the right she could see a through-room, but she by-passed the room and made for the kitchen at the back.

The kitchen was a nightmare. There were old takeaway boxes, baked bean tins, empty beer cans and cigarette butts everywhere. The overflowing sink was full of filthy plates, mugs and even old shopping bags. The thick layer of baked on grease on the cooker was a health hazard in itself. Everything was covered with buzzing flies. Now she felt her eyes being drawn upwards to a cupboard with an old-fashioned sliding glass front. The glass was cracked and grimy, and the shelf beneath it held various jars and cans, but one jar looked as if it contained cheap powdered coffee. The coffee jar lifted itself from the shelf and hung in the air in front of her, at which point the lid opened and the cheap powdery instant coffee poured out like brown dust onto the crowded worktop in front of her. As the jar emptied, she could see something metallic glittering inside.

Margie mentally addressed her self-appointed spiritual guide. 'Christ, Sir Thomas, that's the clearest vision I've ever had!'

She could hear the warm laugh as he addressed her again. 'I was always good at controlling others, Margie, so today, I choose to control thee, but only for the best of reasons my dear, only for the best.'

The voice and apparition started to fade, but there was just enough strength in the connection for one last message.

'Please give my regards to Sir Thomas Hatherleigh, and tell him that I am heartily sorry that he got caught up in my problem. It all happened so quickly and there was nothing I could do for him, but I'm glad it did work out for him in the end. He is happy with Lady Sophie and he has also served my descendant, Sir David faithfully. I am so pleased that he hath taken back his rightful place as Director. That gladdens my heart immeasurably. Give my compliments to Sir David and to your estimable husband. He is a good man who I would have hired in an instant in my day…'

And with that, the voice and the vision vanished.

* * *

'Margie, Margie love, what's happening?'

Baz's voice seemed to be coming at her from afar, but as Margie returned to the world, she could see her husband trying to get her attention.

'Did you get something? Anything?' Baz sounded frantic. 'You've been in a trance and you've been sitting there with your hand stuck out. Did something happen?'

'You bet, Baz. Can you pass me a notepad and pen and I'll give you the info.'

After Margie had written down the relevant information, she told him who'd given it to her.

Baz's face was a picture. 'Bloody Norah, Margie! Who'd believe it?'

Baz absent-mindedly twiddled one of Margie's corkscrew curls while he thought through the implications. 'I'll tell Tommo and the others tomorrow. They'll be gobsmacked. You know Margie love, if this works, it looks as though *Thomas Cromwell* will have done *Thomas Hatherleigh* a big favour. He certainly owes him one.'

Baz kissed Margie and held her close, whispering, 'What a clever psychic you are, my darling girl, and how proud I am of you. You and your new friend have helped save many lives, because even though the virus won't now be let loose in the House of Commons, if it got out from wherever it's hiding it could still kill millions.'

The next day, Baz told Thomas about Margie's psychic vision and he immediately agreed to follow it up. Thomas trusted Margie's gift, and anyway, they hadn't got anything better to go on. Baz tried to dissuade Thomas from joining the operational crew due to his position as Director, but Thomas gave him a withering look. Jack was despatched to sign out side-arms. Although Baz totally believed in Margie's psychic gift, he was still amazed when he Googled *Christina Avenue* and found it in North West London. While Steven organised a search warrant, the TUDOR team crossed to the Mews where they changed into jeans and dark blue sweats with the name 'TUDOR' and the Tudor Rose logo on the back. They loaded, checked and holstered their guns and were soon on their way.

The front door of 47 Christina Avenue was exactly as Margie had described it. Bashing it brought no response, so the team pulled on plastic gloves and Baz used a ram. The house was empty so they made their way quickly along the filthy hall, passing the overflowing bookshelf on the left and the open doorway on the right while heading for the small kitchen.

'Hells Bells!' said Baz with a grimace. 'Margie said it

would be a disaster area!'

Stepping over putrefying food and disturbing a swarm of bluebottles, Baz made for the shelf Margie had described and immediately spotted the coffee jar. As Margie had said, the coffee was in powder form rather than in the granule style of a decent instant. Baz carefully took the jar from the shelf.

Holding the jar at eye level, Baz turned it on its side. It seemed to be about two thirds full. Kelly, Jack, Thomas and Baz peered at the jar while Baz slowly rotated it.

Being shorter than the men and much shorter than the six-feet-four-inch Baz, Kelly was able to study the underside of the jar, and gravity being what it is, something soon started to show up. She yelled at Baz to stop.

'Now jiggle the jar a little, Baz,' said Kelly quietly.

Baz jiggled the jar gently, while Kelly got right under it.

'One more jiggle. *Slowly*! Twist it from side to side. Gently now... gently...' said Kelly very quietly.

Baz rotated the jar very slowly one way and the other.

'There's something metallic in there. It looks like a tube.'

'Right, that's it,' said Thomas firmly. 'We'll get this to Prendergast and he can take it from here.'

Baz slipped the jar into a bag and zipped it up.

Speaking briskly, Thomas told Kelly to come with him to the Health Protection Agency. Turning to Baz and Jack, he said, 'Call your friends at Scotland Yard and get them to turn this place over; there may be nothing else, but we can't take the chance, and I'd feel happier knowing you're supervising the situation. We'll see you back at the office later.'

* * *

If ever the TUDOR team were going to find the Mews bathrooms useful, this was the day for it. Fortunately, the

Mews was also equipped with two washer dryers, so Thomas, Jack and Kelly tossed their operational outfits into the wash, even including their running shoes, before taking long showers and gratefully changing back into their office clothes. There had been so much filth in that house, that even without the addition of a deadly virus, they felt grubby. Kelly congratulated herself on having the presence of mind to keep a hairdryer in her locker.

It was going to be several hours before the scientists at Porton Down would produce results, and while the TUDOR team tried to keep themselves busy, truth to tell, they couldn't put their minds to anything. Baz and Thomas took Ryan on a trip to the stationery room, where they picked out supplies for their offices. When the young PA offered to bring them coffee, they astounded him by yelling at him and telling him they wouldn't touch coffee with a disinfected barge pole, and that he should bring them tea instead!

By lunchtime, Thomas gave up the ghost, walked over to the Mews in search of Sophie, hauled her out of her office and took her to Regine's restaurant for a long lunch. Kelly and Jack disappeared into the local trattoria and Baz took a couple of the new lads to lunch at the Brewery Tap. Ryan was so fed up with the rotten atmosphere that he went in search of Steven, Jessica and Raj and took them to the Six Bells for burgers and chips. Only Julie, Emma, Jason and other junior staff were left, so Emma brought sandwiches up from the canteen and made an office picnic for them all.

Later that day, they were still avoiding real work when the phone call came through. Thomas took it, and the next minute, Prendergast's unmistakable reedy voice came through.

'The metal tube in the jar contained ground rat droppings.' Prendergast coughed as the dreadful strain of being anything other than disparaging got to him. 'You were right, Mr Hatherleigh, the rat droppings *were* infected with the Hantavirus, and it is precisely the quick-acting and highly dangerous strain that you said it would be. It would have caused havoc if it had got out.' Prendergast coughed again. 'By the way, Mr Hatherleigh, how did you find it so quickly? And how did you manage to get your hands on the blood with the antibodies in it?'

'Well, that doesn't matter now does it? Let's say we're all relieved to think that a major crisis has been averted.' Thomas laid his pen down onto his desk in a gesture of finality. 'Thank you, Dr Prendergast, and please pass our thanks on to Miss Crafthole for us as well.'

Prendergast acknowledged the thanks with a grudging and throat clearing response. 'Glad to have helped. Goodbye Mr Hatherleigh.'

'Goodbye, Dr Prendergast.'

Thomas knew that Prendergast wouldn't pass one word of thanks to his assistant, but he'd still felt obliged to do the right thing. He asked Ryan to ring Raj, Sophie and Jessica and to tell them to come across to Millbank. When everyone was assembled, he announced the news.

The Ghastly Prender has confirmed that we did indeed find the virus and the terrorists confirm that there was only ever one vial, so we can safely say that the danger has passed. Congratulations, TUDOR. Good work!'

With that, a loud and resounding cheer rang out while Jack opened the top drawer of his filing cabinet, producing a tube of plastic cups and two bottles of J&B whisky. Opening the first bottle, he cried, 'Jewish booze anyone?'

With the tension at last broken, the laughing team crowded around Jack for a share of the celebratory drink.

Baz said, 'I always wondered what you keep in your filing cabinet, Jacko. I figured it had nothing to do with work!'

8:

Steven And The Budget

For the love of money is the root of all kinds of evil.
1 Timothy, 6:10

A Personal Assistant showed Steven into the Home Secretary's office, where he found Frances Shulman sitting at her surprisingly ornate desk. As expected, her perfectly dressed Permanent Private Secretary, Emson Barotse, was present, but so also was a paunchy guy with thinning reddish hair. Emson introduced the man as Edward Larson from the Treasury, and Steven could see at once that Larson had the self-satisfied smirk of a man whose elevation to high office was pretty recent.

After shaking Mrs Shulman and Emson by the hand and nodding to the new man, he found himself on a straight-backed chair, facing all three of them. Steven had the uncomfortable sensation of being in the dock, but mollified himself with the thought that when he'd been obliged to present unwelcome sets of figures to the Privy Council in Tudorland, he could easily have ended up being thrown into the Tower, while that was now unlikely.

Larson fired the opening salvo. 'The Home Secretary and I have been looking into the budgets for the police and security services, and now we have to deal with yours.' Larson picked up some papers, adjusted a pair of gold-rimmed spectacles and peered at the top sheet, while giving Steven a "what have you got to say for yourself" look.

Steven felt as though he'd been caught scrumping.

Mrs Shulman slipped on a pair of up-tilted spectacles that put Steven in mind of Edna Everage, but she continued to sit quietly and wait for Larson to say his piece.

'Well, Byers, it seems to me that some aspects of your budget are extremely costly, considering what you do for us.' Larson pretended to look closely at his notes. 'How do you explain your IT spend? And what about your telecoms expenditure or your exorbitant salary bill? It seems out of control, if you don't mind me saying so.'

Steven *did* mind. This was turning out to be such an accurate replica of his previous life in Tudorland that he almost found himself asking after the health of First Minister Cromwell and trying to remember to which wife King Henry was currently married. He just about managed to keep himself in the present by clearing his throat and making a start.

'We spend money on IT because it keeps us ahead of the game, and we go to a lot of trouble to prevent our systems from being penetrated by hackers. We need our private messages to stay private rather than become someone else's daily digest, and that even goes for our nosy friends in GCHQ and the NSA. It is interesting to note that the NSA recently complained that the BBI and TUDOR are the only agencies in the world they cannot penetrate, and Mr Hatherleigh told them we intend to keep it that way. So to that end, we recently built and launched our own communications satellite.'

Steven knew the satellite was the main reason for their horrendous telecommunications spend, and he also knew that the costliest part of the operation was now behind them, but he decided to be awkward for awkward's sake and take a poke at the historical laxity of other government departments.

'We can't have some prat leaving sensitive data on the tube, can we? So everything that leaves the office has to be signed out.' He peered at three inquisitors while slightly shaking his own sheaf of papers. 'Needless to say, I've logged this paperwork out for our meeting today, and I will log it back in again upon my return.'

Steven noticed Emson smothering a smile.

'All right, all right,' said Larson with an impatient sniff, 'I understand the need for security.'

Steven waited for the next salvo while Larson began to develop a sneaky feeling that he was going to end up on the wrong foot.

'What about your bloody wage bill?' said Larson. 'You could run the whole of Buckingham Palace on what you spend. And your pension scheme is a disgrace!' The man's face was turning an interesting colour.

Steven responded forcefully. 'The high wage bill is deliberate. Those who put their lives on the line need to be properly remunerated, and they also need a seriously good pension to look forward to when the time comes. If all they can look forward to upon retirement is penury, they'll be tempted to line their pockets by selling state secrets.'

The Home Secretary nodded and commented quietly that this used to happen on a fairly regular basis in MI6, but of course, that was before her time. Steven could have sworn Mrs Shulman was also stifling a grin.

'Similarly, we have some real brain-boxes at TUDOR, and they are engaged in a war – albeit in a cyber war – so we don't want them leaving us for better paid jobs in China and taking our secrets with them, do we?'

91

A secretary came in with a tray of tea, so Steven accepted a cup and smiled his thanks before going on.

'We pay a basic forty-hour week, regardless of the actual hours our people have to work, and we only pay expenses for *genuine* outlay. Our people know they are properly remunerated and appreciated, so they can't fiddle non-existent overtime or expenses. Another point worth bearing in mind is that the Hatherleighs are independently wealthy, so when they travel on TUDOR business, they pay their own way. Business travel can be expensive, especially in Brussels, so their contribution also represents a considerable saving.'

Larson asked about cars and drivers, commenting that maintaining vehicles and keeping drivers sitting around all day was a major waste of time and money. Emson Barotse stared at the ceiling to keep himself from laughing, but Steven's expression was one of pure innocence. 'I absolutely agree, Minister. Most of us come to work by tube, and that includes the Director and senior staff, but when we travel on business, we use a limo firm down the road. Even then, we only use their really big limos when absolutely necessary. For instance, I came here in a perfectly comfortable Hyundai – and yes, the driver is waiting downstairs to take me back after this particular meeting because I don't want to risk walking the streets with the TUDOR budget details on my person.' Steven looked contrite. 'Sorry about that, Sir.'

Larson opened his mouth and shut it again. He knew he was being given the run-around, but couldn't quite see how it how it was happening. The Home Secretary was struggling to keep her face straight.

Larson tried another go. 'The Mews,' he said. 'And the branches in Devon and the Midlands – what are they all about?'

Steven knew he'd have to be very careful because he mustn't allow any information about the Projects slip out. The Home Secretary and her PPS knew all about them, and they had even taken a time-trip back to 1541 during *Operation Oberon,* but Larson was never going to be allowed into that particular loop.

'The Mews is a freehold property which has long since been paid for, so there's no rental there to worry about. We need our rapid response vehicles and a variety of armaments to be in readiness, and that's what the Mews is all about. We now have our own helipad on the bank of the river, but we don't keep our own helicopter, so we borrow or rent one when in need. We also fly heavy gear in and out of the City via London City Airport by using the new Pegasus VTOL stealth-craft with help from the RAF.' Now Steven fixed a *"mea culpa"* look on his face. 'The helipad did cost a bit to install, but it's only a concrete pad, so the ongoing maintenance is minimal.'

'We keep a Harley Street clinic on a retainer though, because it's far better for us to send our staff there rather than having to answer awkward questions at St Thomas's about gunshot wounds and so on, and it ensures that our people get quick and efficient treatment when they need it.' Now Steven swapped the *mea culpa* look for one of seraphic innocence, but even he wondered whether his next statement was going to be a step too far, though on balance he decided that the man was such a twat that he wouldn't see the joke.

'On a mundane level, Sir, we've put free-of-charge high quality hot drink machines into our offices to cut down on the time and cost of tea-making, but we always have boxes of biscuits on hand because they really do improve morale. Indeed, if you came to see us, we would offer you a hot drink in a cardboard mug and an inexpensive rich tea biscuit on a paper plate. We get the biscuits and plates from the Plastic Pound Shop. It may seem paltry, but it makes a surprising difference to the budget.' Now, leaning forward and speaking in a conspiratorial tone as though imparting a juicy piece of gossip, Steven said, 'As you can see, we spend top-dollar on the things that are truly important and very little on appurtenances that others deem vital, so if one of our staff wants to treat themselves to gold embossed wallpaper or a new duck house, they do it at their own expense.'

This had the desired effect of turning Larson an even more startling colour. Indeed, the man's eyes started to bug out so much that Steven wondered if they'd have to take *him* to the clinic before the day was out.

Mrs Shulman harrumphed a couple of times before agreeing that the TUDOR budget was fine as far as she was concerned, while Larson salvaged his self-esteem by stating that the budget allowance would be reduced by ten per cent in the coming year. Larson gave Steven a 'how do you like them apples?' glare before giving Mrs Shulman and her PPS a mealy-mouthed goodbye and making a rapid exit.

Mrs Shulman flapped a hand at Steven as a signal for him to stay behind, but when Emson had shut the door behind the Treasury man, Mrs Shulman turned her gimlet eyes on Steven and went straight for the jugular.

'You're a crafty sod, aren't you, Byers?'

'Why? What did I do?' Steven raised his eyebrows in innocent puzzlement.

'So, what if your next year's budget is reduced by ten per cent?' she pulled off her specs. 'I doubt that you'll be launching any new satellites for a while, *or* building yourself a nice little airport at Maplin Sands. Both TUDOR West and TUDOR North are up and running – including the fact that you provided Carlo with a hillside full of sheep in order to hide whatever mischief is going on there. Your real needs for the immediate future will be miniscule when put against what you did last year, so your ten percent reduction will work out in real terms as an *increase* of something like 480 percent.'

Steven sat quietly while the Home Secretary launched herself into full rant mode.

'Even if the cut was *real,* it's still paltry when set against the monstrous cuts Larson has imposed elsewhere. For Christ's sake, if someone decides to whack the Queen during the coming year, the only protection she will absolutely be able to rely on will be Prince Philip socking the bugger over the head with his umbrella – not that he wouldn't do it of course – but arguing that you are saving the country millions by cutting time spent on washing up cups is complete *rubbish!* You might have pulled the wool over Larson's eyes, but if you expect me to believe your bull...' Mrs Shulman threw up her hands in despair. 'For Christ's sake Byers, how you make me *suffer.'*

Mrs Shulman bent over her desk and gave Steven such a piercing look that he felt he was being given the evil eye.

'And while we're on the subject, if any of your people think I will *ever* drink tea out of a cardboard beaker or eat a cheap biscuit on a paper plate in your offices, you've got another think coming! You can brew me a decent pot of PG Tips and serve it in a porcelain teacup, with semi-skimmed milk, real castor sugar *and* with a fresh slice of good quality sponge cake from Fortnum and Mason, thank you very *much!* Budget or no bloody budget!'

Steven decided to wind the Home Secretary up a little. 'Wasn't it Mrs Thatcher who used to ask her colleagues if they knew the price of a pint of milk?'

Mrs Shulman wasn't silly enough to fall for that one, so she decided to drop her faithful PPS into it instead by giving an enquiring look.

Emson pulled a 'how would I know?' face.

'I bet *you* know, Byers,' scowled Mrs Shulman.

'Eighty-one pence a pint from our milkman, but less from a supermarket, although Kate swears the supermarket stuff isn't a patch on the dairy's milk. She says supermarket stuff comes from unhappy cows and upsets our children, while the milkman's stuff comes from contented cows and makes our children happy. She won't buy anything else.'

'Get out!' screamed the Home Secretary. 'Get out before I come round there and give you a fat smack! I've got work to do, so *bugger off!'*

Steven gave the Home Secretary a respectfully deep Tudor bow before allowing Emson to walk him out of her office. Even as the door closed behind him, they could hear Mrs Shulman muttering. 'Fucking cheeky sod. I'll have that lot in the Tower one of these days, see if I don't. Fat Henry was right – if anyone needs their heads sliced off with a rusty axe, it's that crowd of slippery buggers!'

9:

Emson's History Lesson

Sometimes our light goes out, but is blown into flame by another human being. Each of us owes deepest thanks to those who have rekindled this light.

ALBERT SCHWEITZER

Emson signalled Steven into an armchair.

'Am I imagining it or was Mrs S less belligerent than usual today?'

'She's had Larson round her neck for the past week,' sighed Emson. 'Not every agency has their figures in apple pie order the way yours are, and many don't have their arguments as well thought out. He's slashed some budgets to ribbons and that isn't going to make for effectiveness. She's kept all your little secrets though, because she knows we'll need to rely even more on TUDOR in future, and that's even without factoring in the Project system.

'Is all this cost cutting really necessary or is Larson trying to make a name for himself?'

'Both. Everybody is cutting back these days and we have to do our share, but that idiot is definitely trying to make a name for himself, so his cuts are more draconian than they need to be. Fortunately, Sir David's BBI is new, so there isn't a precedent there yet and anyway, much of their spend will be on electronic surveillance and cyber stuff. They will even run a kind of virtual RAF with drones directed by real pilots in the near future. Amazing stuff really. TUDOR is only concerned with the safety of the realm, but the BBI will follow up on all kinds of things, such as nasty porn and much else that flows around the airwaves, and they'll work more closely with the police than you do.'

Emson grinned at Steven. 'Mrs S is right in one way though, because you Tudorlanders *are* all as slippery as eels, but then I expect you needed to be crafty to survive life in Henry the Eighth's employ.'

'Tom almost didn't.'

'Yeah, that's right. He nearly lost his head when Cromwell's luck ran out didn't he?'

Emson wasn't ready to get back to the business of government just yet, so he asked Steven to tell him about his time in Tudorland, and to explain to him how he, Kate and Thomas had ended up in what they now called New London.

It took Steven a few minutes to roll himself back into a life that was now slipping quickly into the past. He was surprised to find that bits of it were already dropping from his memory.

'When Tom started working for King Henry, the First Minister was Cardinal Wolsey, but Tom mainly worked for Sir Thomas Cromwell. When Wolsey was thrown out of office, Cromwell took over and as he already employed Tom on security matters in England and overseas, he continued to do so. The King also employed Tom directly for his own requirements, especially in Asia Minor and the Holy Land, even though Thomas was really young at that time. Later Cromwell trusted him enough to give him the job of Director of *The Office of State Security for England and Wales.*

'Looking back with twenty-first century knowledge, we now know that King Henry was probably born with some kind of genetic problem which modern doctors suggest may have been *McLeod's Syndrome.* The syndrome is linked to something called *Kell Blood,* which would have been responsible for him having so much difficulty in producing an heir. The syndrome also causes mental instability from middle-age onwards. We also know that the clout on the head that he'd received when jousting would affected his cerebral cortex, so Henry's temper became increasingly unpredictable, as did his decision-making. Added to that, some doctors think Henry was diabetic, which would have made it impossible for the injury he suffered to his leg on that near fatal joust to heal properly, although I've head that it's possible that a bit of bone sheered off and rotted in his leg, thus creating the ulcer that kept breaking open. Added to that, I've learned that a diabetic man can struggle to achieve an erection – and that doesn't help when it's imperative for the man to appear vigorous, and when he wants to produce sons. Henry was an intelligent man, but his ailments were making him increasingly irritable and unpredictable.

'He lost his temper with Wolsey when the Cardinal couldn't persuade the Pope to give Henry a divorce from Catherine of Aragon, but Wolsey cheated the axe-man by dropping dead from a heart attack, possibly exacerbated by a duodenal ulcer. Thomas Cromwell wasn't so lucky, and when he fell out of favour, those who worked for him were also condemned by becoming "collateral damage". As you know, my wife is Tom's sister, and if we had stayed in Tudor London, it's possible that we might also have been executed, simply because we are related to Tom.'

Emson shook his head while taking all this in. Learning history at school was one thing, but hearing it from someone who had lived through it brought it to life in a way that could never happen when watching a programme on the television.

Emson had treated himself to a Nespresso coffee machine, so now he walked to a sideboard and made coffees for himself and Steven. He opened a drawer and extracted a packet of good quality almond-butter shortbread biscuits, giving Steven a conspiratorial grin as he offered him the pack. Steven caught the inference, chuckled and took a couple of biscuits before continuing with his story.

'Sophie had come across Tom's name in a book and realised his death had never been recorded, which meant she could use the Project to remove him from his situation. The Project had been programmed not to cause historical anomalies, so she couldn't rescue someone whose end was known, but as Thomas had simply disappeared from history, she decided to take a chance by lifting him with the idea of dropping him back a few days later in some safe location. In the event, Tom stayed in New London and eventually Kate and I followed, and Sophie's friendship with Margie Baverstock led us to Baz Baverstock and hence to TUDOR.

'You might remember coming to Hatherleigh Farm during the Operation Oberon?'

Emson nodded.

'Well one of our techies at that time was Lucy, and as a result of Oberon, she fell in love with Tom's cousin Charles – the one who everyone calls Carlo. After a lot of difficulty they got together and they now run TUDOR West for us.'

Emson chuckled, 'Mrs Shulman always says there's more nepotism in TUDOR than there is in an African business.'

'She's not racist, is she? I mean, the comment about

African nepotism? What with you having an African background and all that?'

'Nah. Mrs S just speaks her mind. She has a powerful instinct for justice and fairness, regardless of anyone's race or religion, and she hates liars and back-stabbers. Despite her being such a cow, I trust her and I'd rather work for her than serve the needs of someone I couldn't trust.'

Steven nodded and ate his biscuit while still mentally back in his Tudorland era. 'The positions that Tom and I held in Tudorland were far more exalted than those we have here. I had a fair say in the country's budget, while Tom's position was like that of Mrs Shulman, but the situation wasn't the same as it is now. The Privy Council and parliament could put up arguments, but at the end of the day, their only real job was to rubber stamp Cromwell's or the King's decisions, and to find money with which to implement them. Also, the population of England and Wales totalled just over three million, while Ireland was administered separately and Scotland was a foreign country. In modern terms, we were more like the mayor and council of a fair-sized city, but even that doesn't really compare, because England was a major world power even then, and we were surrounded by enemies. We had trouble coming at us from Scotland and Europe and sometimes even further away – such as the Middle East.'

Emson lifted a shoulder and pulled a 'so what's new' face.

'So what's your story, Emson? How did your family get here?'

'My family is Zulu, and Zulus have always been respected in Africa – even by whites and Afrikaners. My parents lived in Zambia, but Zulus aren't native there, so my great grandparents were immigrants even then so to speak. Our tribal homeland stretches from Zimbabwe all down the eastern areas of a South Africa, but my grandfather worked for a white engineer who'd landed a job running a copper mine in Ndola in northern Zambia, and in time, Grandpa worked his way up to the position of supervisor. One day, his boss asked him to accompany him to London for some reason, and when the job was over, Grandpa decided to stay on.

'It wasn't hard for an immigrant to get citizenship in those days because the country needed skilled workers from the Commonwealth, and once he was settled, Grandpa brought my grandmother over from the Zulu lands in South Africa. They worked hard to make a decent future for their children and in time, our dad became an engineer and our mum a teacher, so as you can imagine, they both made sure that my brother and I got a good start. My brother is called Lwezi Barotse, and he's a boffin at RAF Cranwell. He probably designed those drones that Sir David wants for the BBI. By the way Steven, if you ever visit Cranwell on business, ask for *Lew* Barotse, because that's what they call him there.'

Steven nodded while Emson gave him a weary smile. 'You see, Steven, like your family, we're also devoted to Britain, even though what we have to do for our Queen and country isn't always easy.'

Emson Barotse was quiet for a moment. He seemed to be pondering, so Steven sat still and waited. Emson seemed to come to a decision. He looked directly at Steven and said, 'Mrs S has been chatting to Sir David Cromwell and it appears that something is up, and I think that's probably contributed to her current air of distraction. She hasn't authorised anything yet, but I think it might be advisable for Tom to run over to Maida Vale and have a word with his ex-boss.'

* * *

When he got back to Millbank, Steven sought out Thomas and asked if he'd heard anything that involved Sir David Cromwell and the BBI. Thomas nodded slowly, saying he'd picked up a hint of something at Sophie's dinner party. However, in the meantime, Thomas suggested that he and Steven treat themselves to a nice long lunch at Regine's as a reward for Steven saving their budget from annihilation.

'And just for the hell of it, Steven, we'll put the bloody meal on expenses.' Thomas gave Steven a conspiratorial grin. 'Regine told me they've got some decent Volnay on hand at the moment. Fancy a drop? Be like the old days in Tudorland – enjoying a cup or two of good wine at lunchtime.'

'I've never heard of that wine Tom, but if you recommend it…'

10:

The Pigeon Post

Computers are like Old Testament gods; lots of rules and no mercy.

JOSEPH CAMPBELL

A middle-aged Sussex couple were updating their living room when they ripped out an old fireplace and found the bones of a long dead pigeon inside it. That wasn't a big deal as such, but there was a tiny canister the attached to one of the creature's leg bones and it contained a coded message signed by a Sergeant Stott. The couple sent the message to Bletchley Park, but the people there said they no longer did any decoding; suggesting the couple send the message on to GCHQ. Nobody there could decode it either, because without the right decoding book, even modern computers couldn't do anything – so the pigeon continued to keep its secret.

Meanwhile, Sophie was working with Raj on a means of sending messages across time and space, and after reading the pigeon story in the paper, it was inevitable they would call their new invention a *Pigeon*. The apparatus was a wooden box with a small Solabrite battery nestled in a foam-lined niche at one end. The front of the box flipped down to reveal a seven-inch iPad. A metal container filled the rest of the box, the inside of which was coated with a special material that was part of the Temporal Inversion Module system or TIM that worked the Projects. When the box was closed, a little green light appeared on the front to show that a message was in the process of coming in or going out, or one was already sitting in the box. This was similar to the way a telephone answering machine blinks when a message is waiting to be played.

The inner container was large enough to hold letters, a small book, documents, diagrams or photos, but if anything other than paper was put into the Pigeon, it wouldn't work. So while this prevented someone tucking a bomb, poison gas or even a dangerous snake into the box, it meant that the Pigeon couldn't transmit memory sticks or even taped messages. So while this was the most cutting edge gadget of all time, like the pigeons of old, it could only transmit messages on paper.

Sophie, Raj and Jessica were conducting a test by sending a message to the Millbank office, and in order to give their experiment an authentic World War Two feeling, Sophie wrote the message in pencil. Raj popped the note into the inner container and closed it. He tapped his finger on the word '*Millbank*' on the tablet, then tapped the word '*send*'. Then he tucked the tablet back into place and closed the box. The team held their breath. When the light went out, Raj opened the wooden outer box and gingerly lifted the metal lid from the inner metal box. It was empty.

A matching Pigeon sat on a large table in the Millbank ops room, and everyone crowded round it hoping that something would happen. There was a collective intake of breath when the green light came on, and a few moments later, Thomas slowly lifted the wooden lid, let down the tablet and lifted the lid on the inner metal container. Would the letter be in one piece? Surely something as delicate as paper would have become mangled by the journey through matter, then through anti-matter and back to matter once again? The TUDORs held their breaths while they leaned over the table and peered in. There was definitely something inside. It turned out to be a business size envelope with the word Millbank clearly pencilled on the front. Thomas opened the envelope and removed the note. Then he shook his head and sniffed.

'It looks as though Sophie and the silly sods at the Mews have sent us a coded message, but without the key how are we supposed to decode it?'

Steven looked at the note, but clever as he was, he couldn't for the life of him see what the list of numbers was meant to represent. Jack Duquesne peered over his shoulder and a moment later, he started to chuckle.

'I think I can decode it,' he said, 'you see I once had a girlfriend who...'

A groan went around the table.

Undeterred, Jack went on. 'To continue my discourse – and despite the utterly unfair heckling to which I am being subjected, I once had a girlfriend who was into numerology, and this looks like the *Pythagorean code.'*

Jack asked if someone could hand him a notepad and pen, and a moment later, he wrote:

A	B	C	D	E	F	G	H	I
J	K	L	M	N	O	P	Q	R
S	T	U	V	W	X	Y	Z	
1	2	3	4	5	6	7	8	9

He slowly decoded the message, but due to the fact that Steven and Thomas had spent most of their lives in Tudor England, they remained mystified even after the message had been decoded, but the others started to laugh. The message read:

'Allo London, 'allo London. This is Night'awk calling.

Please send another copy of the 'Fallen Madonna with the Big Boobies PDQ!'

* * *

When Raj and Sophie tried the system via T-North and T-West, it worked perfectly, but so far, the messages had only needed to traverse space, while none had been required to cross time. With this in mind, Raj rang Carlo and asked if he and Lucy would like to don their Tudor gear, take a quick trip back to 1541, and pay a visit to Carlo's Aunt Bessie and her farm manager, Jackson. The result of this jaunt was the discovery that the Pigeon worked perfectly across time, and as a result, Carlo and Lucy were delighted to be able to stay in permanent touch with their Tudorland friends from now on.

Steven and Thomas also went back to 1541 and paid a flying visit to Wilf and Janie, also leaving a Pigeon with them. When Sophie saw Thomas donning his beautiful made-to-measure velvet doublet, complete with lace and embroidery trimming, she decided to introduce her husband to the concept of Savile Row tailoring. She thought of the fun it would be to watch a duck rediscovering such familiar water as bespoke tailoring. Meanwhile, Sophie also wanted to test the Pigeon in a different time frame to their familiar Tudorland one.

* * *

Emily was putting a salad together while Sophie was

stirring homemade spaghetti bolognaise when Sophie decided to ask Emily whether she still thought about Shimon or whether she had consigned the lovely Captain Sobieski to history.

'I tried to look upon the episode as a holiday romance,' said Emily, 'the kind of love affair that ends when you return to reality, but in truth is that I'm a long way from coping. The worst aspect of it is that I am in limbo because I don't know whether that's all it ever was or whether there's something more to hope for.'

Emily sliced cucumber into the salad bowl while trying to explain her feelings. 'We live in an age of instant communication don't we? I mean, I have a couple of friends who went to Australia and I can text them whenever I like, but where Shimon is concerned, I feel like some Victorian girl whose man has gone off to fight on the north-west frontier, and I have no idea where he is, what he is doing or whether he still gives me a moment's thought.' Emily brushed away a tear with the back of her hand. 'I feel so miserable most of the time, Sophie. I don't know if you can understand…'

Sophie could definitely understand because she'd gone through an equally intense phase before she knew that her feelings for Thomas were reciprocated.

'So you think that if you went back to the Israel of 1967, you might find Shimon with someone new. Is that it?'

'Well he's very good looking isn't he? His shiny fair hair, baby-face-dimples, happy grin and his great body make him attractive to girls – especially Israeli ones – and they climb all over him. He wouldn't need to sit around for long would he?'

Sophie shook her head gently. 'I guess not. But you're a very pretty girl and you haven't moved on to anyone else have you? So he might still be waiting. I guess it's the uncertainty that makes it hard though.' Sophie looked at Emily's sad face, but she ploughed on, because she still needed to get some idea of the potential strength of this relationship before saying what she needed to say.

'What did Shimon say when you last spoke to him?'

'He suggested that as I am so close to finishing my course that I should go on, because I would regret it later if I dropped out so late in the game. I know he's right, but the situation is getting me down so much that I've even been wondering if I could borrow a Project and fly back to 1967 just for a while so that I could see him. I mean, Sophie, we all know it isn't great to chase after a guy, but even if he has moved on, knowing the truth would bring the situation to an end, wouldn't it? Closure as they say.'

Emily sat down and stared into space while speaking quietly, almost as though to herself. 'You see, Shimon had a lot to do in the wake of the Six Day War, and he also needs time to consider his future. His parents, his sister and her husband run a farm in Galilee so they are settled, but he needs to know they will be safe without him around before he makes any major changes.'

'Is he thinking of coming to New London?' asked Sophie.

'Maybe. He's already told his mother and sister that Mossad might give him a posting overseas, just in case he decided to make the move. He would still want to visit his family from time to time, so I guess it might work out for him in New London – or it might not – I really don't know. It's all a muddle to be honest.' Emily looked sadly into her glass. 'In one way, it would be easier for me to live in 1960s Israel than for Shimon to come here. I would have to adapt to life in a very different country and era and I don't know how important Shimon's family's views are to him, or whether the fact that I'm not Jewish would become a stumbling block.'

At this point, Thomas came in from work, gave Sophie a quick kiss, greeted Emily and went upstairs to change. When he came back down, Sophie gave him the gist of what Emily had told her. Thomas wasn't surprised at the potential religious problems. After all, he'd lived through the early years of the Reformation and he'd also spent time in what he called the Holy Land, so he was aware of both Jewish and Muslim thinking.

'But there's more,' Emily told Thomas. 'I'd need paperwork and a back history if I am to become forty years older than I am now. To be honest, I probably need even for a short visit... and that was something I wanted to bring up with Sophie.'

'What kind of help?' asked Thomas.

'I need a passport of the kind that existed in the 1960s showing me as the age I am now, and I need something to show that I crossed into Israel from Egypt while on holiday there – a stamp in my passport or some such thing – because that's the only way I can get there without appearing on the manifest of an airplane or a ship.'

'We can do that for you.'

'Are you sure? Emily's golden eyes bore into Thomas's vibrant blue ones. He had to admit that being on the end of such an intense look was disconcerting and it gave him some idea of the discomfort he put others to when using his own china blue gaze on them.

'I can ask the guys over at MI6 to help out,' said Thomas warming to the theme. 'A birth certificate wouldn't hurt either would it? And how about a rent book and utility bills and whatnot? That should give those bureaucratic sods over there something to do.'

'Well, okay. If you say so...'

'I do say so. And not just because you fancy a bit of end-of-term nookie, either.'

'Hey Tommy!' laughed Sophie. 'I really don't think Emily is considering a trip to 1967 Israel just to get a decent shag.'

While Emily was still chuckling, Sophie told her there was a reason for inviting Emily to dinner; apart from the obvious one of enjoying her company.

'I might have guessed,' smiled Emily. 'Are you asking me to go to Israel to become a latter-day Violette Szabo? Is this to be a new version of *Carve Her Name with Pride?*'

'What's the girl talking about?' asked Thomas, raising an eyebrow. There were still times when his Tudor background left him in the dark.

'Violette Szabo was a heroine of the resistance during the Second World War,' Sophie explained. 'She did two tours of duty in France and was eventually caught by SS Panzers who handed her over to the Gestapo. The Gestapo tortured her before sending her to a concentration camp where she was eventually shot. She never broke under Gestapo interrogation, she refused to betray the other resistance members and she refused to become a double agent for the Nazis, even though it would have saved her skin.'

'God's teeth,' said Thomas thoughtfully. 'I'm not sure I'd want to hold out under those circumstances.'

Sophie narrowed her eyes before putting a question to Thomas that she'd never thought to ask before. 'Has anyone ever held out against *you*, Tommy? I know that nobody's managed it since you've been in London.' Turning to Emily, Sophie said, 'I've made a point of sitting on the same side as the suspects during some of Tommy's sessions, and it's not a comfortable sensation. When he starts feeding bits of evidence to some poor sod who knows he's been caught bang to rights, I can't help starting to feel sympathy for the baddie.'

Thomas gave a quiet snort.

Turning back to her husband, Sophie asked, 'What happened when you were running State Security in the 1530s?'

Speaking quietly more to himself than to the others, he said, 'You're right Sophie. Nobody stood up against me for long. In my very early days, it sometimes took time to obtain the complete picture, but in time, I learned how to put on the pressure. I never used actual torture, although in some really difficult cases I have to admit that I used a little of what one might call *deprivation*. For instance, when you manacle a person in a standing position against a dungeon wall and leave them there for a day or so, they can't rest, eat, drink or even move away from their position when they need the loo. They become exhausted and filthy – and when they fall asleep, the manacles cut into their wrists and wake them up, and of course, they don't know how long the deprivation is going to go on for. When you think about it though, I was pretty nice to them, because I only ever left them there for as long as necessary.'

Emily looked aghast, but Sophie told her she was perfectly well aware that her husband was an evil monster. Meanwhile Thomas was still mentally back in the 1530s.

'If it became clear that I was dealing with someone innocent, I released them immediately. Indeed, some of those actually ended up working for me. They trusted me, I guess.'

Sophie asked if the baddies broke even when they knew the consequence would mean execution.

'Even then.'

'Bloody 'ell,' said Emily with a shudder.

Both she and Sophie suddenly realised what a tireless investigator Thomas must have been. And still was - despite his current lack of manacles and a dungeon. Emily decided to ask an even more pointed question. 'You had some people executed though, didn't you?'

'Yes, of course. Prison wasn't a punishment in Tudorland, although it sometimes served that purpose for minor crimes – albeit more by accident than design. You see, if it turned out that the accused person had done something insignificant, we'd judge that the time he'd spent in prison was punishment enough and let him go with a caution. Our prisons weren't holiday camps, so those who were inside for more than a few days often became ill, and their families suffered by not having the breadwinner around. If the prisoner was female it was even harder for the family.' Thomas looked into his wine glass. 'If the prisoner was tried and found guilty of a major crime we'd hang him the following day.'

Emily jumped in, 'so if someone posed such a threat to this country right now, today. I mean something that would destroy this country... and if TUDOR considered them too dangerous to be allowed to live?' Emily stopped short.

'You mean now? In New London?' asked Thomas.

Emily held her glass out for a refill.

'Well, we don't have a death penalty now. Not even for treason. And we don't put terrorists into some Guantanamo-type concentration camp either. They might stay in solitary confinement in prison for the rest of their lives, or we might take them to a safe house for a bit while we continue to interview them.'

Sophie asked Emily if she'd seen the remake of Tinker, Tailor, Soldier Spy.

'Yes, I did. And I also saw the recent rerun of the original – the one with Alec Guinness. I think they tried hard with the new version, but it wasn't as good.' Turning to Thomas, she asked him if he'd seen it and if any of it was based on truth.

Thomas nodded slightly. 'Yes I saw it. And Sophie got me a copy of the old TV version. I agree that the earlier one was better, because the film-makers had more time and more scope in which to tell the story. But do you remember how the story ended?'

'The double agent was taken to some kind of private prison. He had wronged a guy called Jim Prideaux, and it was Prideaux who shot him.'

'An accident, maybe? Leaving the baddy exposed in that way?' said Thomas gravely. 'Or perhaps not. Why was Prideaux allowed to get into the area? I understand the idea in the book came from Le Carre's time in MI6 when it was based in Cambridge Circus. It's still called the Circus now you know; even though the they moved to Vauxhall a long time ago.'

Emily nodded, and thought for a moment.

'What about that strange case in the news a few weeks ago? The one about the Parmian guy who fell off the roof at Sainsbury's? I mean, Tommy, what was he doing up there for God's sake? Was that one of your black ops by any chance?'

Thomas set his drink down on the coffee table and sat back, steepling his fingers in a fair imitation of Cardinal Wolsey when he didn't want to answer a direct question. 'You might think that,' he said quietly, 'but I couldn't possibly comment.'

'I'll be doing my shopping in Waitrose from now on,' laughed Sophie.

'You'll find me at Aldi,' gulped Emily.

The evening ended with Sophie asking Emily to come to the Mews as soon as it was convenient, because she had something to show her.

* * *

A few days later, much to Emily's delight, Sophie showed

her how to use the Pigeon.

'You want me to fly to Shimon and see if he'll keep one of these for you and test it out for you?' asked Emily.

'That's the idea,' replied Sophie. 'And then, if you and Shimon are still an item, you can stay in touch with each other via the Mews. As you said, even if it turns out that it is all over between you, at least you won't be chasing shadows any longer, and we'll have given the Pigeon another test run. If you do find that it's all over between you though, don't leave the Pigeon with Shimon. Bring it back to us.'

* * *

That weekend, Emily repeated her previous trip to the Whisky a Go Go, and once more she surprised Shimon at the banquette near the bar. He was absolutely delighted to see her again and he proudly introduced her to his friends as his English girlfriend. Soon they were dancing the night away, laughing and drinking Maccabee beer with his friends. Emily danced with some of Shimon's friends and chatted to some of the off-duty young women. They told her that Shimon was a really nice guy, and despite his baby-faced looks and his huge blue eyes, he was also a good and reliable soldier.

Back at his little house later that night, Emily brought the Pigeon in from the Project. Just knowing they could keep in touch brought Emily's sadness and depression to an end. They spent the rest of the weekend doing touristy things and making love. Emily's immediate plans were to spend Christmas with her father, fly back to Shimon for a couple of weeks, finally returning to New London to focus on her degree. The young couple knew they had a lot to work out, but promised each other they wouldn't be parted for a moment longer than necessary, and at least now they could keep in touch, which made a world of difference.

11:

Calling On Sir David

Patriotism is a kind of religion; it is the egg from which wars are hatched.

GUY DE MAUPASSANT

The area around Little Venice was filled with impressive Georgian houses, and several dwellings in Randolph Crescent had been linked together to create an office system that was now the nerve centre of *The British Bureau of Investigation* or the *BBI*. The main dwelling for the large organisation was a new building in what had been the old factory on the South Bank, and Sir David could often be found there, but today he was in his Maida Vale nerve centre.

The November day was raw and a fine rain had started to fall, so Thomas's driver used his TUDOR pass to enable him to park close to the office while he waited. The camera over the front door picked up Thomas's arrival and the door opened as though by magic. Once through the security system, Sir David's elegant PA, Jill Standish, greeted Thomas with a kiss on both cheeks before leading him up two flights of stairs. They were met by a solid figure walking towards them and holding out a welcoming hand.

Sir David ushered Thomas into his office.

Tom had expected the room to be spacious and it was. He also expected it to be decked out in the dark wood and shiny reddish leather so beloved of senior Civil Servants, but he should have known better. One wall was lined with light elm bookcases filled with legal reference books, and the large desk was of a Scandinavian design. A seating area was light blue, which worked well with the dark blue carpet. A large TV in the corner silently played the BBC news.

'You know Tom, the BBI is big and it's becoming increasingly vital to our national security, but I really miss TUDOR. It was always special, even before you and Sophie joined us and before you brought us the Projects.'

Thomas smiled at his old boss.

'Do you ever find yourself looking back to the time when you worked for my ancestor in Tudorland?'

'I hardly ever think about it now, and things that were important at the time have faded into… well, history, I suppose.' Thomas sat back and thought for a moment. 'I admired Sir Thomas Cromwell, and I would have been proud to count him as a friend, but not as he became in later life – not after he'd lost any semblance of common sense.'

A gentle knock on the door announced Jill's junior assistant bringing coffee, and Thomas smiled his thanks while waiting for Sir David to tell him what was on his mind. It didn't take long.

'There's a new group in the Gulf area who belong to a tribe with their own religion,' said Sir David. 'They've been peaceable up to now, but they have a new leader who has persuaded them to become a bloody nuisance. That would be fine if they kept the problem in-house so to speak, but they want to send their message of power and superiority around the world and they want to do it in a particularly violent manner. They're behind the aggravation that's been going on

117

in the Russian Federation, and needless to say, Putin has stepped on them with a heavy boot, so now they're looking for softer targets. Meanwhile, we've heard something on the airwaves and it doesn't look pretty.'

Sir David had a habit of tugging his ear lobe when he was thinking deeply and he was doing it now. 'Have you ever heard of a Helios bomb?'

Thomas shook his head.

'Apparently, it's pronounced *Hellios* rather than *Heelios*, but whatever it is, the technology originated in the Russian Federation and it has a nuclear component. Are you aware of nuclear power and what that means, Tom?'

'I've read about it, and I've seen films about Hiroshima and Nagasaki and the development of the hydrogen bomb. Are we talking about a bomb of that kind? As I understand it, a modern hydrogen bomb would make London uninhabitable.' Thomas shuddered at the thought.

'I'm not sure what it is yet, but I know it would cause a major drama if it went off.'

'Do we know where the bomb is at present?' Thomas bit his bottom lip while thinking. 'And is there any way of finding it and disabling it?'

'Well the little I've heard suggests that it's being stored in Israel.'

'Israel!' exclaimed Thomas. 'Who would stash a bomb in Israel? It makes no sense.'

'Perhaps that's why they've chosen it, precisely because it isn't an obvious place.'

'So we must suppose that the Holy Land is the target - if not for this bomb, then for something else.'

'It could be, assuming there's more of than one of the infernal things, but our problem is to find the one that's destined for London and we need to spike the bloody thing – and quickly.'

'I'd better have a word with Alec.'

'Alec Blitz of Mossad?'

'Yeah,' said Thomas quietly. 'Mossad will need to know. But if something is going on in the Holy Land, Alec and his team may already have a line on it. I'll see what I can find out.'

Now Thomas decided to ask Sir David for a favour. 'When Frances Shulman asked you to set up TUDOR, you both envisaged a flexible, quick response outfit that could deal with any kind of threat. That's how it was, isn't it?'

'That's right, I guess we saw it as a blend of "Spooks" on the TV and a civilian form of SAS with some police work thrown in.'

'Well, I've been bothered by the increasing amount of cyber stuff that's bogging us down. We have been spending far too much time taking down thousands of dodgy websites. Our techies need to use their brains on innovative stuff; and while intelligence gathering is vital, we can't afford to do it at the expense of everything else. We're too small and I think we're the wrong place for this.

'GCHQ is helpful, but they're up to their eyes in it, so I would like to pass this stuff on to you in exchange for a brief summary that focuses on anything that is likely to be of particular interest to TUDOR. Would you do that for us?'

'Yeah, of course. And anyway, even mundane intelligence might turn out to be of interest to the BBI.' Sir David finished his coffee and then came out with something that was on his mind. 'Tom, I'm glad you've dropped the "Sir" thing now and just call me David. It was different while you were working for me because it encouraged everyone to use the title at TUDOR, but we're equals and friends now. And when you get your own title back again, I won't have to call you *Sir* Thomas, will I?'

'Get my title back? What are you saying?'

Thomas was rewarded with a particularly blank look from his old boss.

* * *

When Thomas came home and told Sophie that Ryan had booked him on a BA flight for Israel the next morning, she'd looked up the temperatures for November in Jerusalem and started to pick out appropriate clothing.

'Israel isn't warm in winter, especially at night, and if happen to go to the desert it could be really parky. I'll pack warm clothes and your good hiking boots. I doubt you'll need a suit though.'

Sophie stuffed two pairs of warm socks into Thomas's boots while asking what overseas travel had been like in his Tudorland days.

'Interesting question, Sophie love. We travelled by sea of course, and the voyage took several weeks, so I needed clothes for the trip in addition to what I needed in the Holy Land itself. My household servants took my cabin trunks down to Tilbury and stowed them on the ship, which was called the *Champion* as I remember. I also remember that we docked at Acre. I already had the status of a knight, so I could have taken an esquire and a troop of men with me, but I preferred discretion. Inns attracted thieves in those days and I was carrying gold, so I needed a safe house in which to lodge. A friend at the Flemish embassy had arranged a connection with a merchant called Ezra who lived in Jerusalem. Ezra turned out to be a man of about my age and he had some connection with the Holy Land intelligence service of the day, so he became very helpful, but when we weren't working, we had a lot of fun. He was a nice guy.'

Thomas stared into space for a while and tried to recall

the weather at the start of the winter. 'I remember it being cold at night when we were away from the city, and of being glad of my warm cloak at the time.'

'Did you and Ezra get up to any mischief?'

Thomas looked a picture of innocence. 'What kind of mischief do you mean, Sophie love? I mean I was there on "business", so there was a certain amount of swordplay and the occasional person who inadvertently ended up dead as a result of getting in the way. But was there any mischief other than business? Well we were young and we needed to let off steam. I remember one occasion when Ezra and I got pissed and broke a valuable ornament in one of his friend's houses. Is that the kind of thing you're talking about?'

'Not really'

'You mean girls?'

Sophie gave a nod.

'Well… I wasn't married at that point, so I suppose there was a girl or two along the way.'

'I'll bloody well bet there were,' laughed Sophie, 'and did you drive them as crazy as you do me? In bed I mean?'

Thomas sat down on the bed and spiralled back through the centuries. He was twenty-two then, very good looking and not yet bowed down by grief or worry. Images of several girls came back to him, but one in particular was edging her way in, and now he found himself talking about her for the first time in two lifetimes.

'Ezra had an elderly neighbour who must have been gay, because unusually for Jews in those days, he had no wife or heirs. Anyway, a few weeks after I arrived, the old boy died and Ezra took over some of his servants, including a young Greek slave girl. Ezra gave her to me as a personal house servant, but she soon became a kind of girlfriend. She used to bring me wine, make sure I had clean sheets, fresh grapes and whatnot.'

Sophie nodded while thinking what advantage-takers young men were, because Thomas had obviously used the poor slave girl for his own purposes as well as enjoying her domestic duties.

Thomas searched his memory for the girl's name. 'She said her name was fairly well known in Greece, but its roots were Persian. What was it?' Thomas bit his lower lip and thought back for a while until it came back to him. '*Roxanne,* that was it! She was tall for a Greek girl and very good looking, and she had the most arresting grey eyes. Her mother died when she was small and her father had little money, so some kind of deal was done between the father and an older woman who wanted to a servant to take back with her to the Holy Land. Roxanne was still a child at that point, but a few years later, the old duck died and Roxanne was sold on to the elderly neighbour. I guess the old girl had liked Roxanne and wanted her to be safe. So she was…'

'Still a virgin?'

'Indeed,' agreed Thomas. 'Like hen's teeth they were, Sophie love. Especially among the servant classes.'

Thomas sat down, his packing temporarily forgotten while he found himself smelling the scent of pine, and seeing the golden stones of Jerusalem through the open window of an airy room. The window was framed by lightweight pale green curtains that drifted around in the warm breeze, and a pretty, dark haired girl lay in the bed laughing up at him while he reached for her.

'Roxanne was grateful for my kindness. I truly loved her and I was sad to leave her behind when I had to return to England.' Thomas sighed quietly. 'Dear me, I'd quite forgotten.'

He stared at the packing with unseeing eyes while his mind was still back in the past. 'I have always loved giving pleasure to the women who shared my bed, and even at

122

that age I knew the tricks of the game, although not as many as I picked up later. I think I made Roxanne happy. She was with child when I left, and there was nothing I could do about it. Ezra said he'd employ her for light work, bringing his food and so on while allowing her to keep her baby and raise it in his establishment. It wasn't an uncommon situation in those days, although it was usually the owner of the household who was the father. I can only say that I hope Roxanne had lived as happy a life as possible under the circumstances.'

'So, you had another child, Tommy, in Israel?'

'I guess so, but I never heard from Roxanne or Ezra after I left, so I have no idea whether she was safely delivered or what the child might have been.' Thomas stood up and took Sophie into his arms. 'It's a long time ago darling, whether it happened over twenty years ago according to my own lifespan or a half-millennium into the past according to the calendar, you're my lover now and I'll never leave you in the lurch.'

'What if you go back in time and bump into Roxanne – and your child?'

'It's done with, Sophie. I would wish her well, but that's all. Roxanne came into my life after I'd been in the Holy Land for a while, and truth to tell, I'd sampled a number of women there even before I met her, including a lovely Essene.'

'Aren't Essenes black?'

Thomas nodded slowly, 'Very black. The Essene girl told me her family had come to the Holy Land from East Africa. She was nice too… but what on earth was her name?' Thomas shut his eyes, tipped his head back and tried to remember. 'Amara. That was it. Amara. Nice name, isn't it?'

'Listen, you arse-pain of a husband, get your passport

and some Shekels out of the safe right now! If you insist on cataloguing all the birds you shagged during your Holy Land trip, we'll be here all night.'

'She had the nicest…'

'Shut up and get your passport before I give you a flea in your ear!'

Thomas pulled Sophie onto the bed and held her firmly. 'Not as nice as yours, though,' he said, turning her on her front. He pushed his wife's hair to one side and ran the tip of his tongue back and forth across the nape of her neck, while rubbing his thumb back and forth across her shoulder blade. Judging by the way Sophie's breath was catching in her throat, the packing would have to wait.

12:

Modern Israel

Strength does not come from winning. Your struggles develop your strengths. When you go through hardships and decide not to surrender, that is strength.

ARNOLD SCHWARZENEGGER

Alec picked Thomas up at Ben Gurion airport.

'Nice car,' said Thomas, admiring the new Volvo.

'I thought it was time I treated myself to a grown-up car, Jeeps get hard on the backside when you're no longer so young.'

Thomas chuckled at the revelation.

'I've booked you into the Mamilla,' said Alec, overtaking a slow-moving lorry. 'It's walking distance from the office and I've got you a map of the city and a few tourist brochures so you'll be able to get around on your own.' Alec gave Thomas a friendly grin. 'Been to Jerusalem before?'

Alec knew nothing about the Projects or Thomas's previous existence in Tudorland, so Thomas told him that this was his first visit.

'Pity you can't stay longer. Jerusalem is an interesting place and it's not short of history. Maybe you'll come back for a holiday and bring Sophie and Rosie with you. I'd be honoured to act as tour guide.'

'I'd like that, and I know Sophie would love to see Jerusalem. We'll definitely do it. Thanks for the offer.'

The first obvious difference from November in New London was the warmth and the sunshine reflecting off champagne coloured stone, but as they started to climb, Thomas noticed several old burned-out military vehicles by the side of the road and Alec explained that they had been left there as memorials to those who died in the War of Independence in 1948. As they approached the city, the ancient city walls came into view, and to his amazement, Thomas found himself picking out several familiar landmarks. Suddenly, the tastes, sounds and sensations of the past rushed sharply back into focus – as did the air of danger that he'd experienced last time round.

After Thomas had checked in and dropped his luggage in his hotel room, they parked behind Alec's office, and soon Thomas was telling Alec the story Sir David had told him.

'Obviously, I've got all our guys at TUDOR asking around, and Sir David's got the BBI's much larger ears to the ground, but it seems that the epicentre of this particular nightmare is right here in the Holy Land.'

'The Holy Land?'

'Sorry, Lapsed Catholic. Must still be indoctrinated,' Thomas said with a smile, silently reminding himself that the country was now *Israel* and that he needed to take more care.

Alec grinned, 'I know what you mean: lapsed Jew in my case.'

Alec said, 'Do you want to go straight back tomorrow or can you stay a while?'

'This is important. I can leave Baz to run the factory for

a bit.'

Alec handed Thomas a shoulder bag while fishing something out of the cupboard. It was a dark red *yarmulke* with a hair clip attached to stop it falling off. Thomas recognised the cap as what Sophie called in a *cupple* in Yiddish.

'You'll need it if you visit the Western Wall or any other Jewish holy places. If you visit any mosques, remember to take your shoes off before going in. Are you happy to wander around by yourself or do you want me to send someone with you?'

Thomas shook his head. 'I'd rather wander around on my own thanks. I'd like to get a feel for the city.'

'Jerusalem is a safe city for the most part because of the heavy security here, but we have our share of pickpockets and mugger-buggers here as in any tourist spot, so leave your temporary Mossad pass at reception and ask them to keep it for you. You can store your passport and any unneeded credit cards in my office safe if you like. Just keep one card and some cash on you. Do you have a travel belt or shall I lend you one?'

Thomas pointed to the belt that he always wore when in unfamiliar territory.

'And with that homily behind us, I'll let you walk back to your hotel while I set things in motion. I'll pick you up about half-seven for a bit of dinner eh?'

* * *

Alec took Thomas to a small Italian restaurant where they had a good pasta dish.

'You must try the St. Peter's fish while you're here. It's very good eating if you like fish.'

'I'm surprised you call it St. Peter's fish. Surely the

127

name comes from Christianity?'

'Everyone calls it St. Peter's fish. It's very nice barbecued the way that bistros do it here, with a dash of olive oil and a fresh salad and a glass of white wine. It's the freshness that does the trick.'

Thomas's mouth was full of pasta, so he just nodded. When he could speak again, he asked Alec why he worked in Jerusalem when Mossad's head office was in Tel Aviv.

'The main office is in Tel Aviv, but they have what you might call branch offices in other places. I run the Jerusalem one while also being the Mossad link with the UK.'

The two men spent the rest of the evening talking shop, and Thomas learned more about the situation in the Middle East in one evening than if he'd taken a year's course in university. Alec wasn't biased and he was surprisingly ready to admit the mistakes that various Israeli governments had made over the years, and those they were still making.

* * *

The next day, Thomas visited the tourist spots and soon he found himself in familiar places. The Dome of the Rock hadn't changed, but the Wailing Wall had, because there was now a clear space in front where there had once only been a narrow alley. He pulled out the *cupple* and clipped it to his hair, cleared security and approached the ranks of religious Jews praying in front of the Wall. He didn't fight his way through the pious ones to get at the ancient stones, but simply stood looking up at the Wall, while sending up a silent prayer.

He visited the Christian areas and walked the Via Dolorosa to the Church of the Holy Sepulchre. He saw the different sections that are now run by the various Christian religions. Thomas recognised the Catholic area and the Greek Orthodox one from before, but the Protestant sector was new to him. He made his way to the Roman Catholic area, knelt and crossed himself before finding a pew. There, he gave thanks for the life he now had and prayed for his family, friends and colleagues, and he asked God for help in his task of keeping his country safe and secure. He lit a candle to 'his' saint – St. Jude – the patron saint of lost causes, because before Sophie rescued him on that fateful June night in 1540, his very life had been well and truly lost.

Thomas wandered through what the Jews called the *Shouk* and the Arabs called the *Souk*, which was the market area of the old town. He peered into ancient shops selling spices, fruit and vegetables, along with colourful tourist tat. It hadn't changed much, and even some of the tourist items were recognisable from his time. Then he grasped a very personal nettle and made his way to the area that contained his old haunts. He hadn't expected to recognise anything, but to his amazement, he began to familiarise himself. Some buildings had gone and others had been added, but even so, the area was far from alien. Ezra's substantial dwelling still stood, although the outer walls were older and grubbier, and a pair of wrought iron gates now fronted the path to the house. He almost found himself looking around for Ezra and Roxanne.

'God's teeth!' he breathed to himself. 'I dread to think what would Sophie say if she saw this?' When he returned to the hotel, he took a bath and had a nap before dressing in khaki slacks, a warm shirt and his beloved sheep-lined bomber jacket. Soon he and Alec were comfortably seated in a small restaurant, where for the first time in half a millennium, Thomas again tasted the delicate white St. Peter's fish, freshly caught earlier that day in the Sea of

Galilee. Alec had suggested a light French wine to accompany the fish without overpowering it, and now they were pouring a second glass.

'The good news is that we're getting somewhere,' said Alec. 'My guys have heard of a group of Drogans, who started out as a small tribe living in an island in the Indian Ocean. It was completely peaceful until taken over by insurgents, who have now decided they don't want to stop at owning Drogana, but also want to take over the world or some such thing. As far as we know, they are operating in an area near the *Caves of Boronia,* which is near a ruined crusader castle called *Bonaventure.* The castle lies in a valley between the caves and a monastery.

'Can we go there?' asked Thomas.

Alec told Thomas he would drive them to a small Mossad branch office in Beersheba, leave the car there and meet a couple of Tamanite tribesmen who would lend them horses. The Tamanite robes and the distinctive Tamanite riding rig would give Thomas and Alec the cover they needed to roam around in the desert.

'Have you heard of Tamanite tribesmen?' asked Alec.

Thomas knew them and he'd used their services before, but he shook his head, so Alec told him about them. 'The Tamanite is an ancient tribe who roams the desert in the same nomadic way as they always have. They aren't Arabs as such, and they were here long before Moses brought the Hebrews out of Egypt. They aren't allied to any side or cause, but they help us because we help them by supplying them with the few things they need from the modern world.

Thomas had also made use of Tamanite insider knowledge in his day, but now he decided to ask a perfectly reasonable modern question.

'Can they use mobile phones in the desert?'

Alec nodded. 'Yeah, we have masts by the main roads,

so if they want to phone, they go to those areas.' Alec topped up Thomas's glass and poured himself another. 'A few of them have given up their old way of life and are living and working here in Jerusalem, and it's through their good offices that we contact the desert Tamanites whenever the need arises.'

'So, you propose to ask the Tamanites to keep an eye on the castle?'

Alec nodded, 'Yes and they have already reported unusual activity in the area.'

Alec suddenly realised he hadn't asked Thomas if he could ride a horse. After all, Thomas might be afraid of riding or he might dislike horses, but Thomas assured him it wasn't a problem.

'Sir David Cromwell is a keen rider and I sometimes join him for a hack around Hyde Park, and we sometimes go to T-West, do whatever business is needed and then take the time to stretch our legs and do a bit of fox hunting.'

'I thought fox hunting was illegal in the UK'.

'If you don't say anything, Sir David and I won't either,' laughed Thomas.

13:

The Desert Monastery

"So I say to you: Ask and it will be given to you; seek and you will find; knock and the door will be opened to you.

LUKE 11:9 (NEW INTERNATIONAL VERSION)

Thomas re-acquainted himself with a style of riding that he hadn't done for a very long time, along with getting used to the Tamanite turban and robes once again. He was glad of the sunglasses this time round, because they made the desert glare easier on the eyes. He tried to remember whether he'd visited the Bonaventure castle on his previous trip, but he'd seen so many castles and monasteries that he couldn't be sure. Something was ringing a bell though, but the memory wouldn't come into focus, so he decided to wait and see what turned up.

An hour of steady riding took them deep into the desert, and another half hour brought an oasis into view. The oasis seemed to be some way up a hill to the right. Just then, Alec stood up in his saddle and pointed to a building that was to the right of the trail, and to some ruins that were dead ahead.

'The castle fell down about three hundred years ago

during an earthquake, and while the Abbey up there was also damaged, the Order rebuilt it with stones from the ruined castle.'

'The name *Bonaventure* sounds French, so was the original Order French?' Thomas asked.

'The original Order *was* French, and the monks still speak an ancient form of French, but also Latin. If the language problem proves awkward, I can get a translator to come down from the university. But frankly, Tom, I'd rather not bring any extra people into the area for the time being, so let's hope we can find someone there who speaks Hebrew.'

Thomas now found himself straddling two worlds. It was the ruined state of the castle that had thrown him, because he now knew for certain that he'd been here before. The old monastery hadn't changed much, though the gardens were a little larger than they had been in his day.

Alex brought his horse to a stop and suggested they drink some water and have something to eat before tackling the monastery. 'Luckily for us, this isn't a closed Order, so we should be able to find someone who can tell us something.'

A half hour later, they were riding into a courtyard where a young monk helped them settle their horses. Another monk went to find the Prior, and soon Thomas and Alec were sitting on a bench in the refectory and drinking lemon tea. The elderly Prior didn't speak any Hebrew – only Latin and ancient French, and this made Thomas even more discombobulated than ever, because the language, clothing, and indeed the monastery, hadn't changed much at all, while *he* had! The last time he'd been here, he'd been a Tudor man in his early twenties, but now he was a modern man in his early forties – as the muscles in his legs and back were reminding him.

Thomas found himself in a real quandary because he

didn't know whether it would be better to jump in and deal with the situation or let Alec call in a translator. Knowing his decision would be crucial, he decided to throw caution to the wind, so he addressed the Prior in his word-perfect Latin.

'*Dic nobis quid tibi videatur in opere circa arce?*'

The response confirmed that there had indeed been some unusual activity around the castle ruins. Now working on Tudorland autopilot, Thomas translated the Latin into his outdated Hebrew for Alec's benefit. Like all Israeli Jews, even secular ones, Alec had learned ancient Hebrew as well as modern Ivrit, so it wasn't too hard for him to understand Thomas's pronunciation.

A young monk approached the Prior and whispered something in his ear, and then at the Prior's nod, the young monk brought forward an old man whom the Prior introduced as Brother Corbu. The old chap only spoke archaic French and some halting Latin, so Thomas used his own Tudor French.

By now, it was perfectly obvious to Alec that something bloody unworldly was going on, but he decided to hold his curiosity in check for the time being. The old monk repeated the story the others had told, and suggested that Thomas and Alec take a look for themselves. He apologised for not offering to go with them, saying it would be hard for him to walk so far over rough ground at his age.

* * *

Riding back down the hillside, Alec buttonholed Thomas and whispered urgently. 'I've always thought there was something weird about you, Hatherleigh, and now I *know* there is. Word perfect Latin? Old Hebrew? Old French? Who the fuck are you?'

'Add old Greek, along with Venetian, Florentine,

Spanish, Flemish, Burgundian, Dutch, old English and a fair bit of Turkish and Egyptian Arabic to that lot, and I'll tell you later,' answered Thomas quietly.

'I sincerely hope you do, Tom, because I don't want to formally interrogate you.'

'I don't want you to formally interrogate me, either. I'm not at my best when I'm tied up in a basement with a bag over my head,' Thomas said with feeling.

Thomas was glad the truth was drifting out, because good as he was at keeping secrets, the situation was beginning to get on his nerves.

The ruined castle covered a fair bit of ground, but as castles go, it was still only small. It seemed to have been built as an outpost to house knights whose job was protecting pilgrims visiting the monastery. The wind had erased some of the evidence of terrorist activity, but there were still a few tyre tracks and an area of disturbance near the centre of the ruins, along with a small cairn of stones that appeared to be recent. But there was no indication of an entrance to anything – or for that matter of the presence of any kind of bomb.

Alec scratched his head, and thinking aloud said, 'There must have been an underground river or reservoir for the castle to have existed here, but I can't see anything now, and the only greenery seems to be around the monastery.'

Thomas stared at the tumbled rocks that had made up part of the keep and nodded distractedly. It was becoming obvious that the only way they were going to find the damned hiding place was to go back in time. He would definitely need to take Alec along, and probably also Shimon for this one, and anyone from TUDOR who could be spared.

Back in Beersheba, they watered the horses and tied them to a post behind the Mossad offices with instructions to the guy on reception to look out for the Tamarites and give them something from the petty cash when they came for the horses. After they'd washed and changed, Alec steered Thomas to a small bar where they sat outside, relaxing in the early evening sun with bottles of Peroni. Thomas took a draft of the wonderful Italian beer and waited for the inevitable, while Alec fixed him with a steely look.

'Interrogation time?' asked Thomas with a slight lift to the corner of his mouth. 'I prefer doing it to others than having it done to me.'

'As the Bishop said to the actress,' grinned Alec.

Soon enough, Alec was so absorbed in what Thomas was telling him that he almost forgot to drink his beer. Alec's black moustache twitched at each unexpected revelation, while Thomas ploughed on and explained how Sophie had acquired the first Project, and how she had rescued Thomas from certain death in Tudorland.

'*The Director of State Security for England and Wales*,' repeated an astonished Alec. 'Fuck me, Tom; you were a top dog even way back then, weren't you?'

Thomas nodded. 'Only Sir Thomas Cromwell stood between me and the King, and in those days, Cromwell ran the country much of the time.' Thomas took another drink before carrying on. 'Life wasn't easy then, though. For instance, I was away on business on one occasion and when I got back, I found my wife and young son had died of the sweating sickness.'

Alec's mouth fell open. 'I had no idea you'd been married before or that you'd lost a child.'

'How could you have known?' said Thomas with a

slight shrug. The memory still saddened him.

'After that I lived alone – albeit with a house full of servants and clerks coming in and out, and I was helped by the fact that my sister Katherine and her husband, Steven, lived next door with their young son, Robert. Thankfully, they didn't go down with the sickness. Anyway, they're all in New London now and we've been back and vaccinated all our friends in Tudorland since then, so that's one worry I can forget about.'

'You aren't talking about Steven Byers at TUDOR by any chance, Tom?'

Thomas nodded.

'Holy King David! So Steven's another Tudorlander?'

Thomas smiled. 'Yep: Steven's my brother-in-law.'

Alec shook his head in wonderment and then finished his drink while Thomas carried on with his story. 'Sophie and I brought Steven and Kate to New London to escape an outbreak of plague, and we all used the strange business in Hidalia to take an opportunity to become immigrants and then fast track to British citizenship. Kate was pregnant at that time, so their youngest lad, Harry, was born in New London. We helped Baz, Sir David, Jack and Kelly by taking them back to 1540 to help with the Westminster Abbey operation, and after that, Steven and I joined TUDOR on a permanent basis. The connection is Baz, because his wife Margie was Sophie's best friend long before any of us came on the scene.'

Thomas waited while Alec went to the bar and ordered more beer and some filled potato-skin snacks before going on with the story. 'As TUDOR grew, others joined us from the armed services and other security services, and then Sir David was asked to open the much larger BBI to cope with all the cyber stuff that's going on. Baz should have taken over as Director of TUDOR, but he didn't feel comfortable with the position, so Frances Shulman appointed me Director with Baz as my deputy.

'Sir David Cromwell?' mused Alec, 'any connection to Oliver Cromwell?'

'David is a direct descendant of my old boss, Thomas Cromwell, via his son Gregory. Thomas Cromwell's older sister married but kept the Cromwell name, and it's her descendant who was Oliver Cromwell. David sometimes jokes that one king cut off the head of one of his ancestors, while another of his ancestors cut off the head of another king 120 years later.

'Incidentally, Gregory Cromwell married Anne Seymour, who was Jane Seymour's sister, and thus joined the Cromwells to the branch of the Tudorland family called Courtenay. The Courtenays were cousins of Henry VIII and they became – and still are – Earls of Devon, so our David is related to all the royals one way or another.'

Alec shook his head in wonderment. 'What a story! I always felt there was something odd about you though. Your formal manner and slight American accent made me wonder whether you were Canadian, and from an old family in Quebec or something, but I could never have guessed this lot, not in a million years.'

Thomas decided to tell Alec about the current batch of Projects. 'Sophie is a clever girl. She's a physicist and mathematician, so she joined forces with Raj and they now keep a host of Projects in a barn in Devon, along with small shuttles behind the old Mews offices.'

'I understood the Mews to be some kind of arms store,' said Alec quietly.

'That too, and we let many of those who work at TUDOR think that's all we keep at the Mews.'

'Holy Moses,' said Alec shaking his head in amazement.

'You know we have two other branches of TUDOR,

don't you?'

Alec nodded. 'One in Manchester and another in the sticks, right?'

'The Devon outpost is at a place called Hatherleigh Farm, and it is run by my cousin Charles who has always been known as Carlo, along with his wife, Lucy. Lucy is modern, but Carlo is…'

Alec cut in, 'Don't tell me – he's another ancient monument!'

Thomas grinned, 'Carlo'd knock your block off for calling him that. He's nine years younger than me, so he wouldn't thank you for calling him ancient!'

Alec chuckled a little while Thomas went on.

'Anyway, that isn't quite the whole story, as we now have another time and place to contend with, and that is 1967 Israel. The connection is a chap called Captain Shimon Sobieski and he's an earlier member of your very own Mossad. Shimon fought in the Six-Day-War, but his arrival in our lives wasn't down to "business" so much as to a mistake made by David's niece, Emily Cromwell.'

This piece of information nearly did away with what was left of poor Alec Blitz's mind.

* * *

An hour later, Thomas and Alec were knocking back burgers in a café called 'McDavid' while Thomas pondered their current problem and Alec struggled to get his head round the TUDOR story.

'I know this sounds daft Tom, but I have a sneaky feeling you've been here before, and I don't just mean Israel. I know you said you haven't, but I can't shake the feeling that this land isn't new to you.'

'I spent eighteen months in the Holy Land doing

business with the Ottomans and Greeks on behalf of King Henry, and doing a bit of spying here and there while I was about it. The year was 1526, I was a young man then, and I hadn't yet met my wife. I knocked off a few people who Henry and Wolsey wanted to be rid of at the time. They both took the same view as Stalin, which was, "get rid of the man: get rid of the problem". So if they wanted someone whacked, it was up to me to do the necessary.'

Alec gave Thomas his white-toothed, piratical smile and lowered his head, while biting his lip for a moment. His deep brown eyes rose to latch on to Thomas's deep blue ones. '*Bonaventure*?' he asked.

Thomas realised that his friend wasn't only bright, he was extremely good at making connections, as any half-decent intelligence analyst should be.

'I couldn't be sure at first, but as soon as we went up to the monastery, I knew I'd been here before and I've even lodged there. I also knew the Tamanites and their ways.'

'I noticed you didn't have much trouble with the horse riding.'

Thomas gave a slight nod, 'Horses were the only form of transport for someone of my class. I still ride when I can and I can still use a sword, throw a knife and pull a bow – useless as skills for now, of course.'

Alec couldn't help noticing that the more Thomas's mind focused on the past, the more his rhythm of speaking slipped back into an older style.

Thomas's blue eyes bore into Alec's brown ones. 'It might behove us to take a trip back in time to visit the castle as it was then. As castles go, it was small and fairly new. The Turks controlled this land and they only allowed small pilgrim castles rather than large fortifications, and anyway the era of big castles was over due to the development of cannon guns that could blow them apart.'

Thomas looked closely at Alec and asked him to keep all this information to himself and not spread it around Mossad.

'Or what?' asked Alec with a teasing grin.

'Or I'd kill you as soon as you'd safely paid for my meal,' said Thomas quietly.

'I'd like to see you try,' laughed Alec. He was still chuckling when it occurred to him that his friend only had one hand resting on the table. A quick check below showed a small but powerful revolver pointing straight at his abdomen.'

'Can't say I like revolvers much,' drawled Thomas. 'I prefer the H&K pistol, but it was all I could get in the *shouk* yesterday.'

'You would too, wouldn't you?' said Alec under his breath.

Thomas's deep blue eyes turned to ice as he looked across the table. 'You wouldn't feel it coming, Mossad or not. If I was forced to take you out, I'd hate it, but our friendship wouldn't stop me. You see, Alec, my job has always been to defend my monarch's realm, and it still is. When you think of it, I had a licence to kill then – and I still do.'

Despite himself, the dashing Mossad man shivered. Thomas's words were reverberating in his brain, and he knew he'd never forget them. "*I had a licence to kill then – and I still do.*" Alec knew that where his country was concerned, Thomas meant business.

14:

The Motley Crew

A lot of times people look at the negative side of what they feel they can't do. I always look on the positive side of what I can do.

CHUCK NORRIS

It was Friday lunchtime and Shimon was relieved to have the rest of the weekend off. His plan was to shower and get something to eat before phoning around to see if any of his friends were looking for company, but first he decided to check the Pigeon. When he opened the inner box, it wasn't Emily's familiar handwriting he saw, but a short note from Sophie saying, *'Please respond.'*

Fifteen minutes later, Sophie was knocking on his door and five minutes after that, they were on their way to the Mews, and Shimon was delighted to find Emily waiting there. Sophie's secretary, Jessica, handed Shimon and Emily a pair of ID cards and told them to accompany her to the TUDOR offices in Millbank.

'There is a meeting scheduled for 15:00 hours,' said Jessica.

'Any idea what it's about?' asked Shimon.

Jessica shook her head. 'I expect we'll hear soon

enough.'

Baz chose to hold the meeting in the briefing room because as he'd told Thomas, 'Everyone and his pet hamster want to be here.'

By two-forty-five, the room was filling up. Thomas was still wearing the jeans and red sweater he'd travelled in, while Alec and Shimon were in uniform. When he came face to face with Alec, Shimon came smartly to attention and saluted. Alec gave him a salute in return and shook Shimon's hand. Alec was fascinated to be confronted with a Mossad man from almost four decades earlier, noticing that the uniform hadn't changed, even down to the Hebrew initials on Shimon's shirt showing he belonged to the *Israel Defence Force*. Alec asked Shimon to stay near him while Emily joined Jessica at the back of the room.

Frances Shulman strode in, accompanied by Emson Barotse. Sir David Cromwell was hard on their heels. Thomas's PA, Ryan Andrews, was setting up a laptop, helped by one of the girls from Steven's office. Carlo and Lucy had flown in from TUDOR West, while Kelly and Mike had done the same thing from TUDOR North.

Baz told everyone to sit wherever they liked and not to worry about seniority, and once everyone was seated, he welcomed them and said that Thomas would start the briefing. Ryan fired up the laptop to show a map of the southern half of Israel while Thomas took his place by the side of the screen.

Thomas said, 'I feel as though I'm in one of those Second World War films, talking to a room filled with young RAF men and telling them about the target for tonight. Perhaps Ryan should pop out and buy cigarettes so we can all light up.'

The mild joke helped everyone relax.

'I'm sorry to say that we don't have as much intel as we

would like yet, but we have an open link to Alec's office in Jerusalem and thence to Mossad HQ in Tel Aviv, so if anything breaks at their end, Steven's assistant, Julie will bring it straight to us.

'Anyway, this is what this meeting is about. We have heard on the grapevine that some kind of bomb is destined to come to London. We know that a small group of Drogans is behind the scheme and that the bomb is currently being stored somewhere in Israel. Drogana is an island off the coast of Saudi Arabia and Drogans aren't Arabs or Muslims, but some kind of ancient tribal group, which has hitherto been peaceable, but they now have a self-appointed leader who wants to show off, and he's decided to make mischief here in the UK. The choice of Israel as part of their offensive programme was an odd one, but Drogans have no historical objection to using Israeli territory and it's closer to Drogana than any place in Europe, so we think it makes some kind of sense to them.'

Thomas stopped for a moment and looked around the room. When he spoke again, his voice betrayed the seriousness of the situation. 'As far as Mossad has managed to ascertain, the Drogans have acquired a single nuclear bomb from the Russians, and the idea is to ship it to London.'

This brought a gasp from around the room.

'It is due to come in by submarine and be offloaded onto a small ship, before being tucked away in some cove, and then transported to the London area. Mossad tell us that the most likely date for the Drogans to start moving the bomb is two weeks from now when the moon is dark.' Thomas put a hand up to quell the unrest that was gathering in the room. 'Apparently, this isn't a nuclear bomb in the normal sense of the word, but we'll come to that in a moment.'

Thomas signalled to Ryan who clicked the image to one

of rocks and tumbled masonry.

'Alec's department got wind of the possible hiding place in southern Israel, beneath a ruined castle called *Bonaventure,*' Thomas pointed to the map. 'The castle fell down in the 1700s due to an earthquake, but there is a working monastery nearby. I flew out to Israel and the following day, Alec and I disguised ourselves as Tamanite tribesmen and rode out to the area.'

There was a murmur at this news.

'Alec has called upon the help of the local Tamanites who are now keeping a lookout for us, and a couple of Alec's men have also joined the tribesmen. An army helicopter is making occasional passes, and a Mossad guy is working in the monastery gardens overlooking the Bonaventure site. He's disguised as a monk.'

That brought a murmur of surprise, but Alec stood up and informed the group that Mossad wasn't choosy about the religion of its recruits as long as they weren't enemy infiltrators. He explained that this chap was a Latin-speaking Roman Catholic who had actually *been* a monk in his younger days. Once he'd finished, he nodded to Thomas, who took over again.

'The castle is small and it was constructed during the Ottoman era to protect pilgrims visiting the monastery and other holy sites. The monks told us that there was once a source of water under the castle, but falling sand and rocks blocked or diverted the underground streams when the earthquake struck. It seems likely that the Drogans have discovered a way of getting under the castle, but we can't find an entrance, and while we could dig up the whole ruin; it would take time and it would also send the archaeological community ballistic.'

Ryan now displayed a close-up of the ruins from a satellite photo that had been taken two hours earlier.

'As you can see, there are tyre tracks and footprints among the castle ruins, although some belong to Alec and me. If you look carefully, you can see the hoof-prints left by our horses. Other than that, there isn't anything to see other than this strange cairn of stones near the northern edge of the site. Baz and I think the best way of finding out what's under the castle is to go back in time and visit it when it was still in operation.'

Thomas nodded to Baz and sat down while Baz signalled Alec to take the floor. Alec stepped forward to take his place, ran a hand through his hair and made a start.

'We are getting intel from friendly Drogans who don't like what their new self-styled leader is doing. They've told us that the device *is* nuclear, but it isn't a bomb as such. It's an *electro nuclear magnetic resonance pulse machine*, or for short, a *Helios* bomb. The device is an updated version of the 1970s electro magnetic pulse apparatus, and it is very powerful. My men think it will be in a protective case, so it will probably be the size of a small fridge and it will be heavy, so the thinking is that it must have been lowered from the back of a vehicle onto wooden tracks and trundled down through some kind of tunnel.' Alec borrowed Thomas's laser pointer and pointed to the cairn of stones. 'We think this cairn marks the spot, because we can't see any other reason for it.'

Raj spoke up. 'Do we know what the Helios would do if it reached here and went off?'

Alec smoothed his moustache and he looked around the room before speaking. 'Apparently, it would knock out all the electricity sub-stations in London and the Home Counties, and it would cause a separation between any computer in the south of Britain and its satellite connection. In short, there would be no communication in the Home Counties and very little further afield either. Gatwick and

Heathrow would close down, and military airports such as Northolt, Manston and even Biggin Hill would be grounded. There would be no electricity, petrol pumps or water supply. Hospitals would continue to operate for a while on petrol-fed generators and they would cancel all non-urgent procedures, but unless the situation could be fixed fairly quickly, they would have to close. Your military would be disrupted and southern England would be plunged back into a medieval world, but with no infrastructure, no time to adjust – and with a large population, many of whom would go on the rampage. Vehicles would run out of fuel, neither mobile or land line phones would work and the police would find themselves dealing with an out-of-control capital city with no means of communication other than police whistles.'

'Great God in Heaven!' exclaimed Jack.

Frances Shulman signalled to Thomas that she wanted to speak, and she did so, slowly, clearly and with feeling.

'Our electricity supply grid is excellent, but parts of it are ageing and that would hold up repairs. We fear that London and other towns would become no-go areas with young louts running around looting at will. We would declare Martial Law and send in the troops, and we'd get on top of the situation in time, but in the short term, the South East of England would become a death trap. It would be like New Orleans after hurricane Katrina but much worse, because London and the South East are a much larger and more densely populated. We have to consider that if we can't get enough clean water into the city, we'd see the return of cholera and possibly such rodent-borne diseases as…'

'The sweating sickness and the plague,' interjected Thomas grimly.

The silence in the room was palpable, while Mrs.

Shulman continued with her briefing. 'I know TUDOR and the BBI will get on top of this one quickly, but Emson and I are already putting a few precautions in place. The Royal family will start their Christmas holiday at Balmoral somewhat earlier than usual – right now, in fact – and the government will disperse. My own department will move directly to the West Country where we have nuclear bunkers and complete office systems on Dartmoor. Emson and I, along with our families and close associates, will take lodgings with Lucy and Carlo. I've heard that it's very comfortable in their home. We will also use TUDOR-West's offices.'

'That's all we need,' muttered Carlo sotto voce, while half rising from his seat and telling the Home Secretary that he and Lucy would be honoured.

Stifling a grin, Thomas got to the crux of the briefing.

'I spent a year in the Holy Land as a young man, but the paradox problem means the earliest that I can travel back is to the late autumn of 1542. However, that does mean that I could get to the castle and look into whatever lies beneath it. I'd want Carlo with me, because he is a Tudorlander, so he speaks Latin and our old French, which means we can communicate with those who lived in the castle and the monastery at that time. I would like to take both Alec and Shimon, and Baz, Jack and Mike. Kelly would have to wear a man's robe as a disguise.'

Kelly smiled to show she understood.

'Is there anyone else who would like to join us?'

The room resembled a school classroom when an outing was proposed, because every man in the room volunteered, and so did some of the women.

Frances Shulman glared at her Parliamentary Private Secretary and told him to put his hand down. 'You're going nowhere so forget it! Even Martinique Mike would have a problem, because blacks were slaves in that era, and I'm not having any member of my staff treated with disrespect. Forget it, Emson.'

It occurred to Emson that the only person who ever treated him with disrespect was the Home Secretary herself, but she treated everyone else just as badly, and it was never racist or personal.

Thomas smiled at the idea of Emson and Mike being slaves. 'Actually, I often used Nubians as troopers in my day, so they could certainly act in that capacity on this occasion, but I wonder whether Emson could look after himself in a shoot-out, especially if we have to do it with bows and arrows?'

'He won't be given the opportunity to find out,' said the Home Secretary in a "that's that" tone of voice.

Emson pulled a face, but acquiesced on the basis that he knew full well he'd be more use in New London than running around the sixteenth century Ottoman Empire disguised as a Nubian.

Thomas turned to Raj. 'Despite the dangers, I will need you along with Sophie and Lucy to operate the encampment and I'll want Steven with us too.'

They all agreed, while Thomas turned to Shimon.

'I understand from Emily that you know the area, is that right?'

Shimon nodded and addressed the room in his lightly accented English. 'I was there during the Six Day War, which was last year to me and thirty-nine years ago to you.' He let that strange fact sink in for a moment before going on. 'In fact, it occurs to me that the entrance to the tunnel could be hidden in the *Caves of Boronia,* because the caves are only a couple of hundred yards from the castle, albeit on the other side of the main road.'

Now Alec jumped in. 'Of course, *Boronia!* I'd forgotten

about those bloody caves. You're right.'

Now Thomas asked Shimon if he knew of a relatively secluded place where they could make camp.

'There is a wadi behind the caves that even shepherds don't visit, because there's no water there. It's hotter than hell in summer, but at this time of year it'll be warm by day and perishing at night.'

'Sounds good to me,' said Thomas while turning to Carlo, 'We're going to need horses - can you supply them?'

Carlo nodded. 'Lucy and I can supply decent mounts, along with their feed and all their other requirements.'

Sir David chimed in. 'You'll need a few extra mounts because I'm coming with you.'

Thomas raised an eyebrow, but Sir David shot him down. 'There's no need to pull that face, Hatherleigh, after five hundred years of my family bossing yours about, I am still pulling rank, even though I am no longer part of TUDOR!'

Thomas put his hands up, surrendering to the inevitable.

Baz stood up and said, 'So are we good to go? How soon can we get off the ground?'

Sophie conferred with Jessica, nodded and said they would be ready to lift-off by about ten the next morning. Lucy agreed that she and Carlo would ferry the horses directly to Boronia, packing them four at a time into their largest Project vans and shuttling back and forth until they had all the mounts and their gear in place. They reckoned the job would take a good few hours.

'So now we must look out our doublets and riding breeches, because we'll be wearing them by the morrow,' said Thomas.

It was then that Baz noticed Emily standing up and waving her arms about.

'What is it, Emily?' asked Baz.

'I think I can save you a great deal of time and trouble - and maybe even save lives.'

'How so, Ems?'

Emily's throat was very dry, but she still spoke up. 'I'm very nervous, Baz. I've never talked in public before.'

'You're with friends here, Emily,' said Baz waving her forward. 'Come up here and go for it.'

Emily made her way to the front of the room, climbed onto a raised area and looked warily at the audience before drawing a deep breath and plunging in.

'My name is Emily Cromwell and I am Sir David Cromwell's niece, and those who've worked in TUDOR for a while will know me.'

This brought nods from some members of the audience and a surprised murmur from others.

'A few months ago, I made a bad mistake – but it could turn out to be a blessing in disguise.'

This brought another murmur.

'You see, when I was still at school I used to help out at the Mews, and as there wasn't anything sensitive there at the time, my presence was no problem, and like any school-kid, I was happy to earn a bit of pocket money. I signed the Official Secrets Act at the time, although I think Uncle only got me to do it to make me feel important.'

A few people smiled at this revelation.

'Later on, I got into in an abusive relationship and Uncle David gave me a key to a back door at the Mews in case I needed a bolt-hole in the middle of the night. In the event, I never used the key, and I forgot about it. Eventually I got out of my bad situation, found somewhere to live and went to Uni, which is where I am now, working for my degree in modern history.'

Emily stopped for a moment and looked up at Baz. He gave her an encouraging smile.

'Part of my course has been on twentieth century Israel, but I struggled to understand the conflicts and I couldn't work out how to help myself. Then, one day, I happened to be unpacking the last of my boxes when I came across the key, so I decided to creep into the Mews at the dead of night, borrow the original old Project and take a trip to 1967 Israel. My idea was to land there soon after the Six-Day-War and look for a villager or a farmer who might tell me something about the conflict.' Now Emily bit her lips, while looking a little sheepish, but she went on with story. 'I reckoned nobody would mind me borrowing the old original Project since the new ones were so much better... if anyone even noticed, that is.'

This information sent a small ripple through the room.

'Well, my history studies might have been coming along nicely, but my maths and computing skills aren't great, so I cocked up the coordinates and landed in an area where there *were* no villages, and I landed *during* the war rather than after it. The Project had landed itself in a nice safe cave, but when I walked outside I almost got creamed by a Jordanian mortar.'

This sent a loud ripple around the room.

'Someone tossed me into a foxhole, dived on top of me and stayed there until the Jordanians moved away. My face was stuffed into the sand at the bottom of the trench so I didn't know who or what was on top of me – and giving me a bit of a grope while he was at it.'

A chuckle went round the room, especially from Jack Duquesne.

'Anyway, the bit that matters is this,' said Emily. 'When I was on my way out of the cave, I tripped over something and I ripped my new trousers, but when I made my way back through into the cave later, I noticed that what I had stumbled over wasn't a natural feature but a shaped slab.

152

My guess is that someone put it there centuries ago – perhaps to hide something they'd wanted kept out of sight. However, the job must have been done in a hurry because the slab didn't quite sit properly in the hole, and if I'm right, the Drogons must have discovered the slab and pulled it up, putting it back unevenly later.'

The murmurs rose to a buzz, while Emily moved over to a flip chart and picked up a marker pen. Turning to Baz, she asked if it was all right to use the pad. Baz gave a nod.

'My Dad is Sir James Cromwell, and if you are all into palaeontology, you will have heard of him because he's the chap people call in when some new fossil comes to light. Anyway, I've always kept an interest in Dad's speciality and it's a subject that links naturally to geology so I can't but help knowing a bit about rock formations, and if I'm right, I inadvertently tripped over precisely what you are looking for.'

This brought a gasp from the room.

Emily drew a line that stopped half way across the page, then a second line beneath the first that continued to run across the page to the edge in a slight downward trajectory.

'The name *"Caves of Boronia"* is plural, is it not?'

A murmur of assent went around the room.

'I've checked out Google Earth and I can see several caves on either side of the one I landed in. They are smaller than the main cave and they are all at ground level, but my bet is that there are more of these long, tunnel-like structures *under* the ground. Such structures are called tubes, and it's possible that the cave that I landed in is directly above a tube that runs in a slight downward angle which would take it *under* the castle.'

Warming to her theme, Emily continued to speak with growing confidence. 'Caves can form when a fold in the rock creates a gap, and if there is earthquake activity, the

153

ground will shift. Over time, water seeps through and the gap erodes, allowing underground streams to develop. Sometimes rivers flow along these underground courses for millennia, eroding them still further as time goes by.

We know that southern Israel is hot and dry now, but it may well have been subject to fierce rainstorms and flooding in an earlier time. Flash flooding can sometimes occur in the desert even today, but further back in time – say close to the end of the ice age – there would have been a lot more precipitation.

Add to this, the rock in the Boronia area may be softer than the surrounding rock, which would make it vulnerable to erosion. Sometimes a tube system ends in a layer of clay that makes it widen out and create a lake. Then water continues to pour in and the lake presses outwards until it finds cracks and outlets that allow the water to travel on, which means the lake stays at the same level for centuries. You see the kind of thing in the *Caves of Drach* in Majorca.'

Emily looked around the room and saw that she had everyone's full attention. 'We know the area is low lying – below sea-level in fact – so the chances are that a water table *did* exist under the castle. That kind of underground lake used to be called "sweet water" because it can be used as a reservoir for drinking and irrigation, as opposed to surface water, which becomes increasingly alkaline due to evaporation over time.

A clue to the situation is the oasis and the kitchen gardens that you see around the monastery, as they must have a similar tube and lake system below, and the monks must have been pumping water from it for hundreds of years. You see the same effect in Masada, where the sweet water inside the hill allowed the Zealots to hold out against the Romans for three years. Interestingly, they even grew salad and vegetables on the top of the hill… which goes to show.'

This brought nods of agreement from those who knew the area.

'We know that Bonaventure wasn't a Crusader castle, so it didn't need to be super strong, and it may well have been slung up quickly using a mix of stone and the local version of adobe, so an earthquake would have brought it down quite easily. Such a quake would definitely affect the underground topography, so it must have dumped sand and stone into the tubes, changing the direction of the underground streams or stopping them altogether. My guess is that a tube runs in a roughly west/east direction from the Caves of Boronia, under the road and beneath the northern sector of the ruins. If I'm right, someone could line the tube with planks, lower something into it and trundle down to a cavern and hide it there in complete safety. The cairn in the photo could be an "X marks the spot" thingy, but my guess is that it was put there to hide an air vent.'

'God's teeth!' exclaimed Thomas.

'Holy Moses!' said Alec, shaking his head.

Shimon stared at Emily in proud amazement.

Alec spoke up. 'I think Emily's done a terrific job, and if she's right, we won't need to travel back in time or take a whole encampment with us. What we now need is to get into that cave and raise that slab PD bloody Q!'

This brought nods of agreement from the audience.

Mrs. Shulman stood up, faced the audience, glared at them and said, 'Whatever you need to do, I sincerely hope you get a move on, because I don't want our green and pleasant land bent out of shape by these bastard Drogons.'

Everyone in the room agreed with *that* observation.

When most of the people had gone, the TUDOR nucleus remained to work out a plan of action, and it was only when this was done that Thomas reminded them that it was Kelly who always chose the names for their operations.

'How about keeping it simple this time, and calling it "*Operation Bonaventure*"? After all, this is something of an adventure and we all hope it will be a "*bon*" one,' said Kelly.

'Sounds good to me,' said Thomas, and so "Operation Bonaventure" was now underway.

15:

Bonaventure Castle

A real friend is one who walks in when the rest of the world walks out.
WALTER WINCHELL

Jack shone a torch down the hole and spotted the tunnel, which had indeed been lined with planks. When Jack shone his torch along the planking, marks came into view that suggested something heavy had been wheeled along it. Soon the team was walking down the tunnel, stooping slightly to avoid catching their heads on the uneven roofline. A few moments later, they reckoned themselves to be under the road that ran between the caves and the ruins. The tunnel started to widen out until it ended in an underground chamber, and when they looked up, they could see that a ventilation shaft had indeed been driven upwards from the cavern. More importantly though, standing in the middle of the chamber, was a grey metal box about the size of a small fridge.

'Okay, that's it,' said Alec briskly. 'Let's get out of here; I'll get the bomb squad to sort this out. I suggest you all get back to the Mews and once you lot are out of the way, I'll tell our people to alert the customs, coast guard and the navy and get them to search any unusual fishing boats or anything else that doesn't look right. We'll have to station people here to catch the Drogons when they come for the bomb.'

'I wouldn't mind being part of that,' said Shimon.

'Me neither,' agreed Jack.

'Let's get the bomb boys to remove the bloody thing first because that will put my mind at rest,' Alec said. 'It seems logical that they'll come for the Helios bomb at the dark of the moon, so that's when we should be here.'

'Funny thing,' said Thomas quietly, 'As you know, Baz's wife Margie is into all things weird and wonderful, and she always says that starting anything during the dark of the moon is a waste of time. So following that logic, if the Drogons try to kick off this operation at that time it shouldn't work for them either.'

'Well let's hope your resident witch is right,' smiled Alec.

* * *

The boffins in Jerusalem confirmed that the Helios bomb was indeed an augmented Russian electro-magnetic pulse bomb with a nuclear component, and that it was more powerful and trickier than the 1980s originals had been. The techies had put the appliance back together again, but with the nuclear works replaced by similar looking, but innocuous metal parts, and Alec and Shimon, aided by several Israeli techies slid the bomb back into its hiding place under the castle.

* * *

Two weeks later, the team set up camp in the *wadi* behind the *Caves of Boronia*. Alec and Shimon were in charge of the operation, with a few trusted members of Alec's team along to give a hand. Not wanting to draw attention to the Projects, Thomas, Jack, Baz, Mike, Kelly and Carlo had flown in to Ben Gurion from Northolt and on to Boronia by helicopter. Raj, Steven and Sophie were holding the fort back in London, now joined by Margie, Lucy, Emily and Jessica who wanted to be there in case of news. In Israel, the members of the Bonaventure team were armed to the teeth. It's cold at night in the desert, especially in December, and it was far from warm in the cave, so both the Israelis and the TUDORs were glad they'd taken Alec's advice and worn warm clothes and good boots.

Sophie had issued the team with the usual safety rings, but also with additional rings that had small, blue gemstones in them. She insisted they all wore them, and that included Alec's Mossad people, but she was strangely close-mouthed about their use.

Soon after eight, a lorry rolled up and turned off the road towards the cave. It parked near the mouth of the largest cave, where several men jumped out and let down a flap at the back. A small forklift trundled off the platform and made its way into the cave, where the driver directed it slowly and carefully past the projecting lump of concrete; then, he turned the forklift 180 degrees. Shimon and Baz jumped onto the driver and Baz covered the hapless man's mouth with duck tape while Shimon dragged him back along the cave and thrust him into the arms of one of Alec's Mossad men, who promptly handcuffed him and taped his ankles together.

Several more Drogons walked into the cave, with a couple of them carrying stout ropes. Like all good plans, theirs was a straightforward one, and it would have worked if Emily hadn't landed a Project in the caves in 1967 and stumbled over the ancient slab, and if she hadn't known all about underground watercourses.

When the first Drogons reached the forklift, they couldn't help noticing that their man wasn't around. Alec understood Drogon, and he heard one of them say that the driver must have wandered off to take a leak. A second Drogon remarked that the driver hadn't chosen a great time for it. Soon the two men were looking around and calling out to the driver.

One of the Drogons was just that bit too alert, so thinking he'd spotted something amiss in the depths of the cave; he pulled out his pistol and cocked it. Another Drogon spotted Shimon half hidden behind a rock, while Shimon simultaneously noticed the light from a torch glancing off the outline of the gun. Shimon leapt to one side and dropped, rolling onto his back and bringing up his own pistol as he went. He narrowly avoided catching a bullet, while spitting out an oath that sounded like 'Layzatzl!'

Baz and Thomas ran towards the Drogons, while Carlo, Kelly, Jack, Alec and the Israelis emerged from their hiding places; a shootout ensued, with the main danger coming from cross-fire ricochets. Jack got off a lucky shot while sheltering behind a handy buttress near the cave's entrance, while Kelly ran forward and winged another Drogon.

Carlo rushed up the tunnel and lashed out viciously with his trusty Tudorland sword, taking a fair-sized lump out of the side of a particularly heavy set Drogon. He followed this by a classic "knight's thrust", which shoved the sword into the man's hip, breaking his pelvis and ending any chance the man had of running away or fighting. Thomas noted Carlo's perfect demonstration of the correct Tudorland method of disabling an enemy, but sadly, this wasn't Tudorland, so the man was still armed. Shimon was the nearest, so he yelled at Carlo to get out of the way, while he quickly put a bullet in the stunned Drogon's head.

Thomas pulled his Tudorland knife from its scabbard,

gripped the point and threw it in a long arc with all the aplomb of a circus performer. It landed squarely in the heart of yet another Drogon. Baz wasn't so lucky, as he was caught by a ricochet that took a lump out of his backside and part of his right hip. The whining and pinging of bullets around the interior of the cave was easing, but not before a bullet had parted Alec's hair and another had smacked squarely into Kelly's chest. Kelly went down heavily, banging her head on a projecting piece of rock and quickly losing consciousness.

The fight moved from the cave, spreading across the road and into the ruins of the castle, but more Drogons were climbing down from pickup vans, and the weight of numbers was beginning to tell. Shimon felt a bullet graze the outer side of his right thigh while Thomas caught one across the top of his left shoulder. By now, the team was pinned down and things weren't looking good. Baz hoped they had enough ammo to damage as many of the Drogon bastards as possible before the inevitable end came.

Thomas silently thanked God for giving him the extra years that he'd spent with his loved ones and friends since escaping King Henry's scaffold in Tudorland, even if this did seem to be the final curtain.

16:

Pandora's Box

To me there has never been a higher source of earthly honour or distinction than that connected with advances in science.

ISAAC NEWTON

Carlo and Thomas picked Kelly up and carried her to the castle where she could at least die alongside her friends; this being a better option than leaving her half-dead where the Drogons would find her. The fact that they had needed to travel to Boronia by conventional plane and helicopter meant that the team didn't have a Project parked nearby and couldn't escape back to New London; nor could they evacuate Kelly.

Worse still, it was becoming clear that however hard they fought and however courageous they were, the TUDORs and the Mossad boys were losing the fight.

Thomas made a mental note that if by some fluke the TUDORs managed to live through this day, they'd never go into a dangerous situation again without an escape Project hidden somewhere nearby.

* * *

By now, the noise of battle was such and the unit so busy trying to survive, that they didn't notice the strange whining and buzzing noise coming from behind the caves. Alec and Baz were sheltering behind some large rocks and reloading their pistols when they started to notice the unearthly racket.

'What the hell is *that!*' yelled Alec.

Soon the noise became hard to miss because hundreds of strange black creatures were flying over the tops of the caves and gathering over the combatants, for all the world like a swarm of malevolent insects. Baz was the first to grasp what was behind the strange phenomenon.

'It's drones, Alec. Hundreds of them.' Still gazing up in awe,' he said, 'I knew the techies were working on something new, but that's nothing unusual in TUDOR so I didn't bother to ask. This must be it.'

The team was still gazing in stupefied amazement at the darkening sky, while hundreds more of the small bat-like creatures flew out and buzzed around over them – but now something even more peculiar started to happen. The bat-drones suddenly loosed off shower after shower of small bullets, but the missiles only smacked into the Drogons, while none were directed towards the TUDOR or Mossad fighters. Baz looked at his hand and realised the ring he was wearing must be sending out a beam that directed the drones away from them. 'So that's what the new rings are for,' he said quietly.

Once the drones had killed or wounded the majority of the Drogons, it didn't take long for the rest to give up the fight, and soon the unnerving plague of small machines turned tail and flew back behind the caves. The now re-energised team rounded up the last of the Drogons, cuffed them and shoved them roughly into their van, giving them a few parting kicks. Shimon was dealing with a particularly feisty Drogon by aiming yet another kick at the unfortunate man's crown jewels while grabbing him by his hair and dragging him to the van, before cuffing him and throwing him on top of his hapless colleagues.

In a day filled with amazing events, an even more astounding sight now materialised from behind the caves. A line of people tottered across the rocky desert – each sporting desert fatigues and Kevlar, complete with what Sophie called 'Wehrmacht style' helmets. The vanguard comprised Sophie and Margie, followed by Emily, Lucy, Jessica, Raj and Sir David Cromwell. The tail comprised Thomas's sister Kate with her husband, 'Exchequer' Steven Byers, who was chatting to Thomas's secretary, Ryan Andrews. The new arrivals all carried semi-automatic pistols or assault rifles and looked as if they were more than ready to finish what the TUDOR team had started. The battered fighters were still gazing open mouthed at this apparition when Margie made a suitably august pronouncement.

'I hate wearing these piss-pot helmets,' she said irritably. 'They muck up my hairdo!'

This revelation broke the tension of the dreadful day.

* * *

By the early hours of the next morning, most of the TUDORs were back in London, but the rest were sitting in Alec's office and warming themselves with mugs of coffee and tucking into buttered rolls. Alec had been on the phone to the hospital for the past half-hour.

'No news yet, I'm afraid.'

A couple of Mossad lads came in with more rolls. Alec commented, 'It was Napoleon Bonaparte who said an army marches on its stomach, wasn't it?'

History buff Jack Duquesne's slow nod showed his fatigue.

'Well,' continued Alec, 'The Israeli army marches on tuna sandwiches and egg rolls, and the lads and girls get very bored with them.'

'I haven't had time to get fed up with them,' said Jack wearily. 'They taste fine to me.'

Disconcertingly, Jack had suddenly morphed from carefree young Casanova to a worried middle-aged man. He and Kelly weren't lovers and they never had been, but they were the best of friends – and truth to tell, Kelly was probably the only woman Jack had ever truly loved.

A young soldier came into the room holding a phone. He handed it to Jack.

The call was from Margie at the hospital in Jerusalem, and she had news.

'Hello Jack; I knew you'd be worried about Kelly, so I buttonholed a doctor. She was wearing her armour, which saved her life, but the bullet smacked her right boob and Kell says it's swollen up like a melon and is now turning fifty shades of blue. She also has a nice lump on her head where she landed on the rock. A scan's shown there's no brain damage, but the doctor isn't happy with the fact that she was unconscious and disorientated, so he wants her to stay in for a day or two under obbo. They said the boob's stabilised and they won't need to drain it or do anything else to it, thank God. Kell's dozy from all the painkillers and she says she has the worst headache ever, but they reckon after a good rest, she'll pull through.'

Jack promptly decided that he'd stay on in Israel and bring Kelly home himself when the hospital released her.

Kelly wasn't the only one at the hospital, so Jack passed the phone to Thomas. Thomas had been the first to be treated and the nurse had fitted his arm into a sling, but he'd insisted on being let out. Now he asked Margie about the others.

'The Mossad guys are being patched up and they'll all be fine, although they'll all have scars for souvenirs. Much of the damage seems to have been done by the ricochets off the rocks in that bloody cave. Baz'll have a deep groove across his bum as a reminder of the operation, but he says he can live with that. He's more worried about Shimon's mental state though.'

'Shimon's *mental* state?' queried Thomas.

'Baz says Shimon's thigh will mend soon enough, but it seems the lad is insistent that he'll find out where the Drogon who shot him lives and he'll go after him. He's even more furious with the one who shot Kelly, although he did manage to kill that one. That's not all though. Apparently, Baz asked Shimon where he'd learned his fighting style as it seemed unnecessarily vicious, and Shimon said he'd copied it from the SS during the Second World War. According to him, the Russians who came through Poland towards the end of the war were bad enough, but they were nothing like the Germans for sheer brutality, so he decided that if he ever needed to fight in close quarters, he'd do it SS style.'

'God's teeth,' muttered Thomas.

Sir David had elected to stay behind, because although no longer the Director of TUDOR, habit made him want to take care of 'his' troopers and to assure himself they were all okay. He surprised the team by assuring them that Shimon would calm down when the adrenaline faded.

'I've seen the same thing happen with ack ack. When under attack, the men open the guns up and they can't stop firing even after they've shot down whatever they were aiming at.'

'I bloody well hope you're right,' said Alec with feeling.

Carlo joined in, 'Sir David's right, Alec. I've seen the same thing when I was in France with King Henry's army.

The blood gets up when men are in a battle and it can take a few hours before it cools. Shimon will be all right when he calms down, you'll see. He does have a certain style though. The kick he aimed at that Drogon's privates must have hurt, mustn't it?'

Alec couldn't help chuckling, while Thomas was looking sour – partly because his own level of adrenaline was falling and the pain on his shoulder was asserting itself.

Carlo spoke quietly and evenly while staring into his own past history.

'It happens that way sometimes, Alec. If you get pissed off enough, it can take a long time for the anger to subside. Shimon will probably always be a ruthless bugger, though. He reminds me a lot of our Tom when he was younger. If someone threatened our family or Tom's friends or looked as though they wanted to damage the King or our country, I doubt anyone could have prevented a massacre. When he settled back down, he showed himself to be a fairly nice guy – on the whole.'

'Hey! Who are you calling "a fairly nice guy on the whole", you young pup! You might have been a soldier for King Henry in France, Carlo, but so was I! *And* I fought in the holy Land! And I'm *still* your older cousin and I need to be treated with respect!'

Carlo's loud raspberry broke the tension, and when Alec asked the team if they'd like more coffee and rolls, they all called for the food and drink in celebration of a job well done, and affirmation of a life to be lived.

* * *

Back in the Millbank boardroom later that week, Thomas was briefing the team with news from Israel.

'Alec says their coastguard stopped a boat that seemed

167

out of place, and when they questioned the sailors, they admitted they were waiting to pick up the bomb. He also said that the Drogon government had now rid itself of the rogue element and gone back to its normal peaceful existence, but we still have to find the rogue element Drogon's contacts in the UK, so let's get on with it.'

Later that day though, Sir David phoned to tell them that GCHQ had picked up a whisper and so had the BBI. Carlo formed a unit that picked up several Drogons who were still hiding in Devon. Their job had been to take the bomb off the submarine and get it to London, while Jack's team picked up the London based ones, who turned out to be camped out in Croydon, which was where the bomb was due to be set off.

The following day, Thomas, Jack and Baz went to Belmarsh and questioned the men, and it wasn't long before the terrorists were brought to trial prior to starting lengthy prison sentences. And so ended *Operation Bonaventure.*

17:

The Pigeon Flies

A bird doesn't sing because it has an answer, it sings
because it has a song.
MAYA ANGELOU

Emily spent Christmas with her father before travelling back to the Jerusalem of 1968, whereupon she and Shimon spent a couple of weeks making love and making plans. While the lovemaking was wonderful, they decided to put the plan-making on hold until Emily had completed her finals. However, things started to change of their own volition when a Pigeon message told Shimon to expect a Project to land in his garage the following evening. When he answered the doorbell, it wasn't Emily on his doorstep but Sophie and Colonel Blitz. Once inside, Sophie told Shimon that Alec had asked her to set up the meeting, but when she asked Alec if he wanted to speak to Shimon in private, he shook his head.

'What I have to say is very simple, Shimon. The offices in Jerusalem are falling apart, the powers that be have decided to sell the plot to a developer, and that is due to happen in about two months from now – in my own time, that is.'

'To be honest, I'm surprised the building's lasted that long, Sir,' said Shimon.

Alec chuckled. 'Yeah, it's probably only the dirt that's holding it together. Anyway, some of my staff have decided to retire and those who are staying are mainly techies, but the powers that be have decided to keep a small branch office in Jerusalem albeit in a new building at the back of the army base – the one just outside the city.'

'I know where you mean,' said Shimon. 'Unless the base itself has moved since my time, it must be at the back of Hebron Square.'

Alec nodded and continued with his story. 'As you know, Shimon, there are two levels of Colonel in the Israeli army, so while I'll still be a Colonel, I will now be promoted to the higher level.'

'Congratulations, Aluf Mishne,' smiled Shimon, using Alec's new title.

'I'm going to need a good second in command, who's bright enough to train as a staff officer, but with the experience and ability to keep his end up in a fire-fight if the need arises. I can only think of one person I'd trust to watch my back in any circumstance and that's you Shimon – despite the fact that you're an absolute ruffian when roused.'

'Colonel, I'm flattered, but you must realise that I have absolutely no idea about IT, communications, computers and all that stuff. I've never even used a mobile telephone...' Shimon felt lame, but it was no more than the truth.'

Sophie interjected. 'Look Shimon, Tommy, Steven and Carlo have managed to adapt, although Tom doesn't drive if he can avoid it because he doesn't enjoy it. Carlo has conquered modern farming methods in addition to everything else that he does, and you'd never think that

Kate and Robbie were ever anything other than New Londoners, so if they can do it you can too. I'm sure Alec can arrange to send you on courses for IT, and Emily will help. Anyway, you won't need to be an expert; you only need to know enough to do your job. You'll probably enjoy it.'

Meanwhile, Shimon was gazing through the window of his little house and talking quietly as though to himself.

'I will come with you because it means that Emily and I can be together without her having to do all the adapting, because now she will change country but not time, while I change time but not country.' Shimon took a breath and looked back at Sophie. 'I can't see myself staying in the past when my friends live half a century in the future.' Shimon stood up and paced the room while thinking furiously, 'I'll tell my sister and brother-in-law the truth, but I don't think I'll bother my parents as they will only worry. I doubt they'd be surprised at me marrying a gentile and they wouldn't be upset by it, but there'd just be too much to explain about TUDOR, Alec and all that. My brother-in-law, Paolo, was in Mossad before he joined my dad on the farm, and Rivka was in the army, so they both know the score.'

'Wouldn't they want to come forward in time?' asked Sophie.

Shimon shook his head. 'Rivka takes care of the kids and our parents and she enjoys working in the farm office. I know Paolo is happy running the farm and the factory, and it would be too disrupting for them and their children to make the change and have to start from the bottom up again. Also, we have the advantage of knowing that their era is relatively peaceful as compared to your time, and I'd prefer to see them continuing to live quietly. They went through enough stress in Europe during the war.'

'I know your family survived in Nazi Poland because of your Arian looks, Shimon,' said Sophie, 'but what about Paolo? I mean, is he brown haired like me?'

Shimon nodded. 'Paolo is dark haired, but he looked similar to the Italians in the area where he lived. He was an only child and his dad had died of cancer before the war, but when his mother saw the way the wind was blowing for the Jews, she persuaded some locals to take Paolo in and pretend he was a distant family member who was helping them out on their farm. Paolo was only twelve at the time and the family took mean advantage of him. He slept in a barn, ate scraps and nearly worked himself to death. However, after the Italians surrendered, the Nazis took over and the SS decided to stiffen the locals by shooting hostages that they grabbed off the street. Paolo's mother was one of the hostages.'

Sophie and Alec winced at the revelation. The holocaust was old hat to her generation – a story told by elderly people who spoke with thick east European accents, but hearing the reality of it from someone as young and vibrant as Shimon brought it sharply into focus.

'The British and US troops came through in the summer of 1943, bringing the war to an end in southern Italy, so Paolo returned to the family home. It had been all but wrecked, and while he figured he could fix it up and stay there, he couldn't settle and the more he thought about it, the more determined he became to get to Israel and to help build the country. He felt – quite rightly – that it's very existence would prevent the disaster we'd all lived through from happening again. He also wanted to be openly Jewish, rather than continue to live as a pretend Catholic.'

'As your family did in Poland,' said Sophie.

Shimon nodded. 'Paolo was only fifteen when the war came to an end, but he planned his escape well. He found work on a merchant vessel that eventually docked in Lebanon, so he jumped ship and started walking south, crossing the Israeli border at night, alone, disorientated and practically at the end of his strength, but someone rescued him and led him to a Jewish family who took him in.'

'Talk about the Good Samaritan!' Sophie exclaimed.

'True enough,' agreed Shimon. 'Look, I'll definitely tell Paolo and Rivka what's going on, and I can see them wanting to take a trip to New London for a look-see, but I know they'll be happier living out their lives in the 1960s.'

Alec put his cup down and said, 'You are clearing the way then.'

Shimon agreed, but he had something else that he needed to ask. 'Colonel, I've been a captain for several years and there isn't much chance of moving up in my era because the hierarchy is too top-heavy. I can also see that I would have a lot to learn in 2019. I can accept that would mean I'd stay at my current rank a while longer, but there must be the hope of a promotion. You see, I intend to marry Emily, so I'll need to earn enough to support a wife and in time, hopefully, a family.'

'It will be no more than three months before you will become a Major,' said Alec firmly, while holding out his hand to shake on the deal.

'I also need to ask Emily formally if she is prepared to marry me and make her life here in Israel,' said Shimon thoughtfully. 'After all, we are making assumptions on her behalf, so I must speak to her as soon as possible.'

'Would she need to convert if she wants to make *aliya*?' asked Sophie, referring to the Israeli emigration process.

'There is no civil marriage in Israel, so we will have to marry outside Israel, and then Emily can become an Israeli resident as my wife, but she can continue to keep her British citizenship or she can become an Israeli national as she thinks best.'

'In that case, Shimon, if Emily accepts your proposal,' Sophie said with alacrity, 'I would like to make the wedding party for you – a kosher wedding that is… in our home.'

'Sophie love, I totally accept your generous offer, but I need to talk to Emily. She has a widowed father in the UK and that may stop her from doing any of this so we can't get ahead of ourselves. There is much for us to think about.'

A few days later, the lovers were snuggled up in Emily's Brentford bed, glad to be out of the winter weather and happy to be in each other's warm and welcoming arms.

'Do you think you could live in Israel darling? With all its problems I mean?'

'It's only fair that I do my share of adapting, but I don't know what use I can be there. I suppose I could teach English or European history.' Emily sighed and flopped back onto the bed. 'I guess something will come along, though…'

Shimon rolled over onto his side and started kissing the corner of Emily's mouth and rubbing a nipple, and that put an end to the discussion for the time being.

18:

Sir James Cromwell

Change is inevitable. Change is constant.
BENJAMIN DISRAELI

James Cromwell was half a head taller than his brother, but slim and slightly stooped, with thinning light brown hair and a pleasantly ordinary face. He often looked a little scruffy, not so much due to academic affectation, but to the lack of a wife and the lack of any incentive to improve his appearance. Indeed, some of his clothing was beginning to succumb to verdigris.

James was no wimp. He had fought hard for his students and for his department over the years, but now he had reached an impasse. The college needed to focus on money-making subjects which would attract wealthy students from Russia and the Orient, and departments such as his were being unofficially redefined as 'interesting but ultimately useless', and to make matters worse, several ambitious bullies were fighting James at every turn. But worst of all was the fact that he knew he had become stale. He still prepared his courses and lectures well, but he'd twice caught himself droning during lectures and boring the students. By rights James should give at least a term's notice, if not longer, but when he told the Master he wanted to leave at the end of summer term, his boss sighed, shrugged and agreed – and then admitted to James that he was also considering giving up the ghost.

James' had long since earned more money than he needed, so over time, his salary had piled up, and when added to the money he'd inherited from his parents and what he would get from downsizing his house, he figured he would be well covered until his college pension kicked in, and he'd still have plenty to put aside for the future. He was keen to put the joys and sorrows associated with his Cambridge life behind him, and to escape the winters by moving to a warm country. He hoped he could use Emily's Brentford flat as a British base, though.

He hadn't yet figured out was what to do about his 'other job' though – the one he'd kept secret for so long. He'd been recruited into MI6 many years ago, when he was still a student, and his travels to a variety of countries in search of fossils had enabled him to act as a mobile listening post, but now it seemed appropriate for him to pay a visit to his commanders and tell them it was time for him to retire.

* * *

Shimon had given his commanding officer his notice, using the excuse that his family needed him on the farm, while Sophie had arranged for Shimon to keep a small Project in his garage so that he could fly back and forth to modern Jerusalem while helping Alec set up the new department. He was finding it disconcerting to work in the same place in two eras, but comforted himself with the thought that it wouldn't be for much longer. Steven Byers had organised the necessary paperwork, so Shimon was now equipped with two 'original' Israeli birth certificates, two Israeli passports, driving licences, medical paperwork and so on. One set would be stored in the TUDOR safe and another would go with him to Israel. If anyone looked into his affairs, they would find an Israeli man who had been born in 1988, rather than a Polish one born in 1937. So now, Shimon could safely move a half a century into his own future.

* * *

Emily knew she'd done well in her exams and was looking forward to being with Shimon, but she needed to talk to her father first, so a couple of days later, she was tucking into a Chinese takeaway with her dad, and he was giving her his news.

'The Natural History Museum has taken my samples, including the fossil cabinets that I had specially made all those years ago. They've also taken my books, apart from a dozen that I particularly want to keep, including a few that I wrote myself.'

'I can't say I'm surprised Dad. I saw the changes going on in my Uni in London and it must be much the same everywhere these days. Let's face it Dad, palaeontology just isn't a money-making proposition, and to use a financial cliché, it's all "bottom line" now, isn't it?'

James gave a slight smile.

'Well, I've also got news, and what I have to tell you will astonish you.'

'Go on love, I could do with a bit of astonishment.'

Emily held her wineglass out for a refill before telling her father the whole story, starting at the very beginning with Sophie's uncle Silas and his invention of the original Project and ending with Shimon and *Operation Bonaventure*. As her story progressed, she was rewarded by the look of utter amazement on her father's face.

'Why didn't you tell me any of this before?' asked James.

'I needed permission to talk about it, and I've only just got it now. Also, I didn't want to bring you any complications and you seemed happy enough here, so I decided to let sleeping Projects lie…' Emily ran out of steam.

'You know, Ems darling, I am no longer miserable about the loss of your mum. I'll never forget her of course, but it's nearly seven years now and the pain has gone. I've dated a few women, and I've slept with a few, but I have always been honest with them about my intentions – or lack of them. I know that I buried myself in my work after mum died and I neglected you when you most needed me. Looking back, I can see that I was thoughtless and selfish and I'm so very sorry for that, but it seems that it's now time for an all-round change.'

James opened a packet of biscuits, sat back and looked into the distance, while saying quietly, 'I don't suppose your Israeli soldier plays chess?'

'Of course he does!' laughed Emily 'He's even won a couple of amateur tournaments against Russian opponents, so I guess he's good at it.'

'Well he must be all right then, mustn't he?'

* * *

Once Shimon had finally moved to 2019, Alec gave him a generous four months' leave.

'You've a shit-load to do, Shimon, and if you and Ems want to get married, you'll need to live in London for a while so you can get a visa and a marriage licence. Has Emily still got her flat?'

Shimon nodded.

178

'What about after that?' asked Alec.

'Emily and I will rent a place in Jerusalem, and her dad's coming with us and he'll take a place nearby. He and Emily want to keep their UK citizenship for the time being, so they'll share the cost of keeping her flat on in Brentford.'

'Will she convert?'

Shimon shook his head. 'Ems isn't into religion, but she says she'd prefer to remain a lapsed Protestant; however, she's very keen that any children we have should be Jewish.'

'You know, it used to be the rule that the mother had to be Jewish for the children to be Jewish, or the kids had to convert when they grew up,' said Alec. 'That's been relaxed to include Jewish fathers now, so there shouldn't be any problem. The only people who won't accept it are the super-religious types, but you wouldn't want to join one of their cults, would you?'

'Not likely,' laughed Shimon. 'I heard that they only have sex through a hole cut in a blanket so they can never enjoy it!'

Alec grinned and shuddered at the idea.

* * *

September in London was warm during the day and nippy at night, but by now, the wedding plans were in full flood. Lucy came up from T-West and trawled the Kensington stores with Emily to help her find a dress.

'I don't want to spend all day heaving a strapless dress into place and neither do I want to look like a lamp-shade,' whispered Emily.

Lucy giggled and then spotted a silky number that she thought would look well on Emily's tall, slim figure. When Emily tried it on, it fitted perfectly and it was comfortable to wear.

'The dress is so lovely, Ems and it looks great on you. I

understand Sophie has hired a DJ and I know Shimon likes to dance, so you can enjoy yourself on the dance floor without worrying that it'll slip down.'

* * *

A couple of weeks before the big day, Sir James Cromwell turned up at Emily's flat.

'Where's your intended?' asked James, giving Emily a kiss.

'He's gone for a newspaper, but he'll be back soon. Sit down, Dad, and I'll make us a cuppa.'

A few minutes later, Shimon came in, shaking raindrops from his golden hair, and when he saw his father-in-law to be, he put his bag down and came up for a hug. When discussing what to call him, James had suggested Jim or Jimmy – whatever worked best, so now Shimon said, *'Alzo Jim, was is neues?'*

Like Shimon, James spoke a variety of languages – both dead and alive – so he had no problem with Shimon's occasional fun-time breaks into Yiddish.

'The house is sold and it won't be long before we exchange,' said James. 'I'll bunk in with David and Helen for a while, but after the wedding, once I'm settled in Jerusalem, I'm going to take a holiday. It's years since I had a real one, and I fancy snorkelling in the Red Sea and dozing in a deckchair for a while.'

'I'll come with you,' Emily quickly said.

'So will I,' laughed Shimon.

'Are we all going on honeymoon together then?' asked James, raising an eyebrow.

Emily spluttered on a mouthful of cake.

'Listen kids, this is my suggestion. Have a decent honeymoon in France or Spain or somewhere, and relax while you can because if I'm any judge, I can tell you that life will soon become very busy for you both.'

'What about you Dad? Will you look for work in Israel?'

'I'm going to take at least a year out. My Hebrew isn't good enough for any meaningful work so I need to take a language course. I might teach again, but if I do, it will be young children rather than students who need to be prepared for exams. I also want to find an illustrator so I can create story books for young people.'

'What a nice idea,' said Shimon thoughtfully. 'If Emily and I have kids, it would be terrific to have a grandpa who makes up stories. Perhaps you could write adventure stories that I would also love to read.'

'How about Indiana Jim and the grumpy dinosaur?' James asked.

'How's it start?' asked Emily.

'Once upon a time, there was a grumpy Stegosaurus called Ernie. Well, Ernie would have been a very happy Steggo, but he had dreadful indigestion, and it was stopping him from enjoying his favourite foods, which were strawberries, string beans, ripe plums and red apples.'

'Did they have plum and apple trees in Jurassic times, dad?' interrupted Emily.

'They do in my book! But to go on, poor Indiana Jim is finding it hard to collect enough Gaviscon to ease Ernie's big belly ache, and the poor man even gets thrown out of Boots for trying to buy a bucket of the stuff, because they think he's some kind of weird drug addict.'

Shimon was laughing his head off, and saying that he and Emily had better get down to having children quickly so he didn't have to wait too long to hear the rest of the story.

19:

A Nice Day For A White Wedding

Falling in love was the easy part; planning a wedding –
yikes!

NANCY NASH

Shimon took a train to the synagogue for the Saturday morning service. In theory, being the Sabbath, he should have walked to Shul, but that wasn't possible in London. Either way, he wanted to thank God for the survival of himself and his family against so many odds, and to ask God's blessing for Emily and himself.

Sir David and Lady Helen went to the cathedral the following day to pray for their niece and the bridegroom.

The nearest thing that Sir James had to religion was a belief in Buddhism, so before he left his Cambridge house, he meditated, chanted and asked the Universe to bless his lovely daughter and her bridegroom.

Shimon had fancied a boy's night out before the wedding, but without strippers or blue comedians, so when Jack came up with the idea of a meal at a kosher restaurant, he jumped at it. The evening reminded Shimon of the nights he used to enjoy at the Whisky-a Go-Go with his army friends; the lads ate everything that wasn't tied down and downed more than a few beers, while telling each other stories about their police and army experiences, which, despite the different countries, cultures and eras they had all lived in, had exhibited the same recognisable forms of bullshit and absurdity. Late into the evening, Baz quietly asked Shimon whether he regretted giving up his single status, and Shimon told him that he had sown a great deal of wild oats in his day, but he was very happy with Emily and he was looking forward to family life.

Sophie sneaked Rivka and Paolo Rosso out of Israel in the middle of the night and dropped them off at Kate and Steven's house, whereupon their hosts bought them wonderful outfits for the wedding and a selection of clothes suitable for a prolonged visit to twenty-first century New London and they wouldn't hear of Emily reimbursing them. Shimon joined his sister and his brother-in-law in the Byers household the night before the wedding, while six-year-old Harry Byers became so disgusted with all the pre-wedding talk that he decided to bunk in with a friend down the road until life returned to normal.

When Lady Helen Cromwell asked James why he only had one small bag to his name when he went to stay at their house, he admitted that he'd thrown everything else out. After telling her brother-in-law that this was no loss, other than to the moths that'd inhabited his wardrobe for so long, Helen promptly wheeled him out to the shops.

Colonel Alec Blitz stayed with Baz and Margie Baverstock, which gave Alec and Baz time to talk over matters of security that could affect both Mossad and TUDOR. To young Taylor Baverstock's delight, Alec was happy to play football with him and on wet days, Alec taught the ten-year-old lad how to play poker.

Carlo and Lucy Hatherleigh and their children moved in with Sophie and Thomas for a while, and the two five-year-old cousins, Rosie and Danny were happy to play together while all the adults took turns in looking after two-year-old Josie.

* * *

Emily had asked Margie Baverstock if fourteen-year-old Shelley would like to be her bridesmaid and Shelley had jumped at the offer. When Margie saw her daughter trying on the figure-hugging aquamarine dress and midi heels, along with some mascara and a bit of lippy, she almost cried. Her baby was growing up fast.

'Christ knows what your father will say when he sees that lot, Shel. He won't want to see you looking interesting to the opposite sex so quickly.'

'That's okay Mum,' said Shelley with a cheeky grin, 'I'll tell I'm a lezzer. He won't worry half as much if he thinks I'm being chased around by a load of muff-munchers.'

'For gawd's sake don't say *that*, Shel!' hissed Margie. 'He doesn't think you know anything about sex. If he thought you knew that stuff he'd have a *thrombi!*'

'You know Mum, when you think about it, we're surrounded by people from the sixteenth century, and now we've got Shimon from the sixties, but Dad's like something out of the Victorian age. Do you think he had a previous life when Queen Victoria wasn't being amused?'

Margie suddenly remembered back to the time when Baz had fallen for her. How he'd luxuriated in her latte coloured body, twirled her corkscrew hair around his fingers and wrapped her long brown legs around his middle time and again. He couldn't get enough of her then – and not much had changed since, although life and children had tended to intervene.

'I don't think your Dad's Victorian, Shel. It's just that

men know what dirty little sods they were as teens, and they hate the idea of a new generation climbing all over their daughters. It's different where sons are concerned. They're happy for the boys to shag anything that comes along – as long as they know how to fit a condom on the end of it.'

* * *

Sunday September the twenty-seventh dawned bright and dry but a little chilly, although the forecast said it would warm up later. Sophie's housekeeper, Valentyna, had brought in a team to help; some were Polish, but others were the grandsons of her West Indian neighbours. The helpers were taking furniture out of the sitting room and storing it in the garage while pushing the larger items against the wall. The centre of the room was filling up with rows of banqueting seats, fronted by a table for the Registrar. A large marquee sat in the garden, with tables and chairs in place and a temporary floor that could be used for dancing later.

The workshop at the end of the garden had originally been built to house the first Project, way back before the 'Abbey affair', but now caterers had installed a mobile kosher kitchen, and they were hard at work. The doors had been fixed back to give the caterers plenty of air, while the workshop sheltered them from the cool early autumn weather.

Thomas had borrowed several long tables from TUDOR, and now three young men were setting up a bar at the back of the sitting room, pouring fruit juice and getting trays ready for the champagne that would be handed to their guests as they arrived.

'Knowing our lot, I can't see much use for the fruit juice – except for the kids perhaps,' sighed Thomas.

'Well in for a penny, in for a pound I guess,' shrugged Sophie with a grin.

'Oh, it'll be fun Sophie love – and Emily and Shimon's friends are ours as well, so what the hell!'

The guests were arriving, with the men arrayed in a variety of smart outfits. The only one wearing a tie was Sir David, while the others sported suits with open necked shirts in a variety of bright colours. Thomas wore black slacks, a black shirt with mother-of-pearl buttons and a light grey jacket. He'd chosen the outfit to remind him of his Tudorland days, when he always attended important functions in sober black or grey doublet and hose, sometimes with a little white or silver embroidery to lighten the effect.

When Baz spotted the outfit, he addressed Thomas out the side of his mouth, using a mock American accent.

'You look like a successful hit man, Tommo.'

'I *am* a successful hit man, Baz.'

This brought a snort of derision from the tall Deputy Director.

Soon the guests were pouring in, and Baz quietly commented, 'If there's a shout today Tommo, either TUDOR will be completely paralysed or the whole wedding party will have to rush across to Millbank and get tooled up.'

'No need, Baz. All the necessary weaponry is stored in my loft, including Kevlar, drones and SAM missiles,' answered Thomas calmly.

'What!'

'When Sir David was at TUDOR,' said Thomas while helping himself to a passing glass of champagne, 'he decreed that we needed a secondary weapon store in case the Millbank or Mews offices were blown up, so it's all here, and I keep the stuff up to date. If there *was* a shout, I think we could cope.'

'Gordon Bennet,' sighed Baz.

Four guests who Sophie and Thomas knew were coming,

but who were a surprise to everyone else, now trotted into the room. Frances Shulman looked fairly human for once, as a hairdresser had given her fearsome carroty frizz a light brown tint and a cut that put her hair into some semblance of shape. The navy skirt and colourful beaded top suited the angular woman well, while her normally non-descript husband, Dennis wore a cream, summer-weight suit and chocolate coloured shirt that made him look unusually smart. Off duty, the Shulmans turned out to be good company. Following the Home Secretary and her husband, were her perfectly turned out Parliamentary Private Secretary, Emson Barotse MP, with his tall, elegant ambassador wife, Thandiwe Barotse. Emson wore a black suit teamed with a dark red shirt, while Tandie wore a dark red dress and a snugly fitted black jacket that complimented Emson's colour choice.

* * *

Raj was working the MP3 and the first movement of Schubert's Unfinished Symphony played quietly while the Registrar prepared her paperwork; then at a signal from Raj, Emily and James appeared at the back of the room.

Sir James Cromwell's new dark blue suit made his tall slim frame appear elegant for once, while Emily resembled a shimmering goddess in her ivory dress. A halo coronet, made of silver and pearl glowed through her fine veil. Behind them walked the lovely young bridesmaid, carrying a bouquet of flowers that matched the larger bouquet that Emily was holding.

Shimon gasped at the sight of his beautiful bride, while Baz gaped open-mouthed at his daughter. It was as though a spell had fallen on the room not quite broken by the murmured congratulations from everyone as they made their way to the front of the room. Shimon wore a dark grey suit that contrasted with the light glancing on his slightly longer than usual pale golden hair and he smiled in utter joy as his bride came to his side. His brother-in-law, Paolo, stood smiling on his other side.

* * *

The kosher meal of smoked salmon and salad, followed by a much-requested chicken soup with noodles, which in turn was followed by roast lamb and finished off with non-dairy fruit pie and sorbet went down well, as did the many bottles of red, white and rose wine. Diabetic Sophie had spent the previous couple of weeks avoiding foods that could convert to glucose, so she allowed herself a portion of desert. She reckoned she would have a piece of wedding cake later, as long as she avoided the marzipan and icing. The younger children ate in the kitchen, with one of the Polish girls helping little Josie to eat her supper.

Then it was time for the speeches.

Lecturer James was completely at ease in front of an audience, so he quickly told the guests how much he respected his daughter who had cared for her sick mother and how he admired the way she'd pulled herself together after her mum had died, and how she'd gone back into education to obtaining her well-deserved first. He said that nobody could have a more loving daughter, and that Emily had a beautiful soul, as had her mother before her. He was happy that she was marrying Shimon, especially since he'd discovered the lad was a half-decent chess player. That brought a few quiet chuckles.

James then told the guests that he was happy to retire and move to Israel to be near the young couple, but that he had something important to tell them. He said that his Cambridge chair had been his 'official job' but that there had long been a second 'unofficial job' from which he was now also retiring. Most of those in the room had no idea what he was talking about, so they were all ears as James started to tell his tale.

'I was recruited into a well-known organisation when I was still a student. Perhaps my somewhat secretive nature had something to do with it, or perhaps my family background counted in my favour, but anyway, it was obvious that my work in geology, palaeontology and pre-history would take me to places that others couldn't visit. In my time, I made frequent visits to the old Soviet Union, and I also visited Communist China, parts of South America, and even such arcane places as Papua New Guinea, Burma and North Korea, always bringing back such information as could be useful to my "control".'

James looked around the room, enjoying the puzzlement that he saw on so many faces. 'I needed permission from my superiors for what I am going to tell you now, but they gave it to me, in part because I am now officially retired, but also due to the nature of the company present here today. Having said the foregoing, there are four people in this room who already know what I have to say.'

James looked across at the Home Secretary, who was playing with a teaspoon and smiling to herself.

'The people who know my secret are my brother David, Mrs Shulman, Colonel Alec Blitz and Tom Hatherleigh.' James was thoroughly enjoying himself as he went on. 'Tom wasn't supposed to be in the know, but he bumped into me one day when I was visiting a man called Johnny Thorn.'

The mention of the head of MI6's name brought pennies dropping all round the room, and now Jack's voice could clearly be heard. 'I'll bet my next month's salary our Jim's a bloody *spook!*'

'Well done jack!' said James as he pushed a stray lock of his light brown hair away from his forehead. 'You'll be glad to know that you won't lose a month's salary because you're quite right. You see, for the past thirty-five years, I have worked on a part-time basis for an organisation that some of you know as *"Six"*. And yes, until my recent retirement, Johnny Thorn was my boss.'

'For fuck's sake,' said Margie loudly, shaking her corkscrew curls in gob-smacked astonishment. 'I knew there was something about the man. He's got that sneaky *"I know things that you don't "* look about him that the rest of you buggers have!'

At this point the room erupted, and it took a while before Shimon could make his own short speech, thanking the guests for attending and handing Shelley a narrow white box, which, when she opened it, made her let out a gasp. The box contained a delicate white-gold necklace, set with tiny diamonds.

'Shelley didn't just walk down the aisle, you see,' said Shimon, directing a smile at the young girl. 'She spent the night with Emily, helping her dress and she made Emily's hair look pretty. And she helped Jimmy get his act together as well. Thank you, Shelley love. The girl dun good!'

Shelley grinned as the room broke into applause. There were shouts for Emily to speak, but she was too choked up to say anything, so she just smiled and waved at everyone.

Shimon was a good dancer and he loved jiving and doing old-fashioned Latin and ballroom routines. Some of the others could also dance, while the rest just bopped around to the music. Yet others sat around, drank brandy, chatted and ate the wedding cake that Shimon and Emily had cut for them later that evening.

The following day, James went to Cambridge to arrange for funds to be wired to Israel for himself and for Emily, while the young couple flew to Tenerife for a proper holiday and a much-needed break after such a busy few months.

And that is how Emily, Shimon and Sir James Cromwell made a start on their new lives.

Part Two

20:

The Gassy Hole

To raise new questions, new possibilities, to regard old problems from a new angle, requires creative imagination and marks real advance in science.

ALBERT EINSTEIN

Professor Tony Price's worries were wearing him out, and now he seemed to be expending even more time and energy on a completely pointless exercise. 'Am I right in thinking that your purpose is anti-terrorism?' he asked, 'because if that's the case...'

Thomas interrupted and told the Professor that the "U" in TUDOR stood for *'unprecedented'* danger, which could refer to anything that posed a danger to the UK. The Professor felt a little easier in his mind – but not much. After all, how could anyone expect to solve *this* particular problem?

'So, what is this about?' asked Thomas, running a hand through his dark hair.

'It's a long story.' Tony Price shrugged, knowing he would have to go over the whole saga again, having already told his story to both the Environment Minister and the Home Secretary earlier that day. It was the Home Secretary who had caught up with him in the corridor after the meeting, and it was she who'd told him to take a cab to TUDOR and to ask for Thomas Hatherleigh or Baz Baverstock.

Tall, light brown haired, pleasant-faced Baz sat down opposite the Professor and pushed his seat back to allow room for his long legs. He looked at the sad and slightly dishevelled young man and told him to take his time.

* * *

'This story started last year in Wyoming where the Professor of geology in the University of Wyoming happened to be looking over some old satellite images of his state, when he noticed that the ground appeared to be rising in one particular area for no reason that he could discern. So with his curiosity aroused, he ran off dozens of satellite images of that area going back over the past forty years, and he studied them carefully, coming to the conclusion that the ground was definitely rising in that spot. When the college holidays came around, he and a friend rented a camper-van, threw some equipment into it and drove out for a look-see. When they got to the area, they saw a strangely rounded hill in a location that was otherwise flat. The Professor's friend took soundings with a portable ground radar machine while the Prof checked the results on his tablet, coming to the conclusion that there was a void under the ground with some kind of gas inside it. They decided that it would be worth drilling an experimental hole into the void, but not knowing exactly what they were dealing with, they decided to operate the drill by remote control while retreating to some rising ground a few kilometres away.'

Professor Price took a tablet from his briefcase, touched a few buttons and gave it to Thomas and Baz, instructing them to start the video. The video showed the drill in the distance, and Baz and Thomas heard the Wyoming Professor's friend calling off the metres as the drill went down, but soon after the drill passed the five-metre mark, there was an almighty explosion and the two guys were blown backwards. They could be heard yelling and asking each other if they were all right.'

Professor Price glanced at his rapt audience before going on with his story.

'Once the dust had settled, it was clear that what had been a mound was now a bloody great hole, and even from a distance, the Wyoming men estimated that the hole was at least four kilometres across. They congratulated themselves on having retreated far enough from the site to avoid their van and themselves from being blown to bits.

When they judged it safe enough, they trudged over the broken terrain and clambered down a shallow slope into the epicentre of the hole, to see what was going on. The Professor soon discovered the cause of the explosion; the area had once been volcanic, and when the ancient lava cooled, it created pockets that filled with whatever minerals had been present in the volcano. These could be metals or chemicals, but in this case, a small pocket had formed that contained both a chemical and a crystalloid coating. It turned out that there were three types of rock, crystal and chemical in the bottom of the hole, and while one was well known, the second was rare but not unknown, while the third type of rock, along with its coating, were a complete mystery.'

At this point, Ryan came in with a tray of coffee and the Professor gratefully took a cup. He told Thomas and Baz that the Wyoming experiments showed the strange rock to be a meteorite of a type that was unknown even within the solar system.

'The problem was that all three crystalloid coatings were the type that gave off a gas when they came into contact with water, which had started to happen when the lava that lay above the void had weathered away enough to allow water to seep through. The three gasses had blended together to form a fourth type of gas, and this it was this hybrid gas that was so volatile. It particularly disliked metal – as per the metal drill. So much so that when the Professor got it back to the lab, and put some of it into a glass case, he bent over the case and saw the gas going for the zip and rivets on his jeans! The Professor learned that the bloody gas didn't like vibration either, so he called it "explodo" until he could think up a more scientific name.

'As luck had it, the Wyoming Professor had a colleague who was working on a compound that could neutralise fires in the oil, chemical and gas industries, and he'd named the compound *Chalkon*. The Professor asked his colleague to get hold of a little of it so they could try it out on the crystals. The Wyoming Prof poured the Chalkon onto the crystals and left it for a month, and when he checked the glass case again, there was nothing left to see.'

Professor Price took a sip of his coffee and smiled grimly at Thomas and Baz, telling them that he filed the article under 'interesting' and promptly forgot about it.

'As it happens, my university is undergoing extensive renovation, so when the academic year ended, I decided to take a sabbatical and have a major clear-out in my office. It was then that I came across some satellite images that showed the same kind of land-rise as the Wyoming one, but this time in the North Lincoln Moor. This intrigued me so much that after looking through every image I could find, I took a day off and went to the Moor for a look-see.' Pushing a stray lock of dark blond hair from his forehead, Tony said. 'I didn't expect to find anything, but when I surveyed the area I became worried, although I decided to keep my concerns to myself until I knew exactly what I was dealing with. The fact that the department would be out of action for months actually helped, because there was no one around to question what I was doing. My girlfriend and I had split up some time earlier, which meant that I could come and go without having to explain myself to anyone.

'Once I had done the calculations and made several trips to the Moor, I realised that this had to be the same phenomenon as the Wyoming one. The area had also once been volcanic and the volcanoes were the same age as those in Wyoming, so the rocks in the area would have been similar, and the meteorite could easily be a piece of the same one that had landed in Wyoming. The rocks and the meteorite would have become buried under kilometres of lava, but this had weathered away, allowing water to seep in.'

Tony's voice betrayed his fatigue, as he pinched the bridge of his nose and went on with the worrying story. 'Without going into too much technical stuff, I realised that the North Lincoln Moor void is under much more pressure than the Wyoming one, and over time it will have thrown out tendrils of gas along thin cracks that travel along under the ground. In short, it now resembles a massive octopus with tentacles sticking out sideways and downwards. I had to ask myself if the thing was likely to blow up, and if so, when this was likely to happen.'

The professor asked Thomas to run his finger across the tablet to bring up the next page. The image was enough to make his hair stand up on end, as it showed a depiction of Kingston-upon-Hull sitting on a south-facing coast, and everything east of the Peak District under the sea, with a new north-facing coast somewhere in the middle of Norfolk.

Baz asked, 'Would this also cause tidal waves?'

Tony nodded and told him to look at the next image. This

showed an area of tsunami devastation that swamped much of the eastern seaboard, washing up the river systems to the point where even the Houses of Parliament, Westminster Abbey and their own Millbank building would be bombarded by detritus-filled water. The tsunami would affect France, Denmark, Holland and Belgium while it sloshed back and forth, and it might even stretch round to the West, damaging Devon, Cornwall and further afield. Much of eastern England and the Isle of Wight would be scraped clean of habitation.

'Of course, the tsunami would eventually recede and those areas could be rebuilt, but much of central England would be gone for good,' said the Professor with a sigh.

'How long before this happens?' asked Baz, in a horrified rasp.

'About five or six years at most,' said the Professor, 'but sooner if some fool drills into it or if a builder inadvertently drills into one of the tendrils. We do get earthquakes in this country, and they can be surprisingly sizable, so if one occurred and if it happened to be stronger than usual...' The young man ran out of steam.

'So it could go at any time,' said Thomas grimly, 'any ideas about prevention?'

'That's exactly what the Environment man asked and I told him there was one thing I could think of, although I couldn't guarantee that it would work – while there was a second idea that would definitely work but which wasn't possible.' Warming to his theme, he went on. 'The first method would be to spray Chalkon over an area of about ten kilometres in diameter, as this would create an impervious barrier and thus prevent any further rainwater from falling onto the area, but of course, it wouldn't do anything about the water that's already dropping down or the rate of expansion of the gas. My estimation is that it will take three or four years for all the water that is currently

197

there to clear its way down to the crystals!'

'That would be cutting it fine,' said Thomas.

Tony waggled his fingers to show he had more to say. 'Well, it would speed things up if I used a carbon-fibre drill in a slow grinding motion rather than a vibrating one, and drilled several holes to a depth of about four or five metres, and then pumped in the Chalkon. This would cut the time down to a couple of years or maybe less before the Chalkon could get to the crystals and neutralise them. Anyway, as I said to the two Ministers, it has to be better than sitting on our hands and waiting for Armageddon. And it would give me time to think of something else.'

Thomas turned to Baz. 'I think we're missing something here, Baz.'

'Yeah, you're right.' Turning to the young Professor, Baz quietly asked. 'What was your other suggestion, lad? The one you said *would* work but which wasn't possible?'

Tony sighed deeply. 'I was dreading this.'

'Why?'

'Well, it brought a lot of sneering and snorting from the Environment man, with comments about *Dr Who* and so on. He made me feel like a complete idiot.' Tony narrowed his eyes while a stray thought crossed his mind... he found himself recalling that the Home Secretary hadn't sneered at all.

'We won't sneer,' said Thomas firmly, fixing his blue interrogator's gaze on the tired man, who went on to finish his worrying story.

'I simply commented that if we could go back in time, to an era when the void was much smaller, we could blow it out and neutralise it with the Chalkon, and nobody would ever be any the wiser.'

At this point Baz sat up, and Thomas jumped up, poked his head out the door and called for Ryan.

'Get me a copy of the Official Secrets Act, pronto!'

* * *

A trip in a Project to the VE Day celebrations in 1945 showed the Professor what time travel felt like, and now he was sitting in Sophie's office with her tiny Yorkshire terrier, Betsy, dozing contentedly on his lap. Thomas had gone back to Millbank, leaving Sophie and her assistant Jannie to make a start on the technicalities.

Sophie asked, 'Have you worked out how far back in time you need to go?'

'Well, not knowing it was possible, I've only done a back-of-envelope calculation, but that puts the optimum at some time during the middle-ages – say from about 1480 to about 1610. It would take several weeks to get through all the number-crunching needed to narrow it down though because the gas doesn't expand at a steady rate, and it changes with time, and then there are the tendrils to consider…'

'Look Tony,' interjected Sophie firmly, 'Go home now, have a good meal and get a good night's sleep. In the morning, pack up your laptop, paperwork and whatnot, along with enough stuff for a week away and I'll send a limo to pick you up at around ten in the morning. The car will drop you at Millbank where Raj and I can help you work on the problem, and you can bunk in with us at Tamerlane Square for a few days. We've plenty of room and Betsy clearly likes you.'

Professor Price gave the dog a gentle tickle behind her ear and watched her stretch out her paws in ecstasy.

Sophie warmed to her theme. 'When Raj, Jannie and I get on to it we'll plough through work that would take you weeks in no time at all, and once we've found the optimum date we can put our minds to the best way of tackling the job.'

The young Professor felt a massive burden lifting off his back, and he made a silent vow to thank the Home Secretary as soon as he could.

199

21:

Sion Park

It is to be regarded that the rich and powerful too often bend the acts of government to their own selfish purposes.
ANDREW JACKSON

'This couldn't come at a worse time,' sighed Thomas. 'I'm off to the States tomorrow while Raj and Sophie will be in Frankfurt for the European Science Fair, but we just can't leave this one hanging the air. We'll have to get Lucy and Carlo to take Tony to Lincoln Moor in the 1540s for a quick look-see.'

Turning to Jack he said, 'The biggest problem that I can see is likely to hit you in Tudorland is the fact that you'll need to get a "Safe Conduct" pass from a clerk in Henry's court in case we run into nosy local sheriffs when we're in Lincolnshire. Young Jannie's used to flying the Projects back and forth to T-West, so Raj's new deputy, Earl, can help Jannie set the correct data into the Project's system and she can act as pilot for you.'

Jack was considering the implications. 'I don't want to go anywhere near King Henry, Tom. He was grateful for our efforts on his behalf during the Westminster Abbey affair, but if the moody bugger happens to be in one of his

200

loony phases, he could easily start spewing out death warrants.' The historian in Jack mentally took himself back to the mid-sixteenth century. He started to brighten. 'You know what Tom, the King was in France during the summer of 1544, so as long as we go to the court in July or thereabouts, we won't have him to worry about.'

'Bishop Gardiner was First Minister by then, and he was an arrogant man and a prat, so we shouldn't have any problems getting a decent legend past him.'

Thomas made a couple of notes. 'I suggest you consult your history books and find a good day to approach Gardiner, while I pull out some old paper and my quill and ink, and write a Tudorland-type request for the Safe Conduct pass.'

Jack was still deep in thought. 'We're going to need a bloody good cover story, Tom. I mean, we can hardly say that we want to dig a hole in the Lincoln Moor in order to save the country from blowing itself to buggery a half millennium hence, can we?'

In the end it was Raj who came up with the workable idea.

'How about going as a delegation from Hidalia visiting Tudor England on behalf of Hidalian foresters who want to collect English tree seeds to bring back to Hidalia. We could pretend to offer English farmers seeds that are new to them in exchange, as a gesture of goodwill. I have a feeling that horse chestnuts and beech trees didn't exist in Tudor times, but one tree they definitely won't have is leylandii, because it's American.' Raj narrowed his eyes while thinking, and suddenly grinned. 'It's a good thing it's October as there are plenty of tree seeds around right now, so all we need do is search around in our local parks and gardens.'

Thomas said the story should work because the Tudorland government were Londoners, and like

Londoners of any era, they neither knew nor cared tuppence about trees.

Jack thought three lodge Projects would do the trick and they could load them with sufficient washing water, food, drink and Tudor clothing for a short visit. Jack still paid occasional visits to friends in Tudorland so he had plenty of clothes from the era on hand. He'd decided to take a new, young intelligence operative called Noel and a lad from the legal department with him on the trip, so he wheeled them round to the theatrical costumers in Shaftesbury Avenue to get kitted out.

Jannie decided her outfit would be 'Hidalian' rather than typically Tudor, so she found a full skirted, silky gown in various shades of pale blue, lavender and white, along with a royal blue, crushed-velvet fitted jacket. She swapped the jacket's boring plastic buttons for sparkly diamante ones and adapted a tiny silver evening bag so it hung from a narrow silver belt at her waist. She couldn't see herself wearing a ghastly Tudor headdress with its cloth hanging down at the back, so she bought a miniature straw hat and stuck bendy, plastic strips with star shapes on their ends to the side of the crown before running a dark blue velvet ribbon around the crown and gluing it into place. When she tried it on, the hat sat in a rakish position with the bunch of tiny stars dancing around above the right side of her forehead. It wasn't 'Tudor' but it looked great. She knew Tudor women didn't have short hair and that her own shortish, deep red hair would look odd to the Tudorlanders, but she decided that she didn't care.

* * *

Late one Saturday afternoon in July1544, the team arrived at the main door of the great room at Sion House. The historian in Jack gazed in wonderment to find himself in the very room in which King Henry would one day be laid on a table in his coffin. He knew that the King's massive body would fill with gas and fluid, and the coffin would burst, leaking blood and body fluids onto the floor to be lapped by dogs, thus fulfilling a curse that someone had reputedly put on him. Today though, the room was set for a banquet.

Jack carefully told a footman who they were and why they were there; the footman asked them to wait while he went off to find a clerk. A number of courtiers were eyeing the newcomers. Tall, blond, handsome Jack in his impractical pale blue doublet and trunk hose immediately captured the attention of many of the women in the room, and while the other two lads also got more than a once over. A gaggle of school-aged girls gazed open-mouthed at Jannie. The sight of someone dressed in a very different style to themselves, but looking so lovely, made them whisper to each other behind their hands. Some were clearly making sneering remarks, which Jannie recognised from her early school days as nastiness born of envy.

At the other end of the hall, a tall, extremely good looking, dark-haired man in a black doublet with a scattering of emeralds on it was also watching the team – and he *definitely* noticed Jannie.

Bishop Gardiner's chief clerk came out and told Jack the Safe Conduct pass would be made up quickly enough, but it could only be signed and have the seal attached the following morning when Bishop Gardiner would be available. He also said he was pleased to be able to tell them that the Bishop had asked the foreign visitors to join the court for the evening's banquet and entertainment.

* * *

Each guest had a specially designated place at the long

tables, so a footman told the team they would have to fit into gaps left by courtiers who hadn't turned up for some reason or another. The lads weren't unhappy at this, as it would give them an opportunity to engage with the locals and ask questions, but while each of the men found themselves among congenial company, Jannie drew the short straw.

The footman seated her on a table to the far right of the room where she was out of sight of the others. A large man on her right had his back to her while he was talking to his friends. To her left sat a dry looking middle-aged man in clerical garb. He had a narrow face and a long nose, which he immediately stuck in the air. A few strands of greasy grey hair showed beneath the earflaps of his black hat. Two younger men faced the cleric across the table. Watching the various dishes arrive at the tables, Jannie decided to do as her diplomat and businessman father had always done when his work took him to Third World countries, which was to become vegan for the duration.

Upon discovering that an unaccompanied young foreign woman had been seated next to him, the cleric decided to demonstrate his importance. He always enjoyed taking the opportunity to bully those who were in no position to stand up to him, and Jannie looked like prime victim material. Taking a breath, the clerical man turned his pale face towards Jannie and rudely asked, 'And who might thou be?'

'I'm Jannie,' she replied politely.

'Who?' said the cleric, speaking even more rudely. The repeated question was designed to make her to dance to his tune by replying a second time, perhaps with some additional explanation, but Jannie had witnessed enough interrogations in TUDOR to be aware of the techniques of intimidation.

Jannie ignored the cleric and focused her attention on

an older woman who was walking slowly up the length of the room. She wore a hideous dress in a colour that Jannie immediately thought of as 'baby-shit brown', and it was topped by a 'church gate' headdress of a type that Jannie had seen in history books but didn't believe anyone had actually been stupid enough to wear. The drab brown dress, combined with a long, pointy nose poking out of the ugly headdress put her in mind of a lurcher peering out of a kennel.

The cleric decided to try again, raising his voice for emphasis. 'I asked thee a question, young woman!'

Still watching the drab-looking woman, Jannie replied quietly, 'And I answered it, middle-aged man.'

By now, the younger and better looking of the bully's hangers-on was trying to hide a smile, but the other one felt the need to ingratiate himself with his master, so he too launched a second attack.

'Knowest thou not to whom thou art talking? This is Bishop Martin Garvin, and he is not accustomed to ill-mannered speech!'

'Neither am I,' answered Jannie with a slight shrug, still looking around the room.

The Bishop decided to go for broke.

'Thou shouldst mind thy mouth!' he shouted. 'We do not need doxies and street-walkers like thee sitting at table with high-born folk.'

Jannie sighed. She had come to the conclusion that the Tudor court in general and this evening's function in particular just weren't for her, so she made up her mind to leave the table to find one of the lads and tell him she was going back to her lodge. It had been fun looking at the Tudor clothes and spectacle of medieval life, but the Tudorlanders themselves left much to be desired. In any case, Martin Gavin's rank smell was rapidly putting her off the idea of eating anything at all. Just for the hell of it though, she decided to say her piece before taking her leave.

'My name is Janine West, I am known by my friends as Jannie, but you can call me Miss West. I live in Hidalia, a country with a long history of alliance with England, due to helping your people on their way to and from the crusades. If you can find a reasonably accurate atlas of maps and ignore that Mappa Mundi rubbish, you will find that Hidalia is in the far east of Europe, adjacent to the far west of Asia.'

She decided to deliberately misunderstand the "doxie-cum-streetwalker" insult. 'For your information, I am not a doggy and I don't live in the street. I am a scientific and technical operative and I work for a government department. I am here as part of a delegation from my country, whose intention is to share scientific information with yours – assuming we can find someone with enough brainpower to take advantage of scientific and agricultural data.' She looked straight into the Bishop's astonished eyes and said, 'Happy now?'

Jannie turned away from the Bishop with the intention of clambering over the bench and leaving the table, but before she could get any further, a heavy clout sent her tumbling backwards.

Two people at the top table had witnessed the performance. The first was a bearded, middle-aged government minister, and the other was the dark-haired man who had taken such an interest in the TUDOR team when they first arrived.

'I think Garvin is about to get above himself,' said the minister. 'The girl is part of an important foreign delegation and it might be worth rescuing her before that idiot creates an international incident.'

The dark-haired man had already decided upon that

course of action, so even as his minister spoke, he was out of his seat and marching swiftly down the side of the room. He reached Jannie just in time to catch her before she bashed her brains out on the ancient floorboards of Sion House.

22:

The Banquet

Once, during Prohibition, I was forced to live for days on nothing but food and water.

W. C FIELDS.

The tall man helped Jannie off the bench, but no sooner was she on her feet when a wave of dizziness overcame her. In an instant, the man caught her and held her fast. She managed to stay just this side of consciousness while her mind registered that the doublet she was leaning against smelled surprisingly clean.

'Did he hurt thee?'

Jannie heard a warm voice and a note of concern.

'He winded me, but I also think I'm feeling funny because I'm hungry.'

'When did thou last eat?'

'I've been busy… I think I had a hot drink first thing, but my last meal must have been some time yesterday morning.'

Jannie buckled again, so the man picked her up and carried her down the room to a spare table that had been set up at the other end. Jannie didn't want this. What she wanted was to get a message to one of the others and return to her lodge, but the man ignored her protests and made for the unoccupied table. Servants came running up to him, so he asked them to find a seat with a back rather than the backless benches that most of the diners were sitting on. A few minutes later, two men rushed up with the right kind of bench, and soon the man was helping the still grumbling Jannie to sit, while he sat down next to her.

Jannie glared at the man. 'I want to go to my lodgings,' she hissed, 'and a toff like you needs to be up there with the lords and ladies, not down here below the salt with me.'

The man could see that Jannie was ready to take any opportunity to escape, so he took hold of her wrist and told her that she would sit down and eat her dinner like a good girl when it arrived.

With no other option in view, Jannie gritted her teeth and muttered under her breath that the next problem was now about to loom over the horizon.

'And what problem is that?' asked her sharp-eared companion.

She noticed a pair of sparkling deep-blue eyes, set in a slightly patrician face, topped by a black velvet hat with a feather in it. Dark curls surrounded the hat. Jannie couldn't help noticing that he looked like a younger version of both Thomas and Carlo Hatherleigh, but with Thomas's serious face and intense blue gaze rather than Carlo's silver-coin eyes and dimpled grin. She came to the rapid conclusion that this had to be another Hatherleigh, which probably meant he would be in a position of power and very likely in some form of intelligence service. She decided that for the time being at least she would fall in with his demands – but on her own terms.

'I won't eat meat, fish, shellfish or fowl. In short, I don't want anything that has lived. I will eat bread, butter, cheese, what you call herbs, cakes and fruit,' said Jannie firmly.

By this time, a team of footmen had arrived and they were bowing respectfully, reinforcing her belief that the guy was some kind of top dog. He told the servants to bring gold or silver platters without worrying about trying to make a matching set, but just to ensure everything was clean. The man ordered a herb-based pottage, along with the things Jannie had asked for, as well as a jug of milk, a dish of clean water and several large napkins. His final instruction was to send for a couple of troopers.

'Oh God, this is so embarrassing,' complained Jannie.

'Dost thou never consume livestock?' asked the man.

'I do,' replied Jannie quietly, 'but I don't know how fresh your goods are or whether the kitchen staff wash their hands after using the loo, and I don't want to get ill.'

'Loo?'

How do I explain this, thought Jannie? She took a deep breath and made a start, 'In Hidalia, a loo is a colloquial term for the place where people relieve themselves.'

'I see,' said the man with a chuckle while giving her a slight bow. 'I understand thy concerns.'

She could see he was ever so slightly taking the Mickey, but that suggested a sense of humour. Meanwhile, a footman arrived with two helmeted soldiers in tow, and her companion stood up to speak to them while still keeping a firm hold of Jannie's wrist.

'Dost thou know the man who calls himself Bishop Garvin?'

The trooper laughed, 'I do indeed, Sir Francis. And his stupid friends.'

The tall man gave a slight nod. 'I have had more than enough of their impertinence this day. I suspect Garvin is taking advantage of the King's absence to show off.'

'We have all reached that conclusion,' replied the trooper dryly.

'Attacking an unarmed girl who happens to be a foreign dignitary is the height of cowardly arrogance, and a spell in the Fleet will teach our self-styled bishop and his friends a lesson or two.'

'How long dost thou want them there, Sir? Bearing in mind there's no trial to speak of.'

'Tell the beadle to give them two months in which to await trial and then to let them go. That will teach them a little respect.'

'Or finish them off,' grinned the trooper.

Jannie's rescuer gave a slight shrug.

When the troopers had gone, Jannie said, 'That's a bit hard, don't you think? I mean gaol and all that.'

The tall man took her question seriously. 'This is not the first problem we have had with Garvin and if it is not nipped in the bud, he and the others like him will aim too high and take too much upon themselves. The King would put a stop to it forthwith, were he here, but when the cat's away, the mice will play.'

Now the man gave Jannie a cheeky smile and said, 'Listen, my skittish little filly, I will let go of thy hand if thou promiseth not to run off.'

Jannie put up her hands. 'Alright, I'll stay put. Anyway, I could do with something to eat.' Jannie looked at the man and said, 'What do I call you? I mean, my name is Janine, but everyone calls me Jannie.'

'My name is Francis.' Francis looked quizzically at Jannie and asked, 'Why are thou not sitting with thy husband, Jannie? Thou couldst have insisted upon it, you know.'

'Husband?' Jannie was puzzled, but then she realised he must be think she was married to one of the team. Shaking her head she said, 'The men are my work colleagues and I'm glad to say, also my friends.'

'So thy husband is in Hidalia?'

Jannie decided she would respond to this fishing expedition slowly, so she shook her head.

'A widow, perhaps?' asked Francis.

Another shake.

'A maiden?'

This brought a small smile.

'A divorcee, then?'

'Sort of,' replied Jannie.

'What might a "sort of" divorcee be?' asked Francis.

'The kind where I had the sense not to marry the dolt in the first place,' answered Jannie frankly.

'I see I shall have to find out more about this,' said Francis. The cerulean eyes were definitely twinkling now.

Now Jannie knew for sure Francis was a member of the Hatherleigh clan. He seemed to have the same the nosy attitude as the rest of them.

'Okay. I'll tell you my entire life story. Will that satisfy you?'

'That would be a good start.' A sudden smile lit up the intelligent face and Jannie couldn't help noticing an interesting warmth gathering itself around her body.

Several waiters arrived with loaded trays, setting down a steaming tureen of what smelled like pea and vegetable soup. The fragrant aroma made Jannie's stomach rumble. This was followed by bread, butter and everything else that Francis had asked for. When the waiters had gone, Francis let go of Jannie's hand, picked up two of the napkins, laying one on her lap while climbing off the bench and tying the other napkin around her neck.

When his fingers brushed the back of her neck, Jannie gasped a little, but despite this unexpected bodily response, she decided to remonstrate.

'Hey,' said Jannie, watching him tie another of the large napkins around his own neck. 'Nobody else is wearing a napkin, why do we have to!'

'They are not eating potage,' answered Francis crisply. 'It drips, and I don't want it on my good doublet or your beautiful robe.'

He's got a point, Jannie thought.

The hot soup was terrific, as was the freshly made bread, but Jannie couldn't work out how to spread the butter onto it without a knife. Francis pulled a dagger from is belt, dipped the end of a napkin into the dish of water and cleaned the blade.

'Where is thy knife?' he asked.

Jannie opened her evening bag and pulled out a key ring with her miniature Swiss army knife attached to it. Francis took the ring and examined it carefully, working the spring steel in wonderment. He opened and closed the tiny knife and inspected the file-come-screw-driver, scissors, tweezers, the penknife and even the plastic toothpick, finally looking at the key and the fob with its pink enamel heart design.

'Fascinating,' he said with a look of amazement on his face. 'Absolutely fascinating – but this will not spread butter, will it?'

Jannie ran a hand through her bouncy copper-coloured waves and shrugged.

'I will do it for thee, then,' sighed Francis, suggesting that it would be a mammoth chore, but even as he joked, he had a strange feeling that this wouldn't be the last thing he'd do for this lovely and unusual girl.

They worked their way through the soup and Jannie drank some of the milk. Francis had insisted she have it in place of wine, as he rightly said that it wasn't good to drink wine on an empty stomach. Jannie was grateful for that. Francis picked up an apple, sliced it and set the pieces down before cracking a few nuts, then taking a slice of apple and dipping it in honey.

'Open up,' he said.

She allowed Francis to introduce her to the new taste, and the sensuality of the action made her insides clench. Something was starting to uncoil, and it was as though the sacred snake of Kundalini was coming to life in her lower chakras. She became aware of sparklers going off in her belly and her breathing becoming slightly laboured. She decided to talk about herself, both to take her mind off the weird spell the man was weaving, and to avoid falling into the trap of mentioning why she and the others were in Tudorland.

Jannie scrutinised a clutch of schoolgirls on a nearby table. They appeared to be kitted out in old curtains, with sheets of cardboard shoved down their fronts. Some of them were clearly pregnant and they were all brimming with youthful confidence. Nodding towards the girls and clearing her throat slightly, she made a start, ticking off items on her fingers as she went.

'Some girls have a hunger for boys from the moment they arrive at puberty, while the others are late developers. Some girls have wealth, style, family connections, parties and music, while others have lives that are filled with schoolwork, homework and housework. I leave it to you to work out which condition applied to me.'

Francis' slight nod showed he understood, while Jannie lost herself in her story. It was only later that she realised she'd never talked about any of this before, but the need to find a neutral subject and the fact that she would soon take leave of this man gave her impetus. She told how she had chosen to stay on at school and get a good education, but with an absent father and only her mother to support the two of them, it was a relief to both her and her mother when she found work as a junior clerk.

Francis queried the fact that a woman could work as a clerk in Hidalia, but Jannie replied that it was not unusual.

Wages had been small, and she split them with her mother, so it was a long time before she could afford to buy modern clothes or start socialising. In time, she made friends with some of the girls at work and started going out with them, and while out and about, she began to attract the attention of young men.

Knowing she would soon be gone from Tudorland, Jannie didn't need to worry about Francis's opinion of her, so she decided not to keep anything back. 'In Hidalia, even perfectly decent men from nice backgrounds expect a girl to have sex with them at the very latest by the third time they go out together, so when I went out with a particular guy on three occasions, and he suggested going back to his place, I agreed, partly to avoid having to fight the guy off, but mainly because I was embarrassed at being a virgin at the age of nineteen. You see, in Hidalia, girls jump into bed in vain attempts to stop men from dumping them – but the men dump them anyway. In the event, I had made a mistake. I never did want that man as a long-term boyfriend, and I felt so rotten afterwards that I decided there and then only to have sex with people I really liked, and not just because some bloke expected it.'

'As it happened, I still didn't meet anyone, but I did make a friend – or so I thought.' Jannie ran a hand over her mouth while recalling the incident. 'Nigel was a management trainee, and as we were the only young people working in those offices at the time, we fell into the habit of joining each other in the kitchen for lunch. He was reasonably good company, and when the time came for him to move on somewhere else, he asked if I would go out with him. I had no real interest in him and it was obvious to me that without the shared interest of work, the friendship

215

wouldn't last, but I agreed to meet up once in a while. In the event, we did hook up once or twice and I thought that would be the end of it. However he sent a message saying he wanted to meet me at his flat because he had something important to tell me.'

'Flat?'

'Rooms.'

Francis could see where this was going, but he kept quiet.

'He didn't have anything important to tell me, and he began to get amorous. Nigel was morbidly obese and far from good looking, but even if he'd been handsome, I had never looked on him as anything other than a friend and I tried telling him that. I picked up my bag and coat in preparation for leaving, but he pounced on me.' Jannie looked thoughtful for a moment. 'I doubt Nigel got much female attention, so I guess this was the only way he could get what he wanted.'

Francis took Jannie's hand and smoothed his thumb over the back of it while giving her an encouraging smile. He knew she needed to get this off her chest.

'Nigel was big, strong and very heavy, so he grabbed me, pulled my clothes off and tossed me onto the sofa. He wrung my breasts like dishcloths and ground his chin downwards on my left breast until the pain got so bad I wanted to vomit. When he got going... with the sex business, it felt as though a horse had fallen on me, and even though I begged him to move to the side and get his weight off me, he didn't. I couldn't shift him, and by then he was so lost in his own pleasure that he couldn't think of anything but himself. I couldn't breathe, and it got so bad that I thought I was going to die there.'

Jannie stopped for a moment while gathering her thoughts together. 'When Nigel finished, he fell off the sofa and lay spread-eagled on the floor, and I took the opportunity to grab my clothes and pretended I was heading for the loo, but I quickly changed direction and raced out of the front door as fast as I could go. Holding my clothes in front of me, I slipped into an alley at the side of the flats, pulled my clothes on and ran home. When I got back, I took a long bath. I was badly bruised and I was pretty sure the bastard had cracked a couple of my ribs because the pain was excruciating.'

Francis had a powerful urge to take this lovely, vulnerable girl into his arms and comfort her, but he did the next best thing, which was to keep quiet and let her finish.

'Nigel must have realised he'd gone too far, because I never heard from him again.'

Jannie thought back and wondered whether she was boring the man, but she decided that keeping him off the subject of the team's visit to Tudorland seemed to be working, so she went on.

'My mother and father were no longer young when they met, and she soon fell pregnant with me, but my dad soon moved on to the next woman, leaving mother to bring me up on her own. He popped in from time to time when he had a bit of money to spare, and he was generous on those occasions, but you could hardly give him a prize for being the father of the year. Over the years, Mother had several boyfriends, but it took a long time before she found one who actually wanted to live with her. By this time, she was in her mid-fifties and the boyfriend in question was much older. He soon turned our home into a one-man home for old people.

The sight of his mashed up, sloppy food, the smell of his pee on the furniture, his filthy old stuff everywhere, his deafness and his loud voice going on non-stop about complete rubbish were unbearable, so I kept out of the way.

Needless to say, I gave my mother money for rent and for the food and laundry, even though I wasn't actually using any of it, while her wages went on that fat old cuckoo. Whenever I got paid, she would want even more money from me, and I had so little left that even buying myself so much as a pair of shoes became an impossibility.'

'As if that wasn't enough, I'd moved up a notch at work and I was earning a little more by then, but then a new manager joined the firm and he was a bully. The bullying made it hard for me to concentrate on my job, but then he started making untoward advances.'

'If that kind of man becomes emboldened, Jannie, it can escalate into assault.'

Jannie was amazed at Francis' acumen. She was also surprised at how comfortable she felt with him. After all, this was a Tudor nobleman, and she was talking about the sexual mores of a far distant time and place.

'My luck finally changed when I ran into a friend who told me about a job some distance away from home, which was due to become available because the secretary who worked there was leaving to have a baby. As soon as I knew the job was mine, I started to look for somewhere to live.

The least expensive option would be to take a room in someone else's house or to share a room with another girl, but I couldn't face it, so I went to my father and asked him for help. He and his current girlfriend knew that I'm neither feckless nor selfish, so they lent me the money that enabled me to set myself up in a rented flat. The wages were much better in the new job, and when my boss realised that I had educational qualifications in technical subjects, she moved me away from clerical work and into technical work. That brought another big jump in my salary, so it wasn't long before I could repay my dad and his lady friend.'

Francis gave Jannie an encouraging nod. The story was

giving him a valuable glimpse into life in Hidalia, so he was happy for Jannie to continue.

'The job is demanding and I'm still getting used to it, and on top of that, the organisation insists that we spend a certain amount of time on sports or exercise to keep fit and healthy. So, what with setting up a home as well, I just haven't had time to go out searching for love and romance.' Now Jannie looked down at the table and voiced something that up to now she hadn't acknowledged to herself. 'I also needed time to process my mother's behaviour. You see, despite having me by accident, so to speak, she had been a good mother while I was young, but she became increasingly sour as time went by. But on top of all that, I needed to stop blaming myself for the Nigel episode.'

'Blaming thyself? Why?'

'When I looked back, I could see that I never really trusted Nigel, I shouldn't have gone to his flat, and if I had followed my instincts and been less bothered about hurting his feelings, he wouldn't have had the opportunity of assaulting me.'

'Thou dids't nothing wrong, Jannie. Thou wert offering friendship to a man who turned out to be a pig and an imbecile – and he raped thee.'

Francis gave Jannie an encouraging grin. She found her gaze being captured by those deep blue eyes and her heart being lifted by Francis's jaunty white-toothed smile. She felt light headed and overheated, but then she became conscious of music playing, and Francis asked Jannie if she would like to dance.

'I love dancing, but I don't know the steps.'

Francis grinned encouragingly, 'Thou'll soon pick them up. It is not hard.'

23:

Revelations

In a more universal deceit – telling the truth is a revolutionary act.

GEORGE ORWELL

Casper's grin could have lit up the room. 'You're the talk of the town, Jannie.'

'Why? Because that Garvin bloke thumped me?'

Casper nodded. 'Partly – but it's your new boyfriend who's the main topic. Apparently, he never sits around with a woman, though he's bonked enough of them, and according to the goss on my table, he's very good at it. The bird on my left told me she'd shagged him once and was longing for an encore, while the one on my right hadn't got around to it yet, but was hoping for an opportunity. They say he can't stand the mindless prattle that court women go in for, so the word in the hall is that he must have a real thing for you.'

Jannie laughed. 'What on earth are you talking about, Casper?'

'Your new admirer, Sir Francis Diall, Baron of Tiverbridge and owner of most of Somerset.'

Jannie realised that she had been so involved in her own

story that she hadn't got round to asking Francis about himself, so other than a gut feeling that he worked in intelligence, she knew nothing about him.

A moment later, Jack and Noel turned up.

Jack gave Jannie a peck on the cheek. 'If you intend throwing a leg over that fit looking geezer, don't disappear into his rooms: take him to the lodge.'

'I don't have any intention of throwing a leg over anyone, Jack, but if I did, why would I take the guy to the lodge rather than to his own room?'

'We need to know where you are, so we can find you if we have to leave suddenly.'

'That makes sense.'

'By the way,' said Jack, 'I've asked some discreet questions about your pal, and I've learned that he can keep his mouth shut. He's the head of intelligence, and by what people are telling me, I wouldn't be surprised if he was related to Tommy and Carlo. I've only seen him from a distance, but he seems to resemble them.'

Something fell into place. Jannie had felt an immediate sense of familiarity when she'd started talking to Francis and now she could see why. Francis was definitely some kind of Hatherleigh, and the fact that he owned land in the West Country confirmed it. The Hatherleighs had originally been a West Country family and Carlo still lived in Devon.

Francis was checking with his superiors, and Jack was keeping a weather eye out.

'Look, Jannie, whatever happens, ask him to come to the big lodge for a late breakfast tomorrow. If he starts to ask questions, tell him you don't know anything and that he must ask us.'

'He won't believe me.'

'That's probably true, but you must insist that he wait until the morning. His curiosity will be piqued. After all, he's a secret bloody agent, so he'll want to know the ins and outs of everything, won't he?'

'Bloody Norah, Jack. I'm not used to this Mata Hari stuff. I might muck it up.'

'You won't. He likes you and that makes him vulnerable.' Still looking towards the knot of men at the top table, Jack said, 'Look Jannie, Noel and Casper will play cards for an hour or so, and they'll be back early. They can keep their lodge window open, so if something worries you, just yell and they'll come in. As you know, the same key works for all three lodges, so it's easy for us to get into each other's if needs be.'

'Where will you be?' asked Jannie, realising as soon as she'd opened her mouth that it was a stupid question.

'Well, I found myself seated with a lovely young lady who wants to teach me to dance. She's not only very pretty, but by Tudorland standards she's a clean freak. She mentioned that she drives her servant girls crazy by demanding baths and hair washes twice a week and wanting clean clothes all the time. They think she's off her head.'

'I suppose they would,' mused Noel, thinking about some of the smells he'd found himself encountering that evening.

'That's not all. There's something peculiar going on in her life and my natural curiosity...'

'Means you want to tickle her fancy and question her at the same time,' laughed Casper.

* * *

A moment later, Francis was back and the lads were bowing and introducing themselves. Jannie was surprised to hear Jack introduce himself as *Sir* Jack Duquesne, but she

222

suddenly recalled that in Tudorland, he *was* Sir Jack as he'd been dubbed by King Henry after the Abbey case.

Soon, Francis took Jannie's hand and led her to lines of dancers. He encouraged Jannie to watch the other women and pick up the steps from them, and they practised the routine for a while before joining the dance team, gliding up and down the room as the sequence progressed.

During the break between dances, the young women who had previously sniggered at her outfit now clustered eagerly about her, showing her the steps and wanting to be her friend. This was clearly due to the interest that Francis was showing, and it reinforced her conclusion that he must be a powerful and important man. They danced again and when the next dance finished, Francis twirled Jannie around, caught her in his arms and held her close. She fitted him perfectly, and he found himself becoming aware that something was going on – and it wasn't mere lust. He had been in love once before and he knew the signs, but it was just his luck that Jannie was due to leave in a day or two.

* * *

Francis offered to see Jannie back to her digs, and on the one hand, she was relieved to have an escort in such an unfamiliar place, but on the other hand, she didn't know what Francis might want when they reached the lodge, or how he would react to the lodge itself when he saw it. There really wasn't any way out of this one, unless she ran back to the hall and threw herself onto the mercy of Noel or Casper and asked them to help. She mentally shrugged and decided to let the dice fall wherever they landed.

She led Francis out through the main door of the house, turned left and walked across the courtyard, past the lines of carriages waiting to carry the revellers home. As they entered the wooded area, the world stilled and quieted. Jannie pulled a small torch out of her handbag. She expected Francis to ask where they were going, and at least to make some comment about the torch, but all he did was take her arm to steady her as they walked along the path. She soon found the place where the path branched, leading to the door in the wall that separated the woods from the walled garden and the ruined house beyond. They followed the contour of the garden wall and then pushed through another door and into the ancient garden itself, where the lodges were hidden. Jannie led Francis past Casper and Noel's lodge and on to her own, flipping a light switch as they entered. Francis gazed around the room but said nothing. Jannie led him to the bench that lined the end of the lodge and gestured for him to sit down behind a glass coffee table. She asked him if he'd like a drink.

In the small kitchen area, Jannie pulled a can of Seven-Up out of the fridge, found glasses and poured out the fizzy drinks. Francis still said nothing. She put the drinks on a tray, along with a small box of biscuits. Now at least, her companion made an enquiry as he peered into the biscuit box.

'Which sweetmeat dost thou recommend?'

'Try the one with the brown stuff on it. It's chocolate and I doubt you'll have eaten it before.'

The 'yumm' noises coming from Francis while he munched his first chocolate biscuit showed that it was going down a treat.

While he was occupied with the biscuits and Seven-Up, Jannie told him she would take him on a tour of the lodge, but he'd have to leave after that. Francis acknowledged this with a nod, being too busy picking out a custard cream to reply.

Jannie showed Francis round the lodge and she even showed him how to use the loo and basin, thereafter leaving him to use it for himself. The tour ended when she led him back along the passage and into her bedroom with its cheerfully coloured double bed, echoed by matching flowery yellow curtains across the small window high above the bed.

Jannie said, 'The blue carpet and blue seating came with the lodge, but this colourful stuff is mine.'

There was small cane sofa tucked into a space beside the chest of drawers, so Francis sat down and arranged his sword and his long legs in a comfortable position. Jannie sat on the corner of the bed facing him. Was he going to try to make a move? And if so, what was she going to do about it? Half of her was longing for him and the other half was terrified at the thought of it. She was on the pill, so that wasn't a problem, but what would a 500-year-old man want from her? How would she cope? She'd told him to go once he'd seen the lodge, but would he take no for an answer? And what must he be thinking about the strange lodge with its electric light and cans of drink?

Jannie waved a hand around the room while letting her hazel gaze fall on the handsome face with its high-bridged nose and vibrant blue eyes. 'No questions?' she asked, 'nothing?'

'I have two.'

Jannie raised an eyebrow.

'Will thy companions try to kill me when I leave here?'

'Whaaat!' exclaimed Jannie. She frowned and shook her head, but then she thought the question through. 'I can see why you might think that, but nobody will try to kill you. When Jack and the lads caught up with me earlier, they told me that you and I were the talk of the town, and this made it easy for the guys to ask others about you. They discovered you can keep your mouth shut, so Jack said I should ask you to keep quiet about today, but come back here tomorrow for a late breakfast and the lads will tell you everything then. They don't want you to quiz me now, but they want to talk to you themselves in the morning.'

'I know about the seeds,' he said.

Blimey, thought Jannie. His spies must work at the speed of light – and I bet he doesn't believe that legend either.

'Well, that's good. And now you've discovered nobody is out to kill you, what's your other question?'

'Is there some way that we can keep in touch once thou hast returned to Hidalia?'

'There is, but I'll tell you after breakfast tomorrow.'

'By the way, Jannie, I'm Frans to my friends.'

Like all Tudorlanders, Francis had a slight American accent with the flat "A's" and rolling "R's".

'Frans? Do you mind if I make that *France*?' asked Jannie, using the long "A" as Londoners commonly do. 'It would feel more normal to me.'

Jannie handed Francis her torch and walked him round to the garden door. When they reached it, Francis took her into his arms and drew her firmly to him, kissing her face gently and nibbling her ear, laughing quietly as the bobbing cockade on her hat brushed his face. He pulled her closely into him while slowly and gently finding her lips and letting his tongue explore just inside her mouth.

Jannie was boiling with desire. Hot flames shot upwards from parts of her body that had never before been activated. Her legs turned to jelly and she clung fiercely to Francis to stop herself from falling while kissing him back with a passion she didn't know she possessed.

'Oh God, Jannie,' breathed Francis, 'I'll not give thee up. There has to be a way.'

And with that, he put her out of his arms, turned and disappeared through the door before she had time to register what had just happened.

24:

Breakfast

Health food may be good for the conscience, but Oreos
taste a hell of a lot better.
Robert Redford.

It was obvious that the day was going to be extremely hot,
so Jannie and the lads were wearing tee-shirts and shorts.
Jannie was laying strips of bacon on the grill while Noel
was cracking eggs, slicing tomatoes and unpacking
sausages when a light knock on the open door announced
the arrival of Francis. He gaped at the sight of Noel and
Jannie in their modern garb, finding it utterly weird to see a
woman with her bronze-coloured hair on view and her arms
and legs visible. Francis himself was red-faced and sweaty
in his heavy Tudorland gear.

'God, you look overheated,' said Jannie. 'Come with
me!' Grabbing his hand, she led Francis out of Noel and
Casper's big lodge, past her smaller lodge to Jack's,
whereupon she knocked on the door and took Francis inside.

'Jack, could you help Francis shower...'

'And lend him something cooler than all that
upholstery, eh?'

'If you can spare it.'

Soon, Jack came back with a much cooler and fresher Francis, whose damp dark brown hair now curled freely around his head. In no time, they were tucking in. Francis marvelled at the way Noel and Jannie were able to produce a hot meal without an open fire, and he fell in love with the Dolce Gusto coffee machine. He had become familiar with coffee in Persia, but this concoction was even nicer. He decided he really liked wearing the pale green "Hidalian" tee-shirt, dark green shorts and flip-flops, and he loved feeling fresh and comfortable in such hot weather.

When they'd finished, Jack helped Jannie stack as many dishes into the small dishwasher as they could fit in, piling up the rest for later. Casper put more coffee into the machine while Jack decided to quiz Francis.

'Can I ask you about yourself, Francis?'

'Of course, and I shall answer truthfully, apart from any requests for specific details about my work.'

Jack smiled, and then asked Francis to tell them about his family background

'My *background*?' Francis had never been asked about his family, but he didn't see a problem; and soon he was lost in his own fascinating history, trying to match the team's modern English.

'My name is Sir Francis Diall and I am the Baron of Tiverbridge, with lands encompassing the whole west of Somerset. The name Diall was thought to be a corruption of de l'Isle, because as far as I know, the Dialls came from France some time in the twelfth century, later being ennobled and awarded land in the West Country.'

Francis went on to tell them that his father had done all the normal things a big landowner does, such as grow crops, draw an income from the tenancies and earn a little extra from copper mining, but the majority of his income had come from wool. Diall senior had been so irritated by the extortionate shipping charges levied on the wool that went to Bruges for processing, that he had ordered a small harbour to be enlarged and dredged so that he could run his own ships. The enterprise had turned out to be an excellent investment, as he soon became a shipper for himself and others.

Francis went on to say that Sir Francis Diall senior had been briefly married to a woman who died within a couple of years, and later to another who lived for a fair length of time, but both wives had died without issue. Later, he'd lived as man and wife with an older woman who wasn't free to marry, because her naval officer husband had gone on a voyage and vanished, and she had no idea whether he was alive or dead.

By then though, both she and Sir Francis senior were getting on in years and neither of them was concerned about public opinion, so they just got on with it. This lady didn't give Sir Francis any children either and by the time she passed away, Sir Francis was in his late sixties. Francis commented that the old boy had wealth a-plenty but no issue, so when he died, he could choose to will his estate to a neighbour, or at worst, the lands would go to the crown. Then his luck changed and he finally fathered a son who would inherit the title and the lands.

Now Francis told them about the maternal side of his family, starting with the fact that his mother, Bella Massingham was, and still is, a beautiful woman and a very nice one. Her father, Sir Edgar Massingham, had owned a great deal of central and eastern Somerset, and as a young man, he had turned his back on the nobility and gentry, choosing to marry the pretty daughter of a wealthy yeoman. Ann Massingham had given him five children, the oldest of which was Bella. Sir Edgar was said to be an excellent man in every way, but he was an inveterate gambler. When young, he could work out the odds for horses or the hands of cards in an instant, and this often made him a winner, but as he got older, his ability waned and he began to lose heavily, chasing his losses until he was on the brink of losing everything. Despite this, reality didn't seem to penetrate, and he still insisted on living the life of a wealthy and sociable landowner, so one day in the winter of 1516 the ever-hospitable Sir Edgar invited his neighbour Sir Francis Diall, to stay for a few days of hunting and fishing.

Now aged fourteen, the ravishingly beautiful Bella was old enough to attend an adult dinner party, and it was during that first evening that Sir Francis fell head over heels in love, but he hesitated about asking for her hand because of the difference in their ages. Bella was far from stupid. She knew her family would soon be thrown into penury and she could see that her mother was worried sick. In addition, Bella couldn't bear the thought of her four younger siblings becoming beggars, so knowing how Sir Francis felt about her, she told her mother that she would accept an offer of marriage if Sir Francis would clear her father's debts.

Bella's mother was horrified at the idea of her daughter selling herself in this way, but Bella insisted, saying that old Diall probably wouldn't live much longer, and then she'd be free to marry whoever she liked. More to the point, Bella actually *liked* the old boy and she wasn't afraid of him. They married and cleared Sir Edgar's debts, and to everyone's joy and surprise, shortly after the early summer pea and bean harvest, Bella announced she was with child.

Sadly though, while Bella was pregnant, Sir Francis had a stroke that left him partially paralysed, but Bella called in nurses to care for him and she ordered a wicker chair to be made with wheels attached so he could be rolled outside on nice days. Fortunately, Sir Francis could still talk, and Bella enjoyed sitting with him and learning from him, while he loved spending time with his kind-hearted and beautiful young wife.

Bella's mother, Ann, had an intuitive feeling that the birth would be tricky, so she moved Bella, Sir Francis and his nurses into the Massingham household where she would be better able to attend to her daughter. This turned out to be a sensible precaution because the birth was very tricky indeed, partly due to the baby lying in the wrong position and partly due to Bella's slight figure and her extreme youth. Bella lost a lot of blood and was very weak after the birth, but her mother's insistence on cleanliness, on keeping Bella calm and quiet, and on engaging a clean and sober young wet-nurse to feed Francis junior, meant that both Bella and the baby survived. The only downside was that Bella could never have any more children.

Then, just as she was getting back on her feet, Bella's family suffered two more blows; Sir Francis Diall had a second stroke that led to his death, and soon after that, Sir Edgar suffered a seizure to the heart, became seriously unwell, and a few months later, a second seizure took Sir Edgar from them. The now the fifteen-year-old Bella, her mother and her fourteen-year-old brother combined the Diall and Massingham estates into one large enterprise. The brother might have been young, but he was a steady lad who had a head for business and a real love of the land, so things started to look up.

Bella had been very sad to lose her husband. He'd been like a wise old grandfather to her and she missed him. She'd been told her mother that sleeping with him hadn't been the sickening chore Ann had feared, because the old man had been very gentle and he knew how to make a woman happy in bed. Indeed, he'd made a point of showing her what life and love were all about, and if she ever married again, she'd insist that any future husband take the trouble to make bedtime a pleasure as old Sir Francis had done. Bella's mother raised an eyebrow at that revelation.

While the family had been very sad to lose Sir Edgar, they were mightily relieved to be free of his gambling addiction. Ann had long since come to the conclusion that winning had never been enough for her husband, and that it was the thrill of the chase that he'd sought. That would have been all well and good for a single man with no family responsibilities, but she had found it impossible to understand how an apparently loving husband and father could take such chances with all their lives and futures. She tried talking to him about it, but he just couldn't see the problem, because he was always certain that sooner or later, he would win so much money that he'd be able to buy Ann a palace filled with gold and silver. Being a normal, sensible woman, Ann didn't want a palace or gold and silver, just security for her family.

It was now that poor Bella suffered her worst loss. Since early childhood, she'd been close to a young man called Will Fortescue. Will was the only son of neighbours who owned a large area of land to the south of theirs in Devon. Will's mother had given birth to several children, but Will was the only one to survive infancy, and now he was a strong young man of seventeen. Men from the nobility usually spent time in the armed forces, and Will had joined up at the age of sixteen to get his tour of duty out of the way, because his heart wasn't into army life. His plan was to do what was asked of him for a year and then get on with his real life. The army could have sent Will anywhere, but as luck would have it, he'd been billeted in Gloucestershire, just to the north of the Diall lands, so while he couldn't reach his parents' land, he *was* able to give Bella and Sir Francis a helping hand.

However, things can go wrong even in the best of circumstances, and shortly after Will arrived back in his regiment after helping to bring in the early harvest, an overloaded wagon broke its axle and slipped its load, which landed squarely on him; a few hours later, Will Fortescue was dead.

When Bella heard of Will's death, she was inconsolable. Family and friends came to the conclusion that her misery was a result of this death coming on the heels of two years of drama and upheaval, but their servants suggested people should look in a *different* direction for Bella's reaction – and for the *real* father of her baby. Ann swiftly sacked the gossips, and rushed to preserve her daughter's good name and her grandson's legitimacy.

When young Francis was three, Bella met and married a yeoman farmer called Henry Cowdrey, and he turned out to be an excellent husband and stepfather, so Francis junior ended up enjoying a happy childhood within his extended family.

When Francis reached his mid-teens, he joined the army – willingly in his case - and he served all over England and in various foreign countries, developing a talent for languages, for gathering intelligence and for acting on it. Eventually the King sent him to Persia to gather information about the eastern lands. Francis sent his reports back to Sir Thomas Hatherleigh, who was then the head of security, but he never got to meet his boss in person. By the time Francis returned to England, Sir Thomas Cromwell had been executed and Sir Thomas Hatherleigh had vanished, and the intelligence service was in tatters. Francis took on the work of putting it back on its feet, reporting to the First Minister, Bishop Steven Gardiner.

* * *

'That's it. That's my story,' said Francis, glad to accept another cup of what he called *"quafay"* after all that talk.

233

'*Quafay*?' Noel enquired.

'I learned to appreciate *quafay* in Persia, but these days I have to wait until a ship comes in bringing me a few *Arabica* beans. I've taught my servants how to grind and serve it with honey and sometimes also with cream.'

Casper made them fresh cups, while Jack voiced his thoughts. 'I want to ask you a weird question.'

Francis indicated that he should go on.

'Would you happen to know Will Fortescue's mother's maiden name?'

Francis narrowed his eyes and bit his lip while letting his mind flow back in time. 'I think so. No, I'm sure. Will's mother's first name was Megan and her surname...' The name fell into place. 'It's Hatherleigh! That's it! Her name was Megan *Hatherleigh*!'

A variety of emotions crossed Francis's face while he made the connection.

Casper said, 'I think we'd better tell the dear boy everything: about us, about himself and about everything else, if you see what I mean.'

Francis said, 'Please call me Frans, or France, if you prefer.'

25:

Back To The Future

How did it get so late so soon? It's night before it's afternoon. December is here before it's June. My goodness how the time has flown.

Dr Seuss

'Just one more question,' said Jack before diving into the TUDOR story. 'Where do you think we come from and how do you think we got here?'

Francis had already given this some thought. 'In theory, the lodges could have been carried up-river in sections and erected here, but I would have received word of that even before they'd reached London, because nothing of this size and complexity could come through without my knowledge.' Francis gazed into the distance, while working towards a logical conclusion. 'I heard many fascinating legends while living in Persia, and one particularly pervasive belief is that of the flying carpet.'

'A magic carpet!' exclaimed Noel.

'In addition, I spent time in Hidalia while on my way back from the East, and while Hidalia is a beautiful country, it's a backward one, while you clearly come from an advanced culture, so if pushed, I'd say you come from much further east – Cathay, perhaps – although that doesn't account for your knowledge of English, albeit your novel way of speaking.'

'Which you are picking up remarkably quickly,' Casper commented.

'Indeed, answered Francis.'

'As you know, we're here on an exchange of tree seeds,' said Casper with a straight face.

'And I'm the court jester,' replied Francis dryly.

The game was clearly up, but before starting to quiz them, Francis had more to tell.

'You see my friends; I was twenty when I left for Persia. I had fallen deeply in love with a beautiful young woman and I had decided to marry her, so I went on ahead to Persia to see if it would be a suitable country for a young bride to live in. When I had discerned that it was, Sybil and her aunt took ship to join me. Their ship didn't arrive, and I eventually received news that it had gone down in a tempest.' A dark cloud passed over the young man's face.

'It took me a long time to recover from the loss and also the guilt I felt for asking them to take the ship, but I gradually recovered. In time, I met a lovely Persian lady who was a few years older than me. It was she who taught me a great deal about life and love. Since my return to England, there have been many women, but none has touched my heart until now. I know enough about myself to understand that my feelings for Jannie aren't a passing fancy, but I am also aware that you must soon return whence you came. I would love to offer Jannie a life here with me, but I fear my country is slipping into lawlessness and possibly even revolution, and soon enough, it will be hard enough for me to ensure the safety of my family without the added responsibility of a beloved wife.

Francis stopped and thought for a moment before continuing his story.

'Henry's war with France has some validity, because intelligence has proven that the French were planning to invade us. We have certainly prevented that from occurring, but rather than finish the war quickly, the King decided to try and occupy the whole of France, and this impossible ambition is impoverishing our country. Henry thinks that charging up and down the battlefield in a suit of armour will bring him popularity, but the days of so-called battlefield chivalry are long gone. What most people want now is peace and enough to eat, and I fear that we will have neither of those things soon.

Furthermore, there is word that once Henry has finished ruining the monasteries, he'll strip the nobility of their landed wealth, and once that happens, nobody will be safe. Worse still, what shape will the future religion take? And who among us will pray what is considered to be the right way from one day to the next?'

Noel found himself grasping something that Jack Duquesne had always known, which was that the Tudor age wasn't a list of boring facts but a time of high uncertainty and danger. Secure in the knowledge that the team weren't out to do him any harm, and relieved to be able to speak so openly, Francis warmed to his subject.

'Henry engineered the break from Rome to divorce Catherine of Aragon and marry Anne Boleyn, but there were further reasons behind his desire for a break with Rome, such as wanting to remove the control that the Vatican imposed upon England and the money it cost us. However, the action has opened the door to the new beliefs that are flooding in from Europe, and the King's opinions tend to change according to his mood. At heart, he's probably still a catholic – just not the kind that suffers being dictated to by Rome.'

'Brexit!' muttered Noel, shaking his head in amazement.

'*Plus ca change, plus c'est le meme chose*,' said Jack under his breath.

'So while ordinary people want things to stay as they were, others kill each other over disagreements as to whether the wine and bread really *do* become the blood and body of Christ when administered by a priest or whether they are no more than mere grocery.'

Francis stopped for a while and sipped his coffee before coming to the end of his story.

'Persia introduced me to people of many religions, some of which are much older than Christianity, and I learned that the countries further east are far more populous than ours and in many ways more advanced. I find it impossible to accept that millions of people are doomed to burn in hell just because they know nothing of Christ or the Pope. And even if it *is* only Christians who are to be allowed into heaven, to what manner of Christianity will the privilege be granted? So one way or another, I can't get worked up about religion, but I am worried about my family. The only thing I can think of is to retain my position at court, where I might gain a better understanding of the way the wind is blowing from one day to the next.'

* * *

The team sat quietly while absorbing all that Francis had told them, but then Jack told Francis the story of TUDOR right from the start to the present time. The time travel aspect of the story didn't shock him overmuch, because it fitted the legends he'd heard in Persia. However, what *did* take him by surprise was Jack's revelation about Francis's antecedents and his hitherto unknown New London family.

'France my old pal, there's no way the old Diall geezer was your father,' said Jack. 'You see, there are situations where a man can make love and he can even produce semen, but the spermatozoa within the semen that carry the means of creating a child just aren't there. I can tell you that the servants' gossip was bang on the money, because we know for a fact that Will Fortescue-cum-Hatherleigh is your natural father. You look like a younger version of Tom and Carlo; you do the same job as them and I'll bet you can be a ruthless bugger when the need arises, just as they are.'

'It has been said,' murmured Francis.

Casper noticed that the dishwasher had finished its cycle, so he emptied it and reloaded it while Jannie put the clean stuff away. Meanwhile, Francis was doing some quick thinking.

'It would attract too much attention if we all troop in to get the pass.' An idea occurred to him, so he turned to Jack and said, 'Would you come with me to collect the pass and then help me take my belongings from my room? I'm a little bothered about leaving my baggage unattended by anyone other than my manservant much longer, as I have a cache of gold hidden there. I would feel happier if it were here with me until I have to leave. I can pick up my horse from the stableman and start back for London later today.'

'Of course,' said Jack.

* * *

They hadn't been back long when Francis noticed a noise outside the lodge and when he stuck his head out the door, he immediately dodged back inside. 'Bandits!' Francis's face was grim. 'Quite a number of them too. It shows how hard this country is getting to control. People like these steal anything they can lay their hands on, and they don't hesitate to kill those who get in their way.'

Ever since the Abbey case, Jack never went anywhere without a pistol, but the other two men rushed to get their guns while Francis snatched up his gauntlets and his sword.

Jannie grabbed a Pigeon and a notepad and pen, and dived under the table where she sent messages to Carlo, Baz and Sophie.

Several scruffy men jumped over the wall and landed on the roof of Jannie's lodge. The New Londoners took pot shots at them, catching two on the lodge and a few more who had got down from the lodge and were now running across the grass in the 'U' shaped area in front of the lodges. Francis tackled one large thug, and the fierce fight only ended when Francis grasped the working end of his sword in one gauntlet-clad hand, and holding the hilt with the other hand, brought the edge of the sword down on the man's head, killing him instantly.

Noel was great at following suspects and overhearing secrets in pubs, but he was slightly built and not a powerful fighter and he'd lost his grip on his gun, but now he found himself unexpectedly grateful for the unarmed combat training he'd so resented having to take. He gave the man a viscous jab with his left elbow, and when the assailant's grip loosened, Noel spun lightly on the ball of his left foot and brought his right leg round in a karate kick, quickly following it up by a leap that landed a kick to the man's face. The thug went down on top of Noel's gun, but not being familiar with modern pistols, it didn't occur to him to pick it up and use it. Casper got behind the assailant and calmly put a bullet through the man's head.

'Thanks Casp, I owe you,' gasped Noel, still catching his breath.

After more shooting, Jack grabbed Jannie and half carried her to her own lodge, while yelling at the others to follow him, and soon a shaking Jannie fired up the Project and flew them to T-West.

* * *

The lodges landed in the docking area of TUDOR West's massive barn, and as the team emerged, they were faced by Carlo, levelling a pistol at them.

'It's all right Carlo, it's only us,' said Jack.

'Who's he then?' asked Carlo, nodding to Francis.

'He's your cousin.'

'What!'

'It's a long story,' said Jack wearily. 'I don't suppose we could bother you for a cuppa? It's been a tough day.'

The air to one side of the docking area started to shimmer, and an old Citroen Cleo settled into place. A moment later, Thomas and Baz emerged.

'Those little cars aren't much fun when you're as tall as I am,' moaned Baz, stretching his back.

Lucy walked into the barn, staring open-mouthed at the team in their mix of summer clothes and doublets, now being joined by the smartly suited and booted Thomas and Baz. Something caught Lucy's eye and a moment later, she saw a ferret-faced man peering out of the door of Jack's lodge. A heavy-set thug pushed past Ferret Face and ran into the barn waving a sword and yelling loudly about witches and black magic.

On autopilot, Thomas reached into Francis's scabbard and plucked out his sword, while Baz faced down Ferret Face with his pistol. By this time, the small man had learned enough about the power of modern guns not to chance his luck, but the big thug's blood was up, so he roared and ran towards Thomas. It had been a good few years since Thomas had been in a serious sword fight, but

241

his Tudorland skills returned with alacrity, aided by his ongoing fencing sessions with Sir David Cromwell. He systematically ground the man down, finally delivering a nasty sideways cut into the neck, after which, Casper and Baz grabbed the man and bundled him into Jannie's lodge. Carlo found some rope and tied up the smaller man, tossing him unceremoniously into the lodge after his companion. Jannie was still somewhat shaken, so Lucy ran into Jannie's lodge and took the controls, flying the lodges back to the Sion summer of 1544, and once there Carlo, Thomas and Baz kicked the two men out the door and slammed it shut, while at the same time yelling to Lucy to get them back to New London.

* * *

Nobody was in the mood for a formal debriefing, so they went across to the farmhouse for something to eat and drink, while recounting their adventures. It didn't take Carlo and Thomas long to work out their relationship to Francis, coming to the conclusion that he was indeed their second cousin, due to the Will Fortescue link.

Later that day, Francis and Jannie hugged each other tightly and said their painful goodbyes before Lucy and Noel flew Francis back to Tudorland to fetch his horse and make his way back to the city. Thomas had given Francis Jannie's lodge Pigeon and showed him how to use it, so now he and Jannie could keep in touch.

26:

The Briefing Room

Yesterday is not ours to recover, but tomorrow is ours to win or lose.

LYNDON B. JOHNSON, PAST PRESIDENT OF THE USA

Baz called everyone into the big briefing room, opening the proceedings by listing the section heads of what Kelly Vance of T-North had now titled 'Operation Jigsaw'. The heads would be Professor Tony Price for the science team, Jack Duquesne for defence, Raj Patel for technical matters, Steven Byers for logistics, Kate Byers and Margie Baverstock for catering, Kelly Vance, Margie Baverstock and Shelley Baverstock for first aide, and Harry Holt for TUDOR backup.

When the TUDORs saw the Wyoming explosion, followed by the images of England after a potential explosion and tidal waves, they knew that the job had to be done. Tony Price had asked if there was anyone in TUDOR who could help with the geological side of things, and that had led to Sir James Cromwell joining the team, joined by Emily Cromwell. Major Shimon Sobieski and Senior-Colonel Alec Blitz of Mossad joined Jack's defence section.

Jack said drones with day and night sights would fly around the camp and the drill site to keep an eye on things, but that they would also post sentries. He said he was bringing in as many troopers from T-North and T-West as they could spare, and that all the defenders should go to the Mews over the next couple of days and pick up the fatigues, helmets, Kevlar and the high quality boots that Sophie had bought in for them. He instructed those who were not officially part of the defence team but who knew how to use a side arm, to carry one at all times and be prepared to use it if necessary. When Sir David realised how short they were of defenders, he insisted on joining the team.

Raj didn't have much to say at this point, but said there would be briefings on the ground as and when needed.

Steven showed projections of the mega-tents, showing that they were designed to keep out all kinds of weather and explaining that they would be set up and fully loaded with gear at T-West so they would only need to be bolted into the ground when they landed at the camp. He showed the layout of the camp, pointing out where the various tents would be, including the HQ, armoury, canteen and so on. He said they were bound to cause some pollution to the river, but it wouldn't be much and it would soon clear away. He also said they were taking a team of Jack Russell puppies along to keep down any rats that may attempt to enter the camp.

Baz brought a groan to the team by announcing that everyone involved in Jigsaw would report to the Harley Street Clinic for inoculations.

Katie and Margie reported that the kitchen would keep veggie food to the left, meat goods to the right and crossover foods, such as fish, cheese and butter in the middle, and they hoped this would suit the variety of religions and food preferences among the team. They also assured the team that there would be hot food at all hours of the day and night. They brought a cheer to the room by announcing that there would be plenty of wine and beer, because they figured if the camp was dry, some ignoramus would smuggle in spirits. Katie said the only person with an actual food problem that they were prepared to cater for was Sophie, so there would be lots of sugar-free jelly, sweetener powder and pills, and custard. At this point, Sir James Cromwell put his hand up and told the girls that he'd recently been diagnosed as having type-two diabetes and could they bring extra jelly and stuff for him too.

Harry Holt said he'd be sleeping on a camp bed at Millbank, while Steven's second in command, Julie Tiller, would be on hand during the daytime and during the weekend. The usual skeleton night staff would be augmented. He also said that if a shout came in, he'd instructed the senior officers at the BBI to get off their cyber-bound asses and cope with it.

Finally, just before the meeting broke for lunch, Thomas strode in and announced that D-Day would be at nine hundred hours the following Tuesday.

27:

Gender Benders

The Moon card often shows up when there is a mystery surrounding the enquirer. Moonlight is deceptive, so the enquirer may find herself on the receiving end of lies and deception, and nothing may be what others are trying to tell her.

SASHA FENTON ON THE MOON CARD IN THE TAROT

At T-West, the massive, domed temporary buildings were ready with their contents stacked somewhat haphazardly inside. Ryan was holding the leads of three excited Jack Russell dogs, which were busily sniffing around, and getting ready for their adventure.

At the Mews, the space was filled with vans and MPVs, while the remaining space was filled with excited, lively people and their luggage. Thomas was on the phone, awaiting instructions from Lucy, which would signal the first of the many shuttle flights from the Mews to T-West, while Sophie, Jannie, Raj and Sophie's long-serving engineer, Kevin, sat in their vehicles with the Project systems warmed up and ready to go.

At T-West, Lucy, Carlo and their engineer, Jeff, were crossing their fingers because lodges and old vehicles that would make up the shield that would surround and protect the camp were set to fly out in one fell swoop.

The moment the word came, Jack and the defence team took off. They flew directly from the Mews to the campsite, fanning out on landing to protect the outskirts of the camp. They were delighted to find that the weather in Tudorland was warm and summery, compared to the cold and stormy autumn weather in New London. Shortly after their arrival, the old caravans and lodges that were designed to create the shield landed more or less in their right places. Extra campervans were gathered together at the top end of the camp, in preparation to moving out to the drilling site the following day.

Two hours later, everything else had landed, and Steven and Raj's teams were trundling misplaced vehicles around to fit them into their proper places. Steven's team suffered some unexpected problems with the water pumps and connections, but by midday the all-important loos were up and running and basic washing facilities were in place. By the end of the day, the shower rooms were fully operational, as were the dishwashers and washing machines. The combination of hard physical work and fresh air, followed by a hot meal ensured that everyone slept well that night.

* * *

The morning of the second day saw the science team making a start at the drilling site, with the Professor, Emily and Sir James peering at laptops while Sir David, Kevin and Raj plodded up and down a grid pattern working with the ground radar.

Part of the problem was the difference in the topography of the ground and the area from the 2019 pattern that was so familiar to Professor Price.

They spent the day searching for something resembling a void, but frustratingly, nothing was showing up. Then, just as the sun was setting, Sir James spotted something on his laptop. It looked like a thin horizontal line of pale blue just edging into the far right of his screen. He called the Professor to take a look.

'It looks as though we are searching too far to the west,' said the Professor, 'we'll extend the perimeter ten meters eastward first thing and focus our search in that area.'

* * *

That evening, those who weren't on watch pulled tables and chairs out of the café, set up the anti-bug diffusers and sat about playing cards or chess or chatting. It was then that Jack decided to tell Baz and Margie about something strange that he'd experienced on the night of the banquet at Sion Park. He'd kept the story to himself thus far, but now he wanted to get some perspective on it.

'As you know, the team didn't sit together at the banquet and I wasn't unhappy about that, because it gave me a chance to chat to the locals, but when we'd exhausted the goss, I turned to a very pretty blond who was seated on my left.'

Baz and Margie laughed, commenting that even if Jack had been dropped into the middle of Antarctica he'd find a pretty girl to befriend. Jack grinned and agreed that it was probably true, but he went on to say that this girl was giving off a strange vibe that he interpreted as some deep kind of sadness.

'I think she opened up to me because she knew I wouldn't be staying long and she felt able to speak out without any fear of repercussions.' Clearly somewhat bothered, Jack bit his lip. Then he took a breath and went on with the story. 'She told me her name was Joanna, that she was eighteen years old and happily married, but after more than a year of marriage, there was still no sign of a pregnancy. Well, there may be many reasons for that, but her next comments struck me as strange. She said that her husband was generous, kind and loving, but the passionate feelings she'd heard other women speak of were a mystery to her.'

Jack pushed a rogue lock of fair hair out of his face and looked slightly uncomfortable. 'Worse still, I couldn't help noticing that she was starting to show a definite interest in me.'

'Yeah Jack, how surprising is that?' asked Margie. 'You're a great looking guy with a cheerful smile and an athletic body. Like all the action-men in TUDOR, you are confident, you emit sexuality – and you're a major flirt. It isn't surprising that a girl as young as Joanna who's married to some kind of non-event bloke would show an interest – particularly if she'd downed a few chalices during the evening.'

Jack nodded. 'Well the funny thing is I wasn't actually making an effort to flirt as such, but I admit that when she started to show an interest... well, I took her hand and licked the tips of her fingers just a little...'

'Cheeky bugger,' chuckled Margie.

'However, the longer I sat with her, the more certain I became that something wasn't right.' Jack bit his lip again, which served to show how disconcerted he had been – and still was.

'After the meal, we danced for a while before wandering off to her room for a cup of wine. Needless to say, once we got to her quarters I took her into my arms, but the feeling that was bugging me now suddenly became stifling.'

By now, both Baz and Margie were thoroughly intrigued.

'I didn't want to frighten her by diving straight into lovemaking, and I wanted to discover the root of my discomfort, so I stroked her and petted her, while asking gentle questions about her life and her marriage.'

Jack screwed up his eyes while he gathered his thoughts. 'It appeared that Joanna's upbringing had been closer to that of a *Victorian* girl than a *Tudor* one. You see, she was an only child and an orphan, and she'd been brought up by a couple of unmarried aunts and an aged grandmother. The family were what you might call "gentility", so she wasn't used to seeing what went on among animals on farms, so what with one thing and another – and very unusually for that era – she'd grown up without any idea about the birds and the bees.'

Baz and Margie nodded to show they understood, but stayed quiet so Jack could continue with the story.

'It seems that when Joanna was fifteen, a wealthy landowning nobleman paid a visit to the household and he took an immediate liking to her. Her family was struggling financially at this time, so the grandmother suggested that Joanna marry the bloke and help the family fill their coffers. Joanna is far from stupid and she knows the lifestyle that's mapped out for girls of her class is marriage and babies, and to be honest she wasn't averse to the idea, so she went along with the arrangement. Truth to tell, she was pleased to be in a position to help her family, while at the same time being married to a nice guy who seemed to care deeply about her.'

Baz went to the kitchen and came back with a couple of more Peronis and a top-up of wine for Margie. When Baz came back, he noticed that jack's expression was surprisingly serious.

'Look I'm not being prurient,' said Jack hesitatingly. 'And I have no desire to talk dirty to you Margie love, but

I know you've studied psychology so perhaps you could help me to understand... and with Baz sitting here, neither of you will misunderstand my motives.'

Baz told him to stop faffing around and spill the beans, regardless of how porno the beans in question turned out to be.

Jack told them that after asking Joanna a few questions he was no nearer to understanding what was going on, but some intuition had urged him to get the girl to take a look at his body and to handle his genitalia, after which he embarked upon a pretty comprehensive love-making session. The outcome was that they both found themselves coming to the unbelievable conclusion that the girl's husband was a *woman*!

'Margie love, I find it hard to believe. But do you think such a thing is possible?'

'I *know* it is, Jack,' said Margie gently. 'There have been several documented cases during Victorian times, but one famous case occurred in the 1920s. In those days, many men had been killed in the First World War, while many others were so badly bashed up or mentally damaged that they weren't able to marry. This caused a shortage of suitors and also a distinct lack of fathers, brothers and cousins in families, so a lot of girls had no idea of what a man's body looked like. It seems that one particularly shy and naïve girl was delighted when a nice young man came along and proposed, but after a couple of years passed by with no pregnancy occurring, she paid a visit to her doctor.

Apparently, some instinct made her do this without telling anyone, including her husband. When the doctor examined the girl, he was astounded to discover that she was still a *virgin*! Gentle questioning brought him to the conclusion that the "husband" might indeed be a woman, so the following day, the doctor visited the household and put his findings to the so-called husband, upon which, he/she burst into tears and admitted the truth. Needless to say, the marriage was swiftly annulled.'

Margie drank a little more wine while continuing to think. 'Believe it or not, there are also hermaphrodites, so that could also be the case.'

'What, people who combine both sexes? Like garden worms?' exclaimed Jack.

'Yeah. There are cases of folk who have small internalised testes, no penis, some kind of vague vagina and semi-formed ovary setup.'

'Bloody-ell,' said Baz, shaking his head. 'So this guy could have been one of those?'

'It's possible, but he could just as easily have been female. I have read of this kind of syndrome being called *onanism,* but that's not really correct. Onanism is ejaculating outside the woman's body in order to avoid pregnancy.

'Otherwise known as "pulling-out-in-time",' suggested Baz with a grin.

'Pre-says-ley,' said Margie in a mock posh voice.

Margie pursed her lips and thought for a moment before asking Jack if he thought the girl might have been a virgin.

'You're absolutely right Margie; she was! It surprised me at the time, but I was too far into it to stop myself or to question it. Margie love, I don't make a habit of it deflowering maidens, but it has happened a couple of times, and I've learned that while some young women suffer a lot of pain when the hymen breaks, others don't. I felt the resistance when I pushed through and she jumped a bit, but she soon got over it and she seemed happy to go on. I'm not showing off when I say this, but I did pay a great deal of attention to Joanna, keeping the pleasure going for her as long as possible by all the means at my disposal. By now, I had figured that she wouldn't be carrying any sexual diseases, so I was happy to do a bit of muff diving. I know it sounds daft, but I felt absolutely compelled to introduce her to reality.'

Jack looked at his lager bottle while thinking out loud and said, 'I have no problem with anybody's sexuality. As far as I am concerned, people can be gay, straight, tranny, bisexual, celibate, promiscuous or whatever they want to be, but I hate the idea of someone being *hoodwinked* – I actually find it disgusting.'

'You're Sagittarian with Scorpio rising,' said Margie. 'That combination makes you loathe deception. You detest those who take advantage of others or pull the wool over their eyes. You hate liars and hypocrites. Despite having girlfriends all over the place, you have a powerful moral compass and while you love to flirt, but you never pretend to offer more than casual love to any woman. Your love of justice led you to study law and to become an intelligence agent.'

'I guess you're right. I never thought about myself that way. I hope I did the right thing by Joanna though.'

'I'm sure you did,' said Baz. 'You opened your eyes to the truth and the rest is up to her.'

'I hope she finds some painless way of getting her "husband" off the hook, though,' Margie commented. 'Homosexuality was a real no-no in Tudorland and gays were routinely hung.'

'Christ, I hadn't thought of that,' said Jack with a shudder.

28:

Operation Jigsaw

*If you set goals and go after them with all the
determination you can muster, your gifts will take you
places that will amaze you.*

LES BROWN

Apart from the sentries, everyone looked north towards the
drilling site, while Tony Price called to the team to sit down
or take cover. Raj worked the drill's remote control, while
the Professor watched through his binoculars, counting off
each metre as the drill went down.

The TUDORs held their breath.

'Two, three, four, five...' intoned the Professor. The
tension was palpable. 'Ten, eleven, twelve...'

As the drill approached thirteen metres, the team felt a
strange rumbling, and those who were perched on the vans
and lodges felt them tremble beneath them. Down on the
ground, the sentries felt the effect even more strongly.

'What the...' said Noel quietly.

The ground at the drill site seemed to rise, and
eventually it became a towering cone of earth, rocks and
dust that hovered briefly before collapsing back down
again. The sound of the explosion reached the camp a few

moments later, while a second explosion threw lumps of granite, ancient lava, soil, dust and gas high into the air. It was a good thing the TUDORs had heeded the Professor's warning or the blast would have thrown anyone who was standing on the vehicles down onto the ground. As it was, at ground level, some of the sentries were knocked off their feet and the smaller, lighter tents came loose from their mooring ropes. It was almost as though the ancient volcano had been brought back to life. Luckily, a slight breeze was blowing the dusty air away from the camp, or the team would have been covered in the choking stuff.

Shock made everyone silent, and they all stood still while gazing towards the distant drilling site. Needless to say, it was Margie who put the whole thing into perspective.

'That'd put any self-respecting terrorist's IED to shame, wouldn't it?'

Once the dust had settled, Thomas, Professor Price, Baz and several others jumped into jeeps and drove to the drill site. The drill was nowhere to be seen, and everything other than one aged dust-covered Volkswagen Transporter had vanished.

'Look at that!' commented Baz. The newer vehicles have vanished off the face, while that old banger has survived.

'German engineering,' muttered Shimon with a grimace.

* * *

There was no longer anything for the sentries to guard at the drill site, but Jack increased security at the camp on the basis that the noise of the explosion could draw unwanted attention from the locals.

The following morning, Professor Price and a few others took shovels and a tanker of liquid Chalkon to the site, taking lots of rock samples from the bottom of the pit before pumping in the neutralising Chalkon. As soon as they were back at the camp, Thomas ordered the senior staff to get the team to strike camp.

Jack's intuition was still bothering him – with good reason – because Sophie and Jannie had spotted some activity showing up on the drone-screen. A few moments later, Sophie's voice could be heard over the camp's loudspeaker saying, 'Riders approaching from the north east!'

* * *

A large raiding party approached the camp and fanned out. One rider slid down from his horse and crept unnoticed into the space beside the supply van at the back of the kitchen. As it happened, the van was slightly misaligned, so it protruded into the perimeter, and it was there that the rider found Lucy walking back to the kitchen. Moving quickly and silently, the man grabbed Lucy and dragged her out towards the sword-waving raiding party. Five months pregnant Lucy found it hard to keep her footing, but when they came to a stop, she found herself held fast against greasy chain mail and with a knife at her throat. She was terrified, but instinct made her keep absolutely still and silent.

Sophie and Shimon crept onto the top of an old campervan, sliding along the roof and tucking themselves down between a pair of old solar panels. Each carried an International L96 sniper's rifle. Sophie smiled slightly to herself at the knowledge that British gun clubs and the old Soviet army knew that women make excellent snipers. It seems to be something to do with the way female eyes lined up with gun sights. For his part, Shimon always maintained that he'd learned marksmanship, and indeed the art of war in general, by watching the Nazis shoot their way through Poland from west to east in 1941 and back again in 1945, being chased by the

Russians who also knew a bit about warfare.

Sophie gave Shimon a slight nod, signalling that she was ready to take the shot. Shimon spotted sunlight glinting off a knife that a second man was getting ready to use on Lucy's baby-filled belly. Shimon hissed quietly, and tipped his head slightly left to alert Sophie to the situation, signalling that he would take out this second man.

Head shots are notoriously difficult, so snipers usually go for the body, but the distance wasn't great and the slight breeze that had been blowing earlier had died away; also, neither Sophie nor Shimon wanted to take any chances while Lucy's life hung in the balance. Within seconds, laser dots were marking the heads of the two assailants, and almost simultaneously, the two rifles cracked. When the man holding Lucy fell backwards, his knife nicked her jaw but mercifully, it didn't cut any of the veins in her neck. The brave girl took to her heels, zigzagging across the open space as she had been taught in her combat classes. The man hoping to use the knife on her belly was also dead.

The few arrows that landed in the camp didn't do much damage, but now the gang leader gave an angry roar and ordered the horsemen to charge. Sophie and Shimon quickly finished off two bowmen while Gunny, the far-from-young TUDOR armourer and ex-gunnery sergeant, showed his paces by picking off two horsemen with his much-loved, aged rifle. Everyone else in Jack's team opened up with assault rifles, while the so-called non-combatants, such as Thomas, Steven and Baz joined in, and even the Professor 'first-blooded' himself by shooting a foot-soldier with his pistol. Margie and Shelley grabbed Lucy and Emily, who was herself in the early stages of pregnancy, and shoved them down between the cooking ovens. Margie yelled at Shelley to look after the girls, while grabbing her helmet, pulling out her side-arm and running out to join the fray.

'Got to help Tommy Thumbscrews and the lads, haven't I!' yelled Margie, 'can't expect them to manage without my help, can I?'

Shelley rolled her eyes; wishing for the millionth time that she had a normal mother, while at the same time being very proud of her irrepressible mum.

The TUDORs tried to avoid hitting the horses, but inevitably some were injured and the noise of screaming animals blended with the general racket. Those who had experienced war in any of the three eras inhabited by the TUDORs weren't surprised at the noise and the smell of it all, but it came as a shock to those who hadn't. Some bullets skidded off armour with the screech of hot metal adding to the row, but some went through and the assault rifles made short work of the chain mail.

The battle was soon over, and now Carlo, Francis and Thomas told the others to keep away while they went out into the field and shot the injured horses. They knew the New Londoners would find this hard to stomach, but as medieval men, it was a natural way of dealing with an impossible situation. Sir David and Steven came out and joined them, bringing ropes, with which they tied the dead and wounded men to the remaining horses and sent the animals off to find their way home.

Several lightly wounded men were still on the field, so after Jack and the others had disarmed them, Margie grabbed one, noticing that he wasn't much older than her Shelley. A bullet had gone through the flesh at the side of his hip, so she frog-marched him to the first aid van where Shelley and Kelly were waiting to deal with the casualties. Shelley disinfected and dressed the wound, showing the lad the pack of bandages and telling him clearly to keep the wound clean. She explained the use of antibiotics and painkillers and made him take some. She gave him a large bottle of water to keep.

Shelley, Margie and Kelly soon fixed up the remaining casualties, and then sent the oldest of the men to Thomas for interrogation. The man seemed to be a gentleman, and when he bowed to Thomas, an automatic response took over and Thomas gave him a Tudor bow in return.

'Why didst thy leader not simply ride up under a white flag and ask us our business here? We would have informed him that the dangerous rocks in that hole needed to be destroyed, as they would in time have destroyed the land hereabouts.'

'That noise frighted our Sheriff, so he ordered us to attack first and leave questions for later.'

Margie had joined Thomas, Baz and Steven and she decided to give the man the benefit of her opinion. 'Your sheriff is a fucking prat,' she said.

'Verily, I would agree with your assessment, but now he is a dead fucking whatever a "prat" might be,' answered the man. 'From our viewpoint that happenstance is an outcome greatly to be desired, as the man who will take his place has a sound head upon his shoulders.'

'Lucky for him he wasn't here today, isn't it?' commented Margie sourly, 'or he wouldn't have any kind of head on his shoulders by now.'

'Tell me, Sir and Madam, where art thou from? And what are those weapons?'

Thomas had his answer ready. 'We're from Hidalia, and the weapons are more advanced versions of your matchlock and flintlock guns.'

'How I would love to take ownership of one of those,' said the man, eyeing Thomas's pistol.

'Well, you can't, so hard luck,' said Margie with a grin. 'Now bugger off home and forget all about us.'

'I doubt I can do that now I have encountered thee, my beautiful Moorish woman,' said the man sadly.

'Moorish woman, for fuck's sake!' exclaimed Margie with disgust as the man limped away.

* * *

Kelly and Shelley looked around to see if anyone needed first aid, but apart from a few easily treated scrapes and bruises, everyone was in one piece, so it wasn't long before the camp was packed away and nothing other than trampled grass and a few dead rats down by the riverside remained to show they were ever there.

* * *

Back in T-West, the team decided to leave the unloading for a while and go over to the farmhouse. Carlo fished several bottles of good whisky out of his cupboard while the girls made tea for Emily and Lucy. The non-pregnant women and girls started to work on their own bottle of whisky. Kelly introduced Shelley to the concept of sipping a small but healing drop of Scotch, which gave Shelley a golden opportunity for winding up her mother.

'Tastes good, Mum,' said Shelley smacking her lips.

'That's all I need,' sighed Margie, 'a daughter learning to be a piss-artist!'

Kelly decided to join the wind-up. 'I think Shel's getting a taste for it, Margie.'

'Her dad'll never forgive us,' groaned the long-suffering Margie.

Carlo and Noel came into the kitchen and put together a supper of baked beans, fried eggs and toast.

'What kind of drink goes best with an after-battle breakfast?' asked Casper.

'More whisky!' was the response.

29:

After Jigsaw

Leadership is solving problems.
COLIN POWELL

Before leaving T-West, Sophie and Lucy gave Francis a box containing small Solabrite batteries to go with his Pigeon, along with paper, pens and a cheap digital camera. The girls showed Francis how to use everything, and they all felt easier now they could keep in touch. Jack had given Francis a heads-up about the future political situation in Tudorland as far as he and his family would be concerned, and this helped Francis to see which faction to court and which to avoid. Jack advised Francis to get rid of any religious books that he had at home or at work, as they would be guaranteed to land him in hot water every time the religion changed, and he also advised Francis to keep his family abreast of the situation.

Later that day, Sophie and Thomas took pity on Jannie by flying France to Tudorland for her, while Emily hugged and comforted the distraught girl.

* * *

Jigsaw had shown the need for more staff in the

Intelligence department and to bring in a new level of seniority called 'Lead Operatives' to guide junior technical and intelligence staff. The Lead Operatives would also share some of the less popular working hours, thus relieving the pressure on the Directors and Seniors. They all accepted that this was only a start, as TUDOR needed to grow, especially where the Intelligence and Data departments were concerned.

T-West scrapped the old vehicles, thus making the Project system leaner and sharper, while Sophie brought in a new and improved range of batteries and solar panels.

Emson Barotse told Steven to hang onto the leftover money from the Jigsaw budget, because he'd need something to fall back on when future cuts came along.

Thomas and Baz brought in a major change by now allowing TUDOR employees to wear casual clothes to work, but insisted that they keep a formal outfit on hand in their lockers. However, Thomas, Baz and Steven decided to continue wearing suits, because they never knew when they'd have to rush out somewhere important.

* * *

Jannie's misery was so obvious that Sophie feared a repetition of the Lucy episode, when poor Lucy had nearly starved herself to death after leaving Carlo in Tudorland, but that was before Sophie and Raj had invented the Pigeons, which meant that Lucy couldn't even keep in touch with Carlo or know his feelings. Sophie understood how Jannie felt, because she was always miserable when parted from Thomas for any length of time. But then she had a brain-wave.

Sophie searched the local junk shops and a few days later, a dilapidated van delivered two old wardrobes to the

Mews. When she'd explained what they were for, Jannie and Kevin treated them for wood-worm, and painted them so they would look like something from Tudorland. The girls fitted the wardrobes with Projects, prepared very precise coordinates and sent Francis a Pigeon. Sophie 'flew' one wardrobe while Jannie flew the other, and they landed against the back wall of a small spare room behind Francis's office. At the appointed hour, Francis watched as the room shimmered and dust flew around, and then the two wardrobes appeared and the doors slowly opened. A moment later, Jannie was in Francis's arms, while he held her tightly and rocked her from side to side as her tears of joy soaked into his beautiful silk-velvet doublet. Soon, they were sipping wine in Francis's office while he told them what was on his mind.

'I intend to take ship to the north of Somerset to see my family, and after telling my parents and my uncle Walter about all that has happened I will contact you so that Jannie can fly out to meet them.'

Sophie nodded and started thinking aloud. 'I expect Tommy and Carlo would like to pay them a visit as well. After all, they know your mother and uncle, and Tommy is convinced your families are related through the various marriages that have taken place over the years – even without the "Will Fortescue" connection.' Sophie thought for a moment. 'Come to think of it, do you reckon they could borrow a couple of mounts and ride down to Devon to pay a visit to Carlo's Aunt Bessie? I know the boys like to keep up their riding skills and they'd enjoy the trip.'

'I remember Aunt Bessie from the old days. She's a lovely lady and I'd love to see her again, so I'll go with them,' said Francis.

Sophie gave Jannie strict instructions to be back at the Mews on Monday morning, then after giving her young assistant a hug, she clambered into her wardrobe and flew back to New London.

Tudorland men were taught that the purpose of sex was to produce children, and they were further taught that women could only become pregnant if they had an orgasm or four. Of course, by this time, Thomas's relatives had learned that this old belief wasn't actually true, but they were still in the habit of giving their ladies a very good time, and Francis had learned a few extra tricks when he'd lived in Persia. It didn't take long for Jannie to discover the intense feelings that could be engendered by a clever and experienced lover, or for Francis to discover what he had long suspected, which was that Jannie was a warm and passionate young woman.

Thereafter, unless Francis was on a Tudorland shout or Jannie was busy working on a New London one, they spent their weekends together, sometimes in Tudorland and at other times in New London. The jury was still out as to when they might get together on a permanent basis – and in which era – but as Jannie said, there were plenty of others like them who could only be together off and on; and for now, it was enough.

Francis's family was understandably astonished at what he had to tell them, but they welcomed Jannie with open arms. They were very glad have advance knowledge of the way things would go in their Tudorland future, and were thankful for the advice that Francis gave them on the best way to navigate the coming storms.

In early February, Lucy went into labour. The snow was falling heavily on the moors, so Carlo rode the tractor into the village and trundled the midwife back to the house. Fortunately, the labour was normal and little Toby was a healthy baby. Danny was delighted to have a brother and Josie loved playing with the new arrival, while Lucy and

Carlo cuddled up and celebrated their good luck.

Three months later, news came through that Emily had given birth to a girl, and that Shimon and Emily decided on a name with no connection to their past or to either of their families. They called the baby Macy, and now, for the Sobieski-Cromwell family, and even for Colonel Alec Blitz, baby Macy represented a fresh start and new hope.

In true Jewish style, Emily had bought nothing for the baby before the birth in case something went wrong, so when the time came, Shimon and Alec rushed to the shops to try out pushchairs, doing pram wheelies round the shop, much to the amusement of the shop assistants. The shops in Jerusalem were used to men behaving like loonies when a new baby came into the world, and the assistants were happy to sell the guys everything that wasn't tied down. The two besotted men bought a ton of baby clothes and soft toys while Sir James Cromwell surfed the Net and bought a pile of children's books in Hebrew and in English so he could read to the new arrival. Needless to say, Emily told them they were all as daft as brushes while Macy slept through it all.

While recovering from the birth, it struck Emily that the silly mistake she'd made when programming the old Project, and landing during the Six-Day-War rather than after it had ended, had led to a wonderful new life for herself, for her dad and for Shimon. Emily hoped that things would work out well for them in Israel, but for the time being she was happy, and that was enough.

30:

Investiture

Following the light of the sun, we left the Old World behind.

Christopher Columbus

The April weather was cool and windy but mercifully dry when Thomas arrived at Buckingham Palace. When they'd cleared security, Sophie, Kate and Steven were led into a large room and directed towards tiered rows of red velvet seats that were reserved for the families of those being honoured. Pages directed the honour recipients along a red-carpeted passage and up a curving staircase, where pike-wielding Yeomen of the Guard led them into a massive room and told them to wait. Thomas felt it surreal to see the same corps of Yeoman Warders that King Henry had created still guarding the monarchy, and for one dislocating moment, he considered slipping home and changing into his doublet and trunk hose.

Soon Thomas was sent into a very large, brightly coloured room. He could see his family on his right, but when he looked to the left, he saw the raised area where the Queen and her small entourage were standing. Thomas approached the platform, and bowed in the modern style before stepping forward again. The Queen greeted Thomas with real delight and motioned him to a cushioned stool. He perched his right knee on the stool, keeping his left leg extended and his left foot anchored to the floor.

'You know how this is done don't you?' whispered the Queen in a conspiratorial voice.

Thomas couldn't help smiling despite the solemnity of the occasion, while a page came forward holding a cushion upon which rested a sword. The Queen took the sword and slowly tapped Thomas first on the left shoulder and then on the right.

Speaking quietly, the Queen asked, 'Were you nervous the last time round, Sir Thomas?'

'I was very nervous then, Your Majesty, but also delighted to be honoured for my service to my King; but I am even more nervous now and even more delighted, because it feels so much more important this time round. It's hard to explain, but you have just returned me to myself again after being out on a limb for so many years. It's as though I'm real again – and I now feel truly safe for the first time since that terrible day in June 1540 when I thought my life was over. I don't know whether that makes any sense to you, Madam.'

The Queen soon put him at his ease. 'Sir Thomas, you've been through a great deal, and it's my opinion that my ancestor made a mistake when he executed Sir Thomas Cromwell and set out to execute you, and I am so glad that I am in a position to put things right for you. We don't often get the chance to right the mistakes of history do we?'

Thomas's sincere nod transmitted his thanks to her Majesty, but there was something more that he needed to say.

'This may also sound strange, but I am also delighted to see King Henry's Yeomen of the Guard in your palace Madam, because to me they symbolise a safe future for the royal family and for our realm. I don't know if you can make any sense of that, either.'

The Queen nodded and said she understood perfectly. Furthermore, she told him she was glad that her Yeomen were giving him such comfort. Then she surprised Thomas by quietly telling him to contact her office in a week or so and make an appointment for a private visit. She said the Prince of Wales wanted to ask him about the court of her ancestor and he had indicated that he wanted to take a short trip back to Tudorland to see it for himself.

Thomas said that could easily be arranged, as the Prince could be passed off as an ambassador from Hidalia. He also assured the Queen that her son would have an armed escort with him at all times.

'I should hope so,' said the Queen. Then she went on quickly, 'I'm sure other members of my family would love to meet you and the rest of the Hatherleigh clan. I know Harry and William would be fascinated to hear about military and other matters as they were in those days.'

'We'd be delighted to give them all the inside information they want,' whispered Thomas. 'It would be a pleasure for all of us.'

The Queen smiled and held out her hand, whispering something to Thomas as she brought the investiture to an end.

When the family met up again, Sophie took one of Thomas's hands and Kate took the other. Their questions tumbled out over each other, but Thomas was too choked up to say anything. Soon, they were in the Palace courtyard with all the other honour recipients, busily taking photos, and then all too soon, the wonderful day was over.

When they were in the car on their way home, Sophie asked the question that had been intriguing her. 'We saw the Queen whispering to you at the end,' said Sophie. 'What was she saying?'

'It appears that she knows about Margie's nickname for me, and the plaque that Jack had engraved and hung in my office; she said, "Goodbye for now, Tommy Thumbscrews"'.

* * *

A few days later, the family and all their friends assembled at Tamerlane Square for a massive party. Everyone ate far too much, got tipsy, and sang songs from the present and from Tudorland days. Then Jannie and Francis arrived and joined Carlo, Kate, Steven and Thomas in teaching the New Londoners the Tudorland dances. Suddenly, Sophie and Thomas's large sitting room was transformed into a Tudor court, as the dancers wove their way back and forth to ancient music that Sophie had loaded onto an MP3.

It was the early hours when taxis were summoned. The helpers had long gone; young Rosie was fast asleep so Sophie and Thomas were alone at last in their pale green and white bedroom.

'Fancy making a k-night of it, Sophie?'

'You were a knight before, so it's hardly a novelty is it?'

'That's what *you* think.' He said, taking her in his arms. 'Now let's see…' he said, giving her ear a nuzzle, 'I may have been a knight before, but you've never been a lady, so let me think… What can I do that's special enough for a new lady of the realm?'

'Lord, give me strength,' sighed Sophie.

'Glad you're asking because I'm feeling young again and particularly frisky.'

'Do the words *sod* and *off* mean anything?' said Sophie in mock irritation.

'Not really,' laughed Thomas, bringing his lips down on hers.

And so our story ends. It was Sophie's Inheritance that started the saga. Sophie had once been so alone, apart from the support of friends like Margie, Baz and a few others, but her decision to save just *one* life from historical destruction had brought her a large family, wonderful friends and a fascinating job.

At the start of the story, Thomas had only a few moments of freedom left before the King's troopers were due to drag him to the Tower, owing to the moody nature of a sick King who wouldn't take responsibility for his own actions. But now, Sir Thomas Hatherleigh was alive and well, with a much-loved family, wonderful friends and a career he was made for. A combination of luck and his own ability had given him back all he had lost. The last piece of the jigsaw had been the return of his title, and he had said to Queen Elizabeth at his investiture – he felt whole again at last.

* * *

Several weeks after this momentous event, a note came from the Palace inviting Thomas and Sophie for tea with the elderly royal couple, and this time the Queen had even more news. She said that she and the Prince had come to the conclusion that Sophie's scientific work had played such a major part in saving the country from destruction that she should be recognised as well. So the Queen had decided to honour Sophie by making her a Dame of the Royal Victorian Order, which would make her 'Lady Sophie' in her own right. Prince Philip said that they had also decided to honour Baz, Professor Price, and the TUDOR Seniors who were involved in the Lincoln Moor operation with CBEs and OBEs. The Prince said it was only right and proper to recognise the men and women who were doing so much for their country.

* * *

The party following these honours was truly joyous, because so many had something to celebrate, but during the evening, it became clear that Sir David wanted a quiet word with Thomas. Thomas took him into his study, closed the door and poured malt into cut glasses.

'Emson wants to retire and write his memoirs,' said Sir David.

'God, it'll feel really strange to have another PPS to deal with after all this time, won't it?'

'Very.'

'Did Emson say who the new one might be?'

'His name is Oliver Chapman and apparently Mrs S doesn't think much of him.'

Thomas couldn't help chuckling. 'That figures. She doesn't think much of anyone.'

Sir David nodded. 'It's not *her* opinion that's bothering me though, it's something Emson said. He told me that the new guy is urbane, good looking, well educated, a good talker, impressive and apparently, discreet, capable and efficient.'

'Sounds perfect,' said Thomas, wondering what else was coming.

'He's all that – apart from one small drawback. You see, Emson's sure the guy's secretly working for the FSB in the Kremlin. The FSB is the successor to the KGB.'

'Surely not!' exclaimed Thomas. 'Can a traitor rise so high?'

Sir David gave Thomas a sour look. 'It happened once before. Have you heard of a guy called Kim Philby?'

'Can't say I have. Who's he? Someone we need to worry about?'

'Mercifully no. Philby was around in the 1960s at the height of the cold war. He worked for MI6, eventually landing a plum job running the Washington DC station. He was so good at his job that he was tipped to become the head of MI6, but he worked with a guy from the CIA who began to harbour suspicions about him. Not being part of the British establishment and not being afraid to blow the whistle, the CIA man spoke up, and it turned out that he was right, because Philby had long since been recruited into the NKVD, which was the forerunner of the KGB, and he'd been passing secrets to the Russians ever since. It seemed that Philby was a prodigious drinker and he lived in a style that the strapped-for-cash British government couldn't finance, so while he might have started out as many did in the 1920s, by believing in the communist system, it later became a matter of money. God only knows how many British and American agents lost their lives because of that bastard.'

'Christ in heaven! So Emson thinks this guy's a double agent like this Philby geezer! What does he want us to do? Allow the bloke to have a nasty accident by falling out of a window in the Bloody Tower?'

'Dunno yet, but I like the Tower suggestion. In your Tudorland days Tom, did anyone actually fall out of a Tower window by accident?'

Thomas took a long sip of his whisky and grinned, 'One or two did lose their footing as I remember. I can't imagine how though...'

'I don't suppose you happen to remember where Henry's men left the axe by any chance?' commented Sir David. 'It might come in handy.'

'I'm sure I could lay my hands on it, but I guess we'll

have to prove the man's a spy and catch him in the act first.'

'Yep, that's about the strength of it.'

'We'd better get back to the party or they'll wonder what's going on,' said Thomas. 'You know what my lot are like for smelling a shout before anyone starts to raise their voice.'

Thomas and Sir David gave each other conspiratorial grins at the thought of another adventure starting to show itself over the horizon...

* * *

But that wasn't quite all... You see, after writing his book, Emson Barotse decided to go on a lecture tour, and it was an unfortunate event at his very first talk that brought Maisie Dixon and Jamie Beaufort into the picture. But all that is for another day and for the fourth book in this 'trilogy'...